Awards and Endorsements for *Together We Empower* . . .

National Indie Excellence Award Winner for Multicultural Non-Fiction, Foreword Reviews' INDIEFAB Book of the Year Finalist in Social Sciences, and 2016 International Book Awards (IBA) winner in the category of Social Change.

"This book tells the compelling story of moving a society from adversity to prosperity, turning roadblocks into opportunities, and helping community members find their voices and become engaged and active members of society, cognizant of their rights and responsibilities as citizens. The resulting changes carry the potential to deepen and widen in their impact. The 3-P approach (people, products, and profits) to development work is unique in its application of business concepts to rural development initiatives to build sustainable and lasting partnerships among all stakeholders."

–Deep Shikha, PhD, Department of Economics
St. Catherine University, Minnesota

"*Together We Empower* illustrates how individual hardships combined with innovations in seed science inspired Suri and Edda Sehgal's personal philanthropy to flow from Iowa to India's most indigent villages, clearing a pathway out of poverty for the poorest of the poor."

–Ambassador Kenneth M. Quinn, president, The World Food Prize Foundation, Des Moines, Iowa

"The selfless activities performed by Sehgal Foundation go far beyond their remarkable achievements related to water. Their new scientific as well as grassroots innovations are effectively addressing the needs of the poor in rural India. I wish every NGO in India operated with the level of professionalism and credibility of Sehgal Foundation.

–M. L. Kansal, PhD, JPSS chair (Hydropower)
Water Resources Development & Management
Indian Institute of Technology, Roorkee

"Despite the adoption of the Universal Declaration of Human Rights, the fruits of development did not reach some sections of the people in India because of bad governance or inadequacies of the systems in place. Social justice in India is a work in progress, and Sehgal Foundation is playing an important role in promoting good rural governance. Social, economic, and political justice, which is the promise of the Constitution of India, are being realized incrementally in the villages where Sehgal Foundation works."

–N. R. Madhava Menon, LLD, IBA chair, Continuing Legal Education, National Law School, India University

"*Together We Empower* documents how Sehgal Foundation has positively transformed and empowered rural communities and farming families. The foundation's talented team is dedicated to measurable results and highly innovative in their approaches to solving complicated issues. The Mosaic Company and its foundation are honored to work alongside Sehgal Foundation to advance agricultural development, water security, and educational opportunities where the needs are greatest in rural Indian villages."

–Kari Niedfeldt-Thomas, senior manager, Social Responsibility; and executive director, The Mosaic Company Foundation

"A revolution in the condition of women that will enable them to lead a fulfilling and dignified life is the need of the hour. The world will be a better place when women are empowered, which is why we should celebrate the spirit of this valuable book."

–Kiran Prasad, PhD, Communication and Journalism Sri Padmavati Mahila University, India

"S M Sehgal Foundation's successful water system innovations, which benefit communities across diverse geographies, show the viability of a market-based model to provide people in need with a sustainable source of affordable, reliable, and safe water. I am quite excited to see that efforts and achievements by Sehgal Foundation are aptly described in this book, a valuable document for others to follow and implement. These initiatives will no doubt be taken up by many social enterprises to impact millions more in need."

–D. R. Prasada Raju, PhD, FNAE, advisor and head, retd, Dept. of Science and Technology, Government of India, New Delhi

TOGETHER WE EMPOWER

TOGETHER WE EMPOWER

REKINDLING HOPE IN RURAL INDIA

SECOND EDITION

MARLY CORNELL

ISBN : 978-81-212-1348-6

Price : ₹ 400/-

First Published in India, 2016

Published by

SEHGAL FOUNDATION

Des Moines - Gurgaon
www.smsfoundation.org

Co-published by
Gyan Publishing House
5, Ansari Road
Daryaganj, New Delhi-110002
Phone: 9811692060
E-mail: books@gyanbooks.com
Printed at: G. Print Process, Delhi.

Cataloging in Publication Data--DK
Courtesy: D.K. Agencies (P) Ltd. <docinfo@dkagencies.com>

Cornell, Marly, author.
Together we empower : rekindling hope in rural India / Marly Cornell. -- Second edition.
pages cm
Includes index.
ISBN 9788121213486

1. Sehgal Foundation. 2. Rural poor--India. 3. Agricultural assistance--India. 4. Rural development--India. I. Title.

HC440.P6C67 2016 DDC 305.5690954 23

"To rekindle hope is to put the *power* in empowerment."

-Suri and Edda Sehgal

Contents

Foreword

Long ago, Mahatma Gandhi said that India's "villagers have lost all hope. They suspect that every stranger's hand is at their throats and that he goes to them only to exploit them." Against such a background, this book about Sehgal Foundation, which provides hope where there was despair, is welcome. *Together We Empower* documents the history and evolution of the Sehgal Foundation from its conception to its fifteenth anniversary and beyond, offering a glimpse into this unique institution and its impact at the grassroots level as well as in academic and policy circles. The foundation's success is due to its approach to development programs that address the greatest needs faced by villages in rural India.

Sehgal Foundation has been at the forefront of many innovations that help manage water resources, improve agricultural production and rural income in some of the country's poorest communities, and empower communities to demand good village governance. I am heartened by Sehgal Foundation's emphasis on individual rights. Without responsible and responsive governance, the fruits of development will not go to the poor. Leading by example and adopting a socially inclusive approach to development, Sehgal Foundation is continuing to emerge as a knowledge institute.

I congratulate the foundation on this timely publication, which serves as an affirming flame in the midst of the sea of despair we often see around us. I wish Sehgal Foundation continued growth and success in achieving rural transformation based on developmental strategies that are pro-nature, pro-advocacy for the poor, and pro-gender equality.

I hope this story will inspire all those who wish to assist and empower rural and tribal families and abolish poverty and hunger. As founder Suri Sehgal so rightly points out, "The only thing that counts at the end is the impact."

M. S. Swaminathan[1]
UNESCO chair in Ecotechnology
M S Swaminathan Research Foundation
Chennai, India

1. Dr. Monkombu Sambasivan Swaminathan won the first World Food Prize, in 1987, for his work spearheading the introduction of high-yielding wheat and rice varieties to India's farmers. He is recognized as a leader in the world's Green Revolution. See http://www.mssrf.org/.

Introduction

The first time Edda Sehgal visited the rural villages in Mewat, where Sehgal Foundation would start its work in India, she looked into the faces of women and was struck by what she saw in their eyes. She said, "There was this sense of total hopelessness. These people had nothing. I wondered how they could exist with so much missing, surrounded by dirt and filth, and not even having clean water to drink. A woman we spoke to said, 'India has forgotten us,' and it was true. India had forgotten these communities."

Not long after Sehgal Foundation work began in Mewat, Edda Sehgal saw those same eyes begin to light up as women and young girls were given the opportunity to learn a skill for the first time in their lives, something as simple as stitching cloth. "This was touching to us. These people were anxious to have opportunities. They liked what they were learning. We knew we couldn't do everything for everyone, but we were at least doing something constructive for some. We were excited, too, to see these young girls blossom."

After more than fifteen years, despite Sehgal Foundation's diverse and expanding work in hundreds of rural villages where incremental progress has been made, these communities remain underdeveloped, isolated, and still forgotten for the most part. "Inclusive growth" is a catchphrase that has not yet lived up to its promise.

The Sehgal Foundation team has learned that, while furthering the well-being of rural communities in India requires patience, the basic ingredients for transformation are already present even in the midst of formidable challenges. This is where hope lies. In order to tackle the generations-old local customs, ingrained myths, widespread illiteracy, and community indifference in a traditionally unequal society, rural citizens and their village-level institutions must be supported and strengthened with the knowledge, skills, and inspiration to take charge of their own destiny. Working alongside communities to achieve these ends is the key to accelerating development in rural India.

Together We Empower is intended as a historical touchstone for the Sehgal Foundation's team members and partners—past, present, and future—who are inspired to assist in empowering rural India. This chronicle is for employees, interns, volunteers, donors, partners, collaborators of every kind, students and teachers of development studies, newcomers to the field of development, anyone interested in corporate social responsibility, and those who may be planning to create their own development foundation.

According to Suri Sehgal, "Development is a path that, while often full of progress, never ends. These insights are offered so others can avoid our mistakes and build on our achievements. Sehgal Foundation will continue to learn as it grows, and will change as it learns."

CHAPTER 1

An Inspired Vision

Dr. Surinder (Suri) M. Sehgal and his wife, Mrs. Edda G. Sehgal, approached development with the belief that every person in the more than 640,000 rural communities across India deserves to have a secure, prosperous, and dignified life. The Sehgals were especially concerned about the millions of small farmers living on arid, rain-fed (rain-dependent) land, who had been bypassed in large part by the Green Revolution[2] and by modern agricultural practices. Those families who live in such impoverished and precarious conditions would be the primary focus of Sehgal Foundation work. Understanding that the exact nature of this work would evolve depending upon a complex combination of social, cultural, and economic factors, the Sehgals were primed for the challenge, open to the possibilities, and ready for hard work.

Suri and Edda Sehgal are American citizens, each of whom escaped dangerous circumstances as children in their countries of origin—Suri from the part of the Punjab in India that is now Pakistan, and Edda from the part of German Silesia[3] that is now Poland.

Suri's personal commitment to social responsibility, community empowerment, and gender equality was implanted early in his life.

---

2. The Green Revolution was a period that began in the mid-1960s with a huge increase in agricultural production that saved millions of people in developing countries from starvation due to the adoption of high-yielding crop varieties and improved farm technologies.
3. The often-divided province of Silesia was once part of the Kingdom of Prussia before becoming part of Germany. After World War II, the Potsdam Agreement divided the region again, designating that only a tiny part of Silesia would remain German. The majority of the region became part of Poland, and a small region became part of the Czech Republic.

When Suri was a child, his father was a follower and associate of Mahatma Gandhi and a community leader in the Indian National Congress. They worked hard for freedom from British rule in India. When the Sehgal family became refugees during the bloody Partition of India in 1947, Suri experienced poverty, hunger, and homelessness firsthand at age thirteen. While separated from his family and living in the streets of Delhi for a time, the young boy found comfort at the feet of Mahatma Gandhi who spoke each evening on the grounds of the Birla House[4] where he was living during the final months before he was assassinated. The great teacher's message in favor of unity and critical of injustice and inequality was deeply imbedded in Suri's mind.

Edda knew similar deprivation as a small child when she and her family became refugees from German Silesia toward the end of World War II and through the years that followed. The couple's common experiences as displaced people living in such compromised circumstances provided each of them with deep compassion for the poor and a strong desire to take an active part in helping those less fortunate.

After earning a PhD in plant genetics from Harvard University, and later a diploma in business management from Harvard Business School, Suri Sehgal became, over the course of his career, "a primary player in the development and worldwide dissemination of high-quality hybrid seed."[5] With Edda, he developed a successful seed business called Proagro Group, headquartered in New Delhi. Part of the corporate mission of Proagro Group, which consisted of four companies, was to improve the lives of the rural poor.

With the profitable sale of Proagro in 1998, the Sehgals used the bulk of the proceeds to establish a philanthropic foundation based in their hometown, Des Moines, Iowa,[6] and a public charitable trust in India the following year—S M Sehgal Foundation (Sehgal Foundation), based in Gurgaon, Haryana. Suri explained, "Undertaking an

---

4. The home of Mahatma Gandhi's benefactor, K. K. Birla.
5. *Maize Genetics and Breeding in the 20th Century*, ed. Peter Peterson and Angelo Bianchi, World Scientific Publishing Company, 1999.
6. Originally called the Sehgal Family Foundation, then simply Sehgal Foundation, the family's nonprofit endeavors in the US were pointed primarily toward India, but other modest efforts were carried out elsewhere in health, education, and conservation of natural resources. Each effort is in keeping with the family's shared and overarching goal of making a positive difference in the lives of others.

obligation to repay the many kindnesses we have received throughout our lives, my family and I established these foundations to put our personal resources to work to make a positive difference in the lives of others."

The choice of Gurgaon district for the Sehgal Foundation headquarters in India was a strategic decision. The location, about thirty-two kilometers southwest of New Delhi in the state of Haryana, was familiar because Proagro Group's operations for the North India Region were based there. Although Haryana is a relatively prosperous state, certain parts are home to some of the poorest of the poor in India, particularly in Mewat.

In contrast to the development occurring elsewhere in the Gurgaon district, time seemed to have stood still in the villages of Mewat. Despite being so close to New Delhi, Mewat was frequently left out of government programs intended to help the poor. The region's low literacy rate, high infant mortality, skewed gender ratio in favor of men, little availability of clean drinking water, widespread malnutrition, lack of healthcare, erratic electric power, and extremely limited natural resources identified Mewat as an area of profound and urgent need. However, attempts by others to develop the region had been entirely fruitless. If Sehgal Foundation could demonstrate success in as difficult and deprived a place as Mewat, the programs could be expected to perform well in other underdeveloped regions.

Sehgal Foundation operations in Gurgaon began in a rented one-story house with offices in the front and two guest rooms in the back. Before long, a move was made to a rented two-story house with more space. The first floor was used for offices, and the second floor served as a guest facility. The furnishings were Spartan, but comfortable. Suri and Edda stayed there when in India.

With the primary office location close to the villages being served, the foundation team could more easily monitor the progress of grassroots projects and make sure deliverables were achieved. Core staff, external experts, as well as international visitors found the location accessible, which was important as global partnerships were further developed.

From day one of the creation of the foundation, the Sehgals were convinced that poverty in rural India was related to large family sizes and the powerless position of women. Rural women had no control over any aspect of their reproductive lives and no easy access to information about reproductive health issues. They had primary responsibility for providing food and water, childcare, and family health—yet they were isolated at home and working in the fields. Women made up the majority of the agricultural workforce in India; however, the manual labor done for their families was not compensated. Discouraged from seeking education, and often prevented from acquiring assets or influence, women continued to have no decision-making power within their families, or with regard to family finances or farming practices. Economically, they were entirely dependent upon their husbands or other male family members.

Growing up with six sisters, Suri saw up close how women had no voice even in well-educated Indian families. His father was so concerned about the public good that his own family was often neglected. Suri noticed how his mother and sisters carried out all the day-to-day responsibilities involved in running their large household.

"Our family was relatively progressive, but still," Suri recalled, "when it came to marriage, education, or selecting a spouse, boys were given preference in all things. A son-in-law was on a pedestal; a daughter-in-law had no recognition. If my sisters had been given the same opportunities I was given, I know they would have done just as well."

Even though the Indian constitution grants equal rights to men and women, keeping women subservient is deeply embedded in the centuries-old patriarchal traditions of the culture. A customary wedding blessing still heard is, "May you be the mother of a hundred sons."

A strong promoter of empowerment for women, Edda Sehgal took a special interest in education for girls and improving healthcare and sanitation conditions in the villages of Mewat. Sehgal Foundation would endeavor to play a key role in empowering women to have a voice in their families and in their communities.

Other contemporary thinkers and influencers shared the views the Sehgals brought to their philanthropic enterprise. United Nations Secretary General Kofi Annan had asserted, "Gender equality is more than a goal in itself. It is a precondition for meeting the challenge of reducing poverty, promoting sustainable development, and building good governance."

Suri and Edda Sehgal's vision for their foundation in India was clear. They wanted their NGO (nongovernmental organization, non-profit) to be effective, credible, transparent, and "built to last." Sehgal Foundation had to be well managed, with the ability to evolve, in order to ensure the enduring impact of productive work in perpetuity.

Their initial plan was for the foundation to serve as a "donor" organization. Rather than developing new programs to confront such deeply entrenched issues, they would provide funds to other NGOs already doing good work. The first projects sought would be in the areas of agricultural productivity and family stabilization. By requiring clearly defined goals, deliverables, and timelines from their NGO partners, the Sehgals hoped to achieve quantifiable results. Projects would be funded and evaluated in six-month intervals, and discontinued if they didn't work out as expected or were not sustainable.

The founders operated with the strong belief that sustainability of a project can only be achieved if driven by community participants, a concept key to continuing development, particularly in light of limited funds. Transferring a concept they knew well in business, the Sehgals understood that just as a company cannot survive without profits, a philanthropic foundation cannot thrive without the equivalent—sustainable results. The deliverables are not the same, but measurable results are required in both situations. Their vision for helping was not based solely on charitable giving, but focused instead on lending a hand to those who would take an active part in their own empowerment.

The first task was to assemble a capable working team to oversee operations. In choosing the initial core staff for the fledgling organization, the Sehgals' top priority was to hire trustworthy individuals. The people in charge would be relied upon for all facets of the foundation on-site.

The first executive director was Arvind Bahl, who had also worked for ten years with the Sehgals as an administrative director at Proagro. Bahl had coordinated major projects during those years and proven his trustworthiness. The rest of the original team included social scientists qualified to monitor the effectiveness of funded initiatives. These people would conduct the search for appropriate projects and partners.

Bahl recruited B. R. Poonia, a skilled sociologist who had worked for more than twenty years with organizations committed to fighting poverty, including CARE India and Trees for Life. Poonia had substantial experience in the rural sector. Originally from a village in Rajasthan, which was similar to those communities with the greatest development needs, he brought the experience and insight to observe programs in action and evaluate how well they worked.

Anjali Makhija was the next team member hired. Her master's-level training in social science and seven years working in organizations with education programs in reproductive and child health made her another ideal fit for monitoring the effectiveness of programs and services, especially those designed for women and girls. Her skill at grassroots team building would be put to use when the time came to develop a field team. Like Poonia, Makhija spoke three languages, including the local dialect in the villages of Mewat where funded initiatives would take place.

This core group, with continuous guidance and participation from Suri and Edda Sehgal, began the process of establishing the foundation's day-to-day operations. They helped define the goals and objectives, took care of obtaining the required approvals and paperwork, and set up appropriate recordkeeping so they could begin soliciting projects. They interviewed representatives of NGOs with similar goals and interests.

Each step in the start-up process was fraught with complications. To begin giving away foreign currency funds, or even to accept donations from others, entailed obtaining approvals and other compliance measures required by India's Foreign Contribution Regulation Act. The foundation was given temporary approval status to take on short-term projects with NGOs in India. However, to obtain approval from India's Ministry of Home Affairs to conduct more substantive work took a lot more time and effort.

The core team reviewed written proposals from NGOs interested in long-term projects in the region. This process included a great deal of waiting. The small foundation team was anxious to take a more active role in countering the abject poverty and pitiable living conditions they found each day in the villages of Mewat.

Lacking even the most basic amenities, the people in Mewat were mired in resignation and despair, and largely disconnected from the outside world. The sense of urgency the Sehgals felt about helping these people, whose circumstances were so dire, was not reflected in any way by the slow-moving bureaucracy. They couldn't help but wonder, "Does it have to be this way?"

The Sehgals felt great respect for the Mewati people's distinctive tribal identity, which had been preserved over many centuries. The majority of the people in Mewat are Meo Muslims, a unique ethnic blend of two major religious and cultural groups. These are Muslim people whose ethnic roots are in Hinduism. The two groups share some of the same caste names. Many Meos follow the traditions of the Pal and Gotra tribal cultures of Hindu Kshatriyas. Hindus and Muslims in Mewat have a long history of harmony and unity, fighting side by side against invaders. They stood together during the 1857 uprising against the British and, in the past, venerated many of the same pilgrimage centers. They still celebrate each other's religious festivals together, though that is not as common as it once was.

Suri and Edda spent several weeks in India during the first year, participating in strategic planning sessions while the foundation goals were defined and approvals came through. Though their home base remained in the United States, and business obligations took them to other countries around the globe, the Sehgals traveled to India each year after that for at least a month or so in the spring and again in the fall to meet with the foundation team and visit people in the villages. Suri and Edda remained in regular close contact with the team and were actively involved in the strategic development and growth of the organization.

Once the required approvals were obtained from the Ministry of Home Affairs, the foundation team was finally able to begin implementation of efforts to strengthen community-led development initiatives to achieve positive social, economic, and environmental changes across rural India.

The team sought potential partners to help fund projects related to developing sustainable agriculture and to address issues of family stability and size. But this undertaking was not as easy as hoped. The selection process took much longer than expected. Unlike southern

India where they found many NGOs doing excellent work, finding credible NGOs in the north was more difficult at that time. Many were businesses lacking any form of transparency. Though the search continued for organizations that could demonstrate their adherence to principles of accountability in their daily operations, the reality became apparent: a large number of NGOs operated with varying levels of deceit. NGOs with government funds earmarked for rural development typically siphoned away the money before it ever reached the intended beneficiaries. Financial mismanagement, bribery, and influence peddling were commonplace in bureaucratic institutions all across India.[7] The rampant corruption that frustrated Mahatma Gandhi in the 1930s was still widespread seventy years later—and continued to cripple the poor. With more than three million NGOs in the country, identifying potentially credible partner organizations was a challenging task.

Continuing their search, the foundation team remained committed to the fundamental principles of honesty, integrity, transparency, and professionalism in its operations. No bribes would be offered or taken under any circumstances. The team fully adhered to and modeled these principles to demonstrate to other philanthropic organizations that it was possible to work honestly, in spite of the highly corrupt outside environment. The foundation team was determined to raise the benchmarks of the development sector in India in terms of expectations and accomplishments. The catchphrase referred to at the time was *Commit Less and Deliver More.* Each person on the team was compelled to demonstrate behaviors at work and in their lives that would influence others positively.

The Sehgals had always found, in business and otherwise, that in addition to strong professional ethics and values, respect for people was a key precept. In practice, certain basic behaviors always bore fruit: treat people with utmost respect; always give credit to people for their contribution, big or small; be fair; strive to create a win-win situation for everyone involved; and be helpful to others whenever possible.

They believed that with well-treated talented people, a company can be assured of good products, which will result in profits—each

---

7. Sal Gentile, "Fighting corruption in India one 'zero rupee' at a time," *The Daily Need*, October 22, 2010. See http://www.pbs.org/wnet/need-to-know/the-daily-need/fighting-corruption-in-india-one-zero-rupee-at-a-time/4405/.

triggering the next. The Sehgals considered these three "p's"—people, products, and profits—a staple in development as well. In this case, the "products" were the programs, and the "profits" would be the positive impact. Putting people first in all situations, Suri and Edda had seen how inspired and productive any team could be when appreciated and given a voice in decision making. Employees enjoyed the freedom of doing their work without threat of shame or harassment for any missteps. Every "mistake" was seen as an opportunity to learn. That was a key factor in promoting a sense of belonging among the staff.

In business, the Sehgals had experienced the power and enthusiasm of those who came together for a common mission. The same potent methodology was now applied to the foundation's approach to helping the rural poor in India. Every person in the equation, every employee, volunteer, donor, as well as each recipient of assistance from the foundation, would be a partner, a member of the team. Teamwork, an underpinning of Sehgal Foundation from its inception, is a steadfast keystone that has continued to motivate people and sustain the organization over time.

The foundation team's first projects addressed two current realities in rural India: large families[8] (the average family size was 7.5 in Mewat at the time) and poor agricultural productivity. The team was careful in screening and choosing NGO partners. Formal agreements clarified expectations and included each project's goals, expected deliverables, and projected timelines. The budget included details on how much money to pay the people implementing the programs in the field. The foundation's core team worked with field trainers from NGO partners who were carrying out programs in more than thirty villages. The team's role was to ensure that training in the community encompassed the intentions of the initiatives.

Some of the first foundation-funded programs focused on empowering young women, such as a program for adolescent girls ages eleven to nineteen, most of whom had never had the opportunity to attend school. Young women were given the chance to learn how to sew, a skill that could produce income. The value of literacy was demonstrated

8. Inclusive of issues related to the role of women.

immediately when the girls did not recognize numbers or letters needed to measure cloth. Female literacy in Mewat was only 4.5 percent, so teaching basic reading and math became essential program components.

Other programs addressed hygiene, care of newborns, and the concept of life goals. A female physician was added to the foundation team to coach and train NGO staff trainers on childcare and reproductive health.

To begin to address the needs of poor farmers, the foundation team sought out global partnership opportunities. Sehgal Foundation provided start-up funding to the Institute of Plant Biotechnology Outreach[9] at the University of Ghent, in Belgium, to create new programs on stress tolerance technologies for crops. The ongoing initiative was led by Dr. Marc Van Montagu, a University of Ghent professor emeritus with whom Suri Sehgal had worked on two corporate boards. Van Montagu appreciated the Sehgals' interest in the complex issues involved in the relationship between subsistence farming and women's reproductive health in India. When a water buffalo and a half acre of land were the only assets a poor rural family had, the family might only be able to eat what they could produce themselves. Improved productivity and more nutritious crop foods would improve the health of the entire family.

In 2001 Suri Sehgal met with Dr. William D. Dar, the director of International Crops Research Institute for the Semi-Arid Tropics (ICRISAT).[10] Based outside of Hyderabad, Andhra Pradesh, ICRISAT was already recognized globally as the most important international research institute working on neglected "orphan" crops, often called "nutri-cereals," including sorghum and millet, for resource-poor farmers in India and other arid and semiarid regions around the world. India's farmers in general had already benefited handsomely from ICRISAT's long presence in the country. The rapid growth of the seed industry in India can be attributed greatly to the availability of elite germplasm (improved seed stocks) bred by ICRISAT.

---

9. Institute of Plant Biotechnology Outreach promotes and assists research programs in fields important to less developed regions, such as nutritional enhancement, conservation and sustainable use of biodiversity for healthcare, tolerance of indigenous plants to abiotic stresses, and transformation of orphan crops. Dr. Sehgal continues to serve on the institute's steering committee. https://www.ugent.be/we/genetics/ipbo/en/aboutus/teamipbo.
10. See http://www.icrisat.org/.

During the meeting between Dr. Sehgal and Dr. Dar, the two scientists reached an agreement that Sehgal Foundation would provide ICRISAT with a multimillion-dollar endowment—a grant for the development of elite (improved) sorghum and millet germplasm. Mewat farm families would also be beneficiaries of this important work in the form of greater crop productivity, more nutritious food, and improved health.

Sehgal Foundation was the first NGO to carry out research work at ICRISAT. As part of this arrangement, the foundation set up an office at ICRISAT and rented some of their land, where foundation researchers conducted studies on maize (corn), a crop not in ICRISAT's mandate. Though corn was not being grown in Mewat, farmers in the southern and eastern states in India would benefit from this work.

Now the Sehgal Foundation had teams working in two locations—the original team working in the villages of Mewat, and a small team of research scientists in Hyderabad. Hyderabad was more than 1,500 kilometers from the foundation's main headquarters in Gurgaon—about a twenty-five-hour train journey or a two-hour flight. The teams maintained contact via telephone and Internet.

When geneticist Dr. M. D. Gupta joined Sehgal Foundation in early 2002, he initiated a corn-breeding program. Germplasm obtained from worldwide sources, and already in the public domain, was checked for its purity and uniformity and multiplied for distribution. A "field day" was held in autumn at the peak of the harvest, and breeders were invited from the public, nonprofit, and private sectors. About sixty breeders and scientists attended to see the field where each row was planted with a different type of seed. Each attendee received a booklet describing the genetic material in each row so they could make selections. Seed samples were available free of charge. The program flourished and field days continued to be held annually.[11] "Mega" field days were held periodically that included at least one hundred participating scientists.

---

11. Thousands of germplasm samples continue to be distributed free of charge for use in breeding programs in public, nonprofit, and private sectors. Dr. Gupta remained as technical director for five years, and then continued on as honorary technical advisor to Sehgal Foundation.

Back in Mewat, a disturbing realization came from listening more carefully to the villagers themselves. A disparity was revealed between the priorities of Sehgal Foundation and the priorities of the people in Mewat. Villagers expressed far more urgent needs than the family planning and agriculture improvement issues addressed by the foundation's narrow focus. Their greater needs were for healthcare interventions and clean drinking water.

While visiting the village of Rangala Rajpur in September 2001, Dr. Sehgal saw firsthand the deplorable water scarcity so prevalent in the region. The semiarid villages of Mewat averaged less than 600 millimeters of rain a year, which all came in a few weeks during the monsoon season between June and September. Over-extraction of water from aquifers and insufficient recharge had caused an ever-increasing depth of groundwater. The lifeline to "sweet" (drinkable) water was further threatened by increasing salinity that had fouled water in 78 percent of the area. Salinity deteriorates the soil quality and limits the choices of crops for farmers. The greater the salinity, the less likely it is for plants to extract water from the soil. High levels of salt destroy soil health and lead to erosion. As groundwater becomes more and more brackish, conditions are increasingly desperate for people, plants, and animals in the region.

For families living in this environment that could not afford to purchase water from tankers (large trucks that deliver potable water), women and girls had to make multiple trips of three or four kilometers each day to bring home enough water for domestic use. This obligation resulted in many young girls being unable to attend school at all. Water-harvesting measures could save women from the daily drudgery of fetching water from long distances and directly help increase agricultural productivity in this arid zone.

Assisting communities with water management fit perfectly with the foundation's strategies on agriculture and on easing the burdens endured by women and girls. Geography played a large part in their predicament. The subtropical region of Mewat is bordered by the Aravalli Range, the hill system that runs through the state. Monsoon rains typically flush freshwater down from the hills. The runoff flows fast from the high ground down over the low-lying areas, where it often mixes with and becomes contaminated by saline groundwater. However, because the geologic formations in the Aravalli hills are very porous and permeable, water in the hills is absorbed quickly if its flow rate is sufficiently slowed. By building a check dam as part of an overall water-augmentation system in the watershed area in Rangala Rajpur, the rainwater runoff would be captured in a large storage area. Rather than flowing into the saline areas, freshwater would instead percolate down to recharge the depleted aquifer, and also refill dry wells.

While Suri Sehgal briefly considered building the dam for the community, he instead recalled the foundation's imperative to help others help themselves, saying, "If we create the dam for them, we will only be creating dependency." So instead, the foundation presented an idea for the community to contribute 25 percent of the cost of this endeavor.

The people of Rangala Rajpur agreed immediately. A pact was made. The community would cover the cost of materials for the final water spillover portion of the dam, a cement and concrete structure to allow the overflow water to be channeled into ponds or wells. The foundation would fund and carry out the first three-quarters of the water-augmentation plan, which entailed creating a 1.5-kilometer earthen embankment for the dam. Construction of the embankment began immediately.

Building a check dam water-harvesting structure in Rangala Rajpur was the first project begun by Sehgal Foundation without collaborating with any other NGO. Some other projects would eventually run parallel with programs carried out by the foundation's NGO partners as well. As the Rangala Rajpur project moved along, the team initiated some small-scale, focused pilot projects in several other villages. They dug and deepened wells; held agricultural extension programs and trainings; conducted education sessions on health issues, such as HIV/AIDS, tuberculosis, immunizations, and menstrual hygiene; and sponsored youth recreational activities.

A caveat imposed on the Sehgal Foundation team, and reinforced by Suri Sehgal at every opportunity, was that any small-scale projects be evaluated based on cost, deliverables, and impact. The team used the catchphrase *Small Interventions, Big Impact* to reflect their preference for small "fulcrum-like" projects with the community that made a big difference, the same way a small rudder changes the direction of a ship.

Though Sehgal Foundation was still assisting communities indirectly for the most part as a donor organization supporting the activities of others, Suri and Edda Sehgal paid careful attention to a larger development picture in making targeted donations from Sehgal Foundation. Contributions were made on a holistic scale as the foundation established partnerships with a growing network of visionary organizations reclaiming the agriculture and ecology resources of India, and assisting in rural development, crop improvement, biodiversity projects, and conservation efforts.

Seed money was provided for the development of the Dharma Vana Arboretum on the outskirts of Hyderabad, where endangered species of trees and plants of the Deccan Plateau were being collected and preserved. The arboretum, when completed, would also serve as an ecotourism site, welcoming everyone from local schoolchildren to international visitors.

A large grant went to Ashoka Trust for Research in Ecology and the Environment (ATREE), based in Bangalore, Karnataka. ATREE is actively involved in conservation of biodiversity, protection of the environment, and sustainable use of natural resources in the Western Ghats and Eastern Himalayas. ATREE is building a critical body of knowledge about India's ecosystems.

Sehgal Foundation in the United States provided funding to establish the William L. Brown Center at the Missouri Botanical Garden in St. Louis, Missouri. Named in honor of Suri Sehgal's mentor and friend, plant geneticist Dr. Bill Brown, the center's mission is to "study, characterize, and conserve useful plants and associated traditional knowledge for a sustainable future."

Trees for Life International (TFL), based in Wichita, Kansas, received a large donation to support its Global Circle of Knowledge program. TFL had been active in India since the early 1970s in education and in promoting tree plantings.

Suri Sehgal reached out to other nonprofit organizations and individuals in the United States who were already doing work in India or were interested in alleviating poverty in India. Recognizing that there were many other people in the United States who were originally from India, he cofounded the India Development Coalition of America as a platform for the exchange of ideas among like-minded Indian-Americans interested in sustainable development in India.[12]

The foundation team in Gurgaon was drawn more and more toward projects and programs they could be directly involved in implementing. As they visited the Mewat villages to monitor foundation-funded projects carried out by partner NGOs, they became familiar with NGO field teams as well as the intended beneficiaries. The foundation team wondered why meaningful results were not forthcoming. They couldn't help but think that they could utilize resources more effectively and accomplish more if they could directly carry out the programs themselves.

Sociologist Anjali Makhija initiated an experimental family life education project that focused on health and hygiene for families, and reproductive health for women. Her small pilot project yielded more noticeable participation and productive results than larger programs with similar goals being provided by the foundation's NGO partners. Field staff from other NGOs did their best, but they were sometimes thwarted by their own organizations from doing the agreed-upon work or they only paid for a portion of the work. As it turned out, some funded organizations were not as transparent as the foundation team had hoped.

The Sehgal Foundation team noted that other NGOs typically thought in terms of short-term projects rather than long-term or more comprehensive strategies. Giving away money to support others carrying out narrowly defined grassroots projects held less and less appeal. The team wanted room to define their own strategies and evolve more as an organization. They were frustrated with the lack of measurable progress and their limited reach. The foundation's highly skilled staff was like a team of horses being held back and not allowed to run.

The time came for the foundation team to consider a shift in strategies. With wholesome fundamentals and always open to continuous improvement, the Sehgal Foundation team was primed and ready to begin working directly with communities in Mewat to put programs

12. See http://idc-america.org/.

into action that would demonstrate value and provide evidence of impact. The way to accomplish this strategic shift was to bring together the best and most committed experts on development and consider the possibilities. The Sehgals had always been entrepreneurial—thinking big but being realistic, carefully balancing risk with opportunity, thinking long term but never neglecting the short term. Suri Sehgal was known for taking a good look at the big picture before making any decision. By the middle of 2002, the big picture was becoming clearer.

CHAPTER 2

Underpromise and Overdeliver

The people of Mewat had plenty of experience with individuals and organizations showing up and promising great things, but delivering very little. People came often over the years with religious or political agendas, or with an offer to "help" them in some way. Known to be suspicious and not particularly welcoming to more strangers making familiar promises, the people of Mewat were deeply skeptical. The government and some NGOs had labeled Mewat "development resistant" and concluded that even trying to educate Meo people was a "waste of time."

The foundation team gathered development documentation of this sort from government sources and other groups that previously attempted to address poverty in the Mewat region. At best, earlier programs were ineffective; at worst, they were exploitative. Reports provided long lists of recommendations about what needed to be done in Mewat, but no ideas were offered on how to actually achieve the desired results. These details were reviewed and studied carefully by Sehgal Foundation's new executive director, Rajat (Jay) Sehgal, through the fall of 2002 as the foundation team gathered together for brainstorming sessions to discuss the shift in the organization's strategy.

Jay Sehgal, nephew of the founders, had been promoted to the role upon the retirement of Arvind Bahl. Jay had proven his skills and leadership acumen while working for more than a decade at Proagro. He had worked at the foundation for about a year, serving as an information technology consultant. Jay had no concrete experience or training in rural work, but he took to his new role with energy and enthusiasm, anxious to "get his hands dirty."

Jay spent several months going into the villages each day with members of the foundation team to meet local people, hoping to get a feel for their needs and interests. By now, the staff included a few people hired from local villages who served as a field team.

Though he was not new to issues of poverty, Jay felt like the new kid on the block during those visits. He had visited similar villages when he was a child and had worked in several local villages during his years at Proagro. The poverty and filth were not unfamiliar to him. But now he approached the circumstances he witnessed with far more probing questions and concerns as he tried to figure out what exactly was being accomplished by partnerships the foundation had with different NGOs working in Mewat. He was there to learn. The field team provided valuable coaching and offered insight into the character of the region.

The foundation team walked from house to house, determined to behave respectfully in every possible way with the people of Mewat. Sociologist B. R. Poonia instructed Jay in advance, "If you are offered water, you drink it. You may suffer later with gastric distress, but you must remember: if you refuse what these people offer, it is the same as refusing them."

Jay recognized the enclosed feel of the village environment. The streets were narrow. A brick path of sorts, about five feet wide, circled a cluster of homes and marked the boundary of each village or hamlet. Trash-littered paths inside the periphery branched off to different houses. Care was taken to avoid stepping in muddy wastewater. The team made their way around the occasional cow or buffalo tied to a post in front of a house, or a child squatting to defecate in the path.

Most of the homes were not particularly well built. Some were made of mud with a thatched roof and no windows. Typically a mud stove stood in the corner of the main living space, and all four walls were lined with *charpois*. These cot-like beds, also called *manja*, had four wooden legs and a sleeping surface made of woven hemp or jute ropes. Some houses had adjoining outdoor spaces, like a small room with low walls, for the family buffalo, with straw stored there as well. Homes often had a small paved veranda in front. The people sometimes brought charpois or plastic chairs outside for visitors to sit.

Jay Sehgal introduced himself only as Jay and left most verbal exchanges to the rest of the team. If invited inside a home, the team accepted any courtesies graciously. If the villagers sat down on the floor, so did the team. Whether the meetings with families were held inside, or outside on the veranda, conversations were only with the men. Gestures of hospitality were extended by the male head of the family. Women did not speak in mixed company. The women on the team, including the physician, usually moved a few feet away to speak quietly with female family members.

Team members typically drank anything they were offered in the villages, whether it was water, tea, or *chaas* (a savory yogurt-based drink), and listened carefully to whatever the villagers shared with them. Jay never experienced ill effects from anything he was given.

Visits were cordial; the people were hospitable. Jay was a little surprised to find the people so accommodating, in light of hearing how "closed" villagers might be to outsiders. He said, "The people smiled and welcomed us."

Conversations with villagers were casual efforts to get to know people. Visiting team members asked simple questions, such as, "How many children do you have?"

In Ghaghas, the first village Jay visited with the field team, only two of the 300 households had latrines. People used the surrounding fields as open-air toilets; children defecated anywhere. The village schools were nearly deserted. Every family talked about their desperate need for water. In addition to scarce drinking water, there was often no water for bathing, cooking, or sanitation purposes. Lack of clean water was a serious health issue as well, because so many infectious diseases in India are waterborne. Conversations between the women villagers, sociologist Anjali Makhija, and the female physician were often about the care of newborns, how to have safe deliveries, or how to help a sick child.

The more Jay saw and heard, the more he understood the dissatisfaction shared by the field team at what they considered insufficient progress in providing real help to the villagers. The need was enormous. He agreed with his colleagues, saying, "We've got to do more."

While visiting with partner NGOs about initiatives the foundation funded in Mewat, NGO staff members were usually anxious to impress foundation representatives with the work being done. The team listened to their exaggerated summaries of successful interventions with young people. There was little observable evidence of the achievements claimed.

The frustration felt by the entire foundation team was verbalized by Anjali Makhija when she said, "We can do this better ourselves!"

That sentiment grew with each subsequent meeting. What the partner NGOs were doing in the villages did not correspond to the business credo espoused by the Sehgals, which they also applied to development: always underpromise and overdeliver. What the team observed in Mewat was the other way around. There was plenty of *over*promising and *under*delivering.

All these issues, learnings, and frustrations were discussed in depth during the brainstorming sessions with the full staff. Lively conversations were about how they could have a greater impact in Mewat if Sehgal Foundation itself would directly implement all programs. The team was challenged and invited to think big and imagine the possibilities. If the foundation accepted responsibility for all direct programming, what was the area of greatest need? What might the selected programs look like? Which issues would be addressed first? Would the villagers be motivated to contribute to and participate in projects of partnership with the foundation? How would the team ensure that a real difference was being made with the initiatives attempted?

The team discussed what they had already observed from several small-scale pilot programs they tried: in each case the needs were so great, they appeared to be endless. How would they choose which initiatives were most important?

To use the resources of Sehgal Foundation to the greatest effect without being spread too thinly, Suri Sehgal stressed that the best strategy was to focus on programs with the greatest demand from the community—those that would have the greatest impact, and where significant accomplishments could be made. Once success was achieved in any given area, the next step should be taken to build on that success. Hence another catchphrase was born: *Success Builds Success*. A crucial ingredient to any true success would be an investment in the outcome on the part of the people in the communities of Mewat.

Ongoing struggles had developed with the check dam water-harvesting project begun in Rangala Rajpur in 2001 that were a cogent reminder of the need for a tangible commitment from individual communities for any project carried out with them. The effort had stalled, but the project provided the foundation team with useful insight into the minds of village leaders and brought to light some types of complications that could derail a development initiative.

An important lesson for the team was that the villagers' enthusiastic agreement to take part in a project was not the same as having the means or intent to actually follow through. Sociologist B. R. Poonia and the project implementation team had continued over weeks and months to ask the community to fulfill its part of the bargain. But the rainy season came and went, and the work wasn't completed. Village leaders said they were serious about wanting to carry out their part of the agreement, but they had no money. Maintaining the foundation's position that the community must contribute, the team suggested that community leaders approach the local Member of Parliament (MP) to issue funds for the project from the Local Area Development Fund. Under the Member of Parliament Local Area Development Scheme (MPLADS), a member of parliament could suggest that the district collector release funds, in specific amounts under specific guidelines, on behalf of the constituency for work to be done.[13]

Sehgal Foundation staff mediated a meeting between the MP and the community leaders. The MP sanctioned the required funds, but the money was not released. Bureaucratic hurdles and complications kept the project in limbo for the time being.

A complex water-augmentation project proposed the same year in Ghaghas was handled differently. That project and all future projects with expenditures would require communities to follow through with their portion of a project *before* the foundation would start work on the greater portion. The community's commitment had to be tangible. As strategy discussions continued, the team kept these learnings in mind while thoroughly considering any program choice.

---

13. See http://mplads.nic.in/.

Water management would be a key program. Water management was an obvious need in every village—every visit to every community included a conversation about the need for water. Water scarcity in the region had become much worse in recent decades due to over-exploitation of the groundwater, ecological degradation, and the unmanaged water supply. Collection, conservation, storage, the equitable distribution of water, and the link between drinking water and health were discussed at great length. The entire region needed rainwater-harvesting systems, groundwater recharging, more check dams and ponds, ecological regeneration, resource planning, and the all-important strategies for engaging the community in the responsible management of their water supply in the first place.

Improving agriculture and farming practices held the most promise for an income-enhancement program in Mewat district. Agriculture was the main form of income for 58 percent of the population. People in Mewat had been living the same way and planting their crops the same way for centuries. The only asset for most of these rural villagers was their land, and the usual plot size was very small.[14] Two-thirds of the farms had no groundwater for irrigation and few sources of underground sweet water. The brackish water in most areas was not fit for irrigating the main crops that could be grown in the region. The bordering Aravalli hills run parallel to the monsoon winds, ensuring that rainfall is always sparse. Farmers without any other source of irrigation could be wiped out financially in a year if there was little or no rain, and few job opportunities existed elsewhere in the area to help supplement their income.

An income-enhancement program would have a concrete goal of raising farmers' income levels by a specific percentage within a defined time frame. Objectives included improving farmers' business skills, introducing higher-value crops, and using farming practices to increase crop productivity and diversification. To achieve the defined target, the foundation team facilitated start-up activities to develop linkages

---

14. Per the Census of India 2011, the total population of Mewat was 1,089,263, of which 88 percent was rural. Forty percent of households were landless, 40 percent owned less than 2.5 acres, 8 percent owned 2.5 to five acres, and 12 percent owned five to twenty-five acres. There were no large landowners.

between farmers and markets to add to farmers' share of the retail price for their produce. Early efforts to form a Fruit and Vegetable Growers Association in the village of Ghaghas already looked promising. Income-enhancement possibilities would be strengthened by the promotion of environmentally sound and sustainable farming practices.

No other NGOs were working on issues of agricultural development or water management in Mewat. Sehgal Foundation had a perfect opportunity to make a difference in areas of its greatest expertise as well as the communities' greatest need.

Since government was (and still is) the largest delivery system for healthcare and education in the country, Sehgal Foundation would act only in the role of catalyst for the promotion, awareness, and access of services that already existed in those areas, and occasionally would fill gaps at the village level when possible. The foundation team would help create linkages to curative care and mobilize local communities to seek out health services they were entitled to use. An education program in rural health could be designed to promote preventive care, with information on good nutrition, hygiene, and safe health practices.

Similarly, in education, the foundation team would provide assistance to government schools in the form of small interventions to help facilitate student enrollment, and the retention of girl students in particular. Though the team agreed that creating awareness about the relationship between having a large family and not having enough food and water would be a valuable deliverable, the idea of encouraging young girls to postpone marriage, delay childbirth, and have fewer children had been quashed rapidly. Such topics remained taboo in the predominantly conservative Muslim community. In addition, adolescent girls had no choices or power in their own families. They could only do what their parents allowed. None of the parents in Mewat wanted their daughters learning about birth control or other "sex" education topics.

The team suggested addressing the barriers with this issue in more indirect ways as part of a family life education program similar to projects the field team had already been experimenting with alongside NGO partnerships. The program could include sessions with parents and community elders that demonstrated the connection between large family size and poverty, during a comprehensive discussion about the costs, risks, and benefits associated with family size.

In these forums, the consent of elders would be sought for the participation of girls in programs that taught useful skills. Sewing and tailoring centers, similar to those already created in partnership with NGOs, could serve as a platform for multiple purposes, becoming expanded forums for empowering young women and building their self-confidence and communication skills.

Each program that was proposed and selected had to be created with sustainability in mind in order to make the most impact. These were seen as opportunities to create viable models with potential for a wide reach across India.

Having decided on four possible programs (water, income, health, and education), the team discussed how to narrow the number of villages being served at one time, from thirty or more at that time, to only four. A limited number of programs in a limited number of villages sounded sensible. Criteria for choosing the four villages to work with were discussed in detail. The method for the selection of four villages had to address several factors the team considered essential for the maximum success potential.

The most important criterion for selection was that villages had active *panchayati raj* (local government) bodies with an honest and pro-development *sarpanch*, the elected head (similar to a mayor) of the *panchayat* (village council), and elders and leaders who were favorable to development. Many panchayats were barely functional, and some were resistant to any type of change. The field team visited dozens of villages while monitoring the family life programs. They had worked directly in a few villages and already had some ideas about which villages might be more interested in partnering with the foundation.

Accessibility was the next criterion in the village selections. The communities chosen had to be reachable on navigable roads by Jeep or motorcycle, so the foundation team working within the community would not be hampered by distance or access barriers. The team tried to think of every possible advantage to ensure the greatest chance for fruitful interactions with villagers.

A third factor was sweet groundwater availability, or the potential for building more check dams to slow monsoon rainwater flowing down the Aravalli slopes and direct it to areas at the bottom of the hills, where it could percolate into the ground to recharge the aquifers. Only sixty-three of the more than 500 villages that were part of Mewat at that time had sweet groundwater.[15] The sweet water in those villages was being depleted rapidly because the adjoining villages with saline groundwater needed it as well.

To address the over-exploitation of the sweet water, Sehgal Foundation adopted an approach whereby the limited sweet-water pockets located in the foothills would be recharged by slowing runoff from large catchment areas higher in the hills and directing it to sweet-water pockets. This would check (slow or stop) the depletion of sweet-water pockets and, at the same time, check the recharging of saline groundwater that caused salinity encroachment over sweet-water areas. The four villages chosen had to be located close to where water-augmentation systems could be constructed in watershed areas of the Aravalli hills.

Though some difficulties had occurred with the first two check dam water-harvesting projects, this technology was essential for the future of Mewat. Sehgal Foundation would not allow anything to stop progress in that direction.

Population size was the final factor in the choice of communities. Villages in Mewat ranged from a few hundred to more than 10,000 people. Trying to work in a village of 10,000 sounded unmanageable. For real impact to be possible, the team agreed on a midsize number. Villages with about 3,000 people sounded reasonable.

Four possible villages that met the identified criteria were suggested: Agon, Dhaula, Ghaghas, and Goela. Each had three or four neighboring villages or hamlets that could benefit as well from their proximity to the chosen villages. The goal of this concept was to create a cluster of up to twenty villages with a community center close enough to each village to be used as a convenient meeting place.

Now that specific programs and village partners were being discussed, more expert opinions were needed. Plans were made to bring together Sehgal Foundation staff from both Gurgaon and Hyderabad to

---

15. Prior to 2005 Mewat district included 512 villages. Some villages were transferred to nearby districts when Mewat was formally made the twentieth district of the state of Haryana, comprised of 431 villages.

meet with key representatives from prominent nonprofits doing credible development work in rural India. The goal was to present the foundation team's intention to change development strategies, and find out if other specialists and stakeholders in development would endorse the ideas that came out of the team's brainstorming sessions.

The gathering was held in November 2002 in a conference room at the India International Center in Delhi. About half of the twenty attendees were from Sehgal Foundation, including Suri and Edda Sehgal, staff from Gurgaon and Hyderabad, and a consultant hired to mobilize resources in the United States. The rest of the attendees were development industry representatives knowledgeable in the areas of information technology (IT), water management, agriculture, education, and rural health.

Excitement could be felt as participants were energized by fresh ideas and new possibilities over the two-day event. The first day began with Suri Sehgal presenting a review of what Sehgal Foundation had been doing since 1999. A frank discussion included the obstacles and hurdles the team had faced and the important learnings thus far. A diagram displayed connections between the key issues to be addressed by four proposed programs. Illustrating the complex combination of social, cultural, and economic factors, Suri identified the proposed new model as "Integrated Sustainable Village Development."

Many examples were cited to show how key issues were intertwined. Water scarcity in a village meant that girls missed out on education because girls had to stay home and help their mothers fetch water or care for younger siblings while their mothers sought water. With no water in the schools, those children who were able to go to school had to go home by the middle of the day to get a drink of water. They rarely returned. Daily sanitation and wastewater issues at school or at home were an ongoing health threat since so many illnesses were caused by contaminated water. Water, education, health, opportunities for girls . . . the overlap was multifaceted with each issue and extended to agriculture issues as well, such as the shortage of water for crop irrigation, poor crop production, and the resulting lack of income. All of these factors kept small farmers in poverty. An integrated approach was needed to confront these seemingly intractable issues.

Foundation team leaders presented the rationale behind their program ideas. Each initiative was thoroughly discussed. A communications plan to mobilize communities in Mewat was described along with strategies to engage individual villagers as role models and volunteers within their communities. Plans included the pursuit of IT connectivity to bring the villages into the twenty-first century in terms of access to knowledge and resources.

By midday on day two, experts were talking about overarching issues in village development, not just one aspect or another. Conversations now centered on how to achieve genuine impact and measure results. Enthusiasm was mounting as experts in the wider team could envision far more progress being made by establishing targeted, integrated grassroots programs within a few specific villages.

By the end of the meetings, a list of recommendations had been developed and approved by the entire team as a blueprint for the work to be done over the next few years. The formal decision was made: Sehgal Foundation would no longer be a donor-only organization promoting the activities of others. The foundation would be an active "implementing" organization.

With that, a jubilant cheer erupted in the room: "YES!!"

The team agreed to "learn by doing, and then evaluate how well we do." Successes and learnings would continue to be observed and built on as the organization moved forward. An added intention in every effort was to collect experiences and share knowledge with others interested in development. This move marked a shift from what the team had originally considered a "needs-based approach," referring to needs perceived by the foundation team, in favor of the new Integrated Sustainable Village Development (ISVD) model, now termed a "service-delivery approach," to meet the needs identified by the villagers themselves. The new model was designed to integrate all aspects of village development.

Before the meetings came to a close, the team identified the four program subjects to be implemented in four villages: (1) water management, (2) income enhancement through sustainable agriculture, (3) preventive health, with an emphasis on sanitation and hygiene, and (4) family life education, focused on educating adolescent girls on reproductive and child health. Each program would be designed to be replicable, scalable, and sustainable, with the goal of demonstrating satisfactory levels of transformation (impact) in four villages within four years. Projects would depend upon available funds. Costs and timelines would be carefully tracked. The most effective and sustainable programs would then be expanded to more villages.

To spur on the goals of the ISVD model, the team created a catchphrase, *Four, Four, Four,* representing four villages, four programs, and four years to demonstrate results.

As the phrase was announced, the room again erupted in cheers.

CHAPTER 3

Building Trust

In the 1930s Mahatma Gandhi had advocated for the panchayati raj system as the preferred decentralized form of village self-governance. He and Jawaharlal Nehru shared the view that poverty would be addressed more effectively by putting power into the hands of the people in the form of local village councils. Prime Minister Nehru formalized the establishment of these panchayati raj institutions throughout India in the 1950s.

Village councils were not seen as a political body until years later with the launch of the Integrated Rural Development Program (IRDP) in 1978. The IRDP assigned a budget to each district to generate self-employment opportunities for the rural poor. Assistance was provided in the form of government subsidies, bank credit, and loans from financial institutions to help lift people above the poverty line. Acquiring income-generating assets, education, training, and upgraded skills benefited individuals as well as the community. That aspect of the program was in keeping with Mahatma Gandhi's view that self-reliance was necessary for rising out of poverty. However, much of the assistance never reached the villages, including many in Mewat. Panchayats were often inactive and in some cases nonfunctional.

The 73rd and 74th Amendment Act of 1993, passed by India's parliament, was an attempt to revitalize rural local government. This landmark legislation provided constitutional status to the panchayati raj institutions. The Act mandated regular timely elections for locally elected bodies with the inclusion of disadvantaged groups, including women, lower caste members, and indigenous populations, and called upon the federal government to enact further legislation to devolve power and resources to local district panchayats so they could actually function as local government bodies.

Panchayats were now able to make plans for and implement their own development activities, receive regular financial aid, play a central role in providing public services, and create and maintain public goods. They could play an active role in political parties and within voluntary agencies. Unfortunately, the transfer of power (the functions, functionaries, and funds) to the panchayats did not occur consistently as required by the Indian constitution. A wide variation still exists across the states in how the devolution of power reaches and affects local government.

Self-help was addressed more directly by the creation of *Swarnajayanti Gram Swarozgar Yojana* (SGSY) in 1999. This initiative was intended to engage villagers in self-help groups (SHGs) to work together to develop and use their skills and abilities to maximum advantage to generate greater income. Clusters of people could come together based on their aptitudes and interests. NGOs and others provided training and assisted in funding each cluster's microenterprises.

Despite the existence of these programs and amendments, the villages in Mewat did not benefit. In addition to reasons already noted, many government programs suffered due to a lack of effective delivery systems. Control of any funds was in the hands of the bureaucracy. People did not necessarily know how to tap into their benefits, and panchayats remained fairly dormant. All these issues formed the backdrop for the work the foundation team faced in an effort to engage local villages in their own development.

The most important goal for implementation of any program in Mewat was to establish Sehgal Foundation as credible with the people in the selected communities. After so many years of neglect and betrayals, villagers had to be convinced that Sehgal Foundation was a trustworthy organization. Transparency was essential for building trust. Approval and consent from elected members of the panchayats were needed before any foundation programs could be launched in the communities. So the first place to try to create a mutually respectful rapport that could lead to trust was with the panchayats in the four villages—Agon, Dhaula,[16] Ghaghas, and Goela—that were chosen based on the selection criteria for the Integrated Sustainable Village Development model.

Sehgal Foundation's multidisciplinary team doubled in the coming months as more program leaders were hired to launch the new model. Many of the new staff members lived in or came from villages in Mewat. A few had previously worked with the foundation's NGO partners in the area. Grassroots implementation teams and program leaders were required to speak the same dialect as the villagers for good communication and responsiveness in complex communities that were both highly deprived yet culturally rich.

Field staff members were well trained and supported in all aspects of their work within the communities. When building any team, Suri and Edda Sehgal considered it essential that everyone on staff have "connectivity and mobility." Employees were reimbursed for monthly cellphone use and offered interest-free loans to buy vehicles. People hired from the villages would otherwise be less able to afford these vital tools. Many of the women purchased scooters or motorbikes.

In some cases, personal behavior changes were required from field staff. Young men hired from the villages had been raised to believe it was disrespectful to speak before elders in their community. They had to recognize that respectful conversation with elders was appropriate and necessary for good communication in their new positions.

Young women trainers had a tough time at first in the role of professional female. They had to endure taunts and criticism for stepping out of their homes and engaging in unconventional roles and activities. The bravery, persistence, and higher vision of these young women role models would gradually be rewarded over time with admiration from the community. But those early days of personal growth were challenging. One young woman remarked in retrospect, "In order to lead the community, we had to first bring about our own inner transformation. After all, we were brought up in the same culture. At Sehgal

16. Rangala Rajpur was eventually substituted for Dhaula as a result of redistricting; the team was already working there quite a bit.

Foundation, we were taught to remember what Gandhiji[17] said: 'Be the change you wish to see in the world.'"

People from the area had never before known of an organization that believed in taking care of their own employees. Jay Sehgal's leadership style was in full agreement with the founders' approach. Like Suri and Edda, he brought his business practices to social services. He encouraged creativity and independence in the team along with good planning and communication. He took a straightforward approach to problem solving, bringing the staff together to involve everyone in discussions. Empowering team members was consistent with the work with villagers in Mewat. He explained, "We must feel confident first, if we want to empower others."

Jay found that, at the end of the day, some decisions were his alone to make; but by using the "consortium" approach with the core management team and with the field teams, most decisions were arrived at during discussions, and the staff was involved and invested in the outcomes.

B. R. Poonia, whose job title was now leader of community mobilization, was responsible for meeting with the sarpanch and panchayat in each of the four selected villages to explore and mobilize potential partnerships. The core team attending each meeting consisted of Poonia, sociologist Anjali Makhija, and executive director Jay Sehgal, in addition to specialists in water management and agriculture, and a female physician. The combination of experts involved in each meeting varied occasionally. Sometimes another social scientist or a representative of a different NGO came along. A second female physician was hired in 2003.

Treating people with courtesy and respect was the highest priority in efforts to develop relationships within the communities. Care was taken to approach the local elected officials with great consideration and to listen carefully to whatever they had to say.

Members of the team introduced new people, shook hands, asked many questions, and paid close attention to whatever thoughts and opinions were voiced. The meetings were often held outside under

17. Mahatma Gandhi. The honorific *ji* is added to his name in affection and respect.

a shade tree. Sarpanches provided chairs to the team to show their respect, but Poonia had again advised the team ahead of time to sit on the ground with the villagers to further minimize barriers between them. Pooniaji (the respectful honorific *ji* now added to his name) led the discussions during the first meetings in each village.

Jay Sehgal was a silent observer for the most part in the early meetings. He was a bit nervous and not yet fully conversant in the local dialect. In some situations, Pooniaji instructed him ahead of time not to speak. Jay trusted Pooniaji and followed his advice.

After the initial greetings, Pooniaji began each conversation by asking questions about whatever was going on in the village. The elders were asked what they thought about family life education instruction that had been presented to young women in their villages. The team wanted to get a feel for what the people in the community knew about the programs—good and bad.

A typical exchange with village elders began this way:

"What happens in the Family Life Education sessions?"

"They teach girls sewing and stitching."

"Do the girls learn anything useful? Is the program beneficial or not?"

"Oh yes, girls can fix our clothes at home now."

Some elders were less positive about the programs, even though they agreed their families had benefited. In each situation, there were occasional naysayers. This was not a surprise. A few elders in the community admitted being fearful that if their young people learned too much, they might "stand up" against their elders and religious leaders.

The team members assured elders that any programs proposed or embarked on by Sehgal Foundation would have no religious components. The message that Sehgal Foundation was not affiliated with any religion or political viewpoint had to be reiterated again and again.

To find out people's greatest concerns and interests, Pooniaji asked, "If we start programs in your village, what do you most need?"

As people began to think about their true needs, they tended to suggest big projects—a hospital, English language schools, a high school for girls, but always, most importantly, water. Access to water was the most crucial need in each village.

Follow-up questions aimed for specifics, such as, "What exactly do you envision?"

Managing expectations was critical. Pooniaji was careful not to suggest that the foundation could or would provide all the necessities suggested. He was clear that he and the team would take the ideas back to the foundation to see what was possible. He explained that the goal was to work *with* the community within the bounds of the foundation's expertise, and not to do things *for* the community. He assured them, "Whatever we do, we will do together."

The team quickly learned they had to be careful and selective about who accompanied them on visits with panchayat leaders. On one occasion a particular NGO representative who came along made several promises to the people that he had no ability to keep, saying he would "take care of" the issue being discussed. Though such promises, sometimes even made by team members, were usually the result of an enthusiastic desire to help, such wishful assurances could easily sabotage the foundation team's efforts. People of Mewat had heard plenty of what turned out to be empty promises from other NGOs.

The team began enforcing a policy that no one could come with them into the villages until briefed and reminded ahead of time about what to do or say and what not to do or say. Everyone was basically told, "Make no promises. The people will describe many needs and requirements, but you must not give them false hope. If we promise, we must deliver. Building trust is paramount."

As ideas for potential programs were discussed further in meetings with panchayats and villagers, suspicion and resignation in the people was obvious, as though they were thinking, *Hamari kaun sunta hai?* (Who listens to us anyway?) To address their concerns and suspicions head-on, team members answered villagers' questions with as much clarity and detail as possible, careful to keep in mind, almost like a mantra: "Underpromise and overdeliver."

The important concept of partnership was another topic that required frequent reminders. For goodhearted people, who wanted so much to help, to be in the company of those whose needs were so desperate, the temptation was strong to want to fix problems *for* people. The foundation team had understood this and insisted from the beginning that any venture had to be a partnership to be successful. Joining *with* villagers was the only way for villagers to assume ownership over the results of the work. That lesson was underscored for Jay Sehgal early in the process of visiting villages when he thought he could easily solve a street trash problem by supplying rubbish bins for each block. The idea seemed simple enough to him at the time. However, upon returning to the village the following week, he found the neighborhood children using the bins for swings.

Pooniaji explained to Jay, "We cannot expect to solve any problem, no matter how seemingly simple, without fully engaging the people involved."

Jay said later, "I learned to rely on the wisdom of the community mobilizer."

People had to be part of the decision-making process in order for them to care about an issue in the first place. They had to understand all the circumstances involved in a project and the solutions being offered. In addition, the best results could only be assured if the people involved not only believed in it but also participated in the implementation of the outcome. Pooniaji described the process as needing to be "end to end" to make sense. This was the same concept Suri Sehgal frequently referred to as "closing the loop."

The trash-can effort was swiftly abandoned. That loop had not been closed.

The same lesson was underlined by obstacles that had emerged in the attempt to provide that first check dam for the village of Rangala Rajpur. Another monsoon season came and went before the work eventually continued with the assistance of partial funding from the local government. But again the project was left unfinished as costs escalated.

The foundation was fortunate to have the skills of an on-site engineer to handle water projects directly. Lalit Mohan Sharma, another former Proagro employee of many years, was strongly influenced by Sehgal Foundation's vision. He had been a volunteer on weekends since the organization's beginning and had been involved in each water project. When he first saw the vulnerability and suffering in the villages of Mewat, he wanted to do whatever he could to make life easier for these people. Though he was a civil engineer with a master's degree in technology management and systems and a postgraduate diploma in construction management, Lalit thought he should become a social worker for the foundation. However, he was called upon as a consultant and coordinator of all the foundation's water construction projects, including designs for the check dam water-augmentation projects in Ghaghas and Rangala Rajpur. Suri Sehgal considered him an excellent fit and was happy when Lalit agreed to take a position as the leader of the foundation's Water Management program in April 2003.

As it had from the beginning, water dominated every conversation as the greatest need in each village. In some villages there were water connections outside the houses, and water was available for an hour or two at a time. However, frequent failures and pipeline leakages rendered the system unreliable. Villagers had to find other sources of water, usually from some distance away.

Lalit was concluding a meeting with a group of women in the village of Karheda about the construction of soak pits for the safe disposal of domestic wastewater, when an elderly woman stood to speak. She said that getting water in the first place was far more critical than its disposal. Her village's piped water supply was unavailable for weeks at a stretch, requiring women in her community to walk four kilometers to Ghaghas to fetch water. The woman's face contorted in pain as she said, "Being old, I am not able to walk and carry water so long. So I take water from a nearby source (a village only one kilometer away) that is somewhat saline. But this saline water causes diarrhea and other problems. I can't drink tea of my liking as boiling milk with this saline water spoils the milk."

With that, her tears came.

Lalit recalls, "I was deeply shaken that whole day. I kept thinking, *What is the use of my being so qualified and holding the position of program leader of Water Management if I cannot help these people have access to potable water?* I decided to do something innovative to create a local source of potable water."

For immediate relief in Karheda, Lalit and the water team developed three wells over the next few months and diverted the infrequently piped water supply into those wells. People in the village helped with the digging. Now they could fetch water from those wells when their water was turned off. Though this was not the long-term solution, the same elderly lady told Lalit afterward how thankful she was to Sehgal Foundation. She said to him, "Every day in my prayers, I pray for God to bless you all."

He said later, "These were the most motivating words of my life."

Lalit was now committed to finding more solutions for solving water problems for people living in saline groundwater villages. Successes from the work by the Water Management team would later bring multiple honors to Sehgal Foundation.

The team proposed a new design plan for a water-augmentation system in Ghaghas and explained the plan in detail. Decades before, the Government of India had built a small check dam in the nearby foothills. Over the years, the wall of the dam structure, which was made of soil, had washed away due to water pressure. A new check dam would be an effective first step in helping to recharge the aquifer. The villagers would be required to contribute a small percentage in cash or in-kind goods or services, equal to approximately 20–25 percent of the cost of this endeavor, and they had to take part actively in that or any other project undertaken on their behalf.

Suri Sehgal had participated in some of the early conversations with the panchayat and saw the expressions on the villagers' faces when he explained why they would have to pay a percentage of the cost of a new dam. An elder said in disbelief, "You said you came to help us, and now you are asking us to contribute money?"

The elders did not like the idea of any demand being made of them. A senior admitted, "We have only been taught to take what is given to us. We only know how to take."

Suri Sehgal, or "Dr. Suri" as some villagers and staff had begun calling him, reminded the people again that Sehgal Foundation had not come to Mewat to do things *for* them—but to work alongside them, *with* them. His voice was kind but firm as he repeated, "If you don't contribute, we won't build it. If you contribute, you will own it."

The team was prepared to demonstrate how the village money would be safeguarded. They assured the elders that any money collected would only go toward the agreed-upon project. A village-level institution would be established to keep track of the assets involved.

Over the next several months, Pooniaji continued to speak with the Ghaghas elders, further explaining why it was in their best interests to participate in a project to benefit their community rather than to just "take." He reminded them that Sehgal Foundation was there to help them help themselves. He explained again and again that villagers would not place value on something merely given to them. They would only place value on something they felt they owned, by being part of creating the outcome. He illustrated his point with an action they could have taken, but did not, related to their own nearby check dam, which had been damaged for ten years. No one in the village had done anything about it in that entire time, even though their need for water was so dire.

Pooniaji asked the villagers, "Why did you do nothing? Why didn't you care about the dam?"

The answer was, "We didn't create the dam; the government did. Why should we do anything?"

Pooniaji pressed his point further, explaining that the villagers did nothing to repair the check dam because it was *given* to them. When the government built that check dam in the nearby foothills, responsibility for the dam's upkeep was essentially handed over to the people. The dam would either be sustained by the community, or it would be ignored. When it was damaged, no repairs were ever done. The dam was ignored.

He explained, "You see, if you pay in some way for a new check dam, that same thing will not happen again, because *you* will own it. *You* will care about it, because *you* will have placed an investment in it."

The elders remained unconvinced. The people wanted the water, but they did not want to play a part in building the dam. The community could not see why they should take any responsibility for the dam. In their minds, it was the government's responsibility, and the government never came back to repair it.

Ghaghas villagers continued to believe that it was the government's duty to provide for their needs, even when that didn't happen. Villagers had no buy-in with the original check dam from the beginning. The loop had not been closed.

There even appeared to be an expectation on the part of many villagers that Sehgal Foundation would build a new check dam anyway, as part of their new Water Management program, whether villagers helped or not. But the foundation's message remained firm: the dam would be built only if the community contributed and participated.

Sehgal Foundation would always do what was promised, but the foundation's help was only promised in exchange for a true partnership. That partnership included villagers' cash or in-kind contributions toward materials for any endeavor undertaken on behalf of their development. Though these villagers could see no reason or method to help themselves, the foundation team was confident that the people of Mewat would eventually get the message and follow the path to development. The process was slow, but the team was committed to countering the villagers' self-destructive mind-set of dependence.

B. R. Poonia understood how helpless and often hopeless the villagers felt. He could appreciate their concerns. He had grown up in a similar situation where water was scarce. He recalled his childhood in the 1950s, in the early years following India's independence. Everyone in his desert village in Rajasthan had always taken great care to capture every drop of water. Each family harvested rooftop rainwater—something rarely seen now in Mewat.

Prior to India's independence from British rule in 1947, the government had played no part in helping people in the villages obtain water or meet any of their other basic needs. In "old India," people were more independent by necessity. Everyone had to do whatever they could to get by, with no expectation of help from the government or anyone else. How expectations had changed since then!

A subtle shift had slowly eroded the sense of community spirit and responsibility in many of the poorest communities during the decades after India gained its freedom from British rule. In the heady glow of freedom and egalitarian ideology, leaders told their people all the wonderful things the government would now do for them. India's citizens would be provided with water, electricity, education, and so on. Wells and tanks would be installed; schools, check dam structures, and roads would be built. But such lofty promises were impossible to keep. In such a highly diverse and stratified society, eliminating social and economic inequities was no quick or easy task. The form of peaceful democratic socialism Nehru envisioned did not come about with changes made in a few laws. The people of Mewat remained deeply mired in their long-term abject poverty.

The Government of India attempted to provide water and electricity connections and basic health and education centers, but most services in the villages remained erratic and inadequate. A more all-encompassing approach was needed to mobilize people in these communities to understand that they could do for themselves what no outsider could do for them. Taking a step back, the field team continued their conversations on these topics with the panchayats, with groups of village women, and with any special-interest group in the communities.

A vivid reminder of the necessity to "close the loop" occurred the same year in conjunction with a project Sehgal Foundation initiated with the help of the Rural Development and Self Employment Training Institute (RUDSETI)[18] to provide vocational training for young people. RUDSETI had identified high-demand trades, such as general business development, computer hardware management, beauty care, and air conditioner and refrigerator repair.

Using the RUDSETI profile designed to identify competencies and talent with various skill sets, interested young people from one village were assessed. Four candidates were chosen who matched profile requirements for training in computer hardware management. However, none of the four young men accepted for training ended up following through with the course. In evaluating the process related to this initiative, foundation staff concurred that a lack of self-confidence on the part of the four candidates was the primary reason for their lack of effort.

However, other aspects of the program were recognized as additional factors in the young men's change of heart. No study had been done to determine if they could actually access the jobs in the identified need areas if they were subsequently hired after training. There was no transportation available from Mewat to reach job opportunities that were located at a distance. Closing the loop in this case would require better counseling and preparation for the training, and more advance legwork to make sure the team understood the associated practical and logistical challenges.

Every project that didn't work out as planned nonetheless offered useful information that was applied to new initiatives moving forward. These were the growing pains of an organization committed to development, and a team unwilling to give up on the long road toward empowering rural India.

---

18. See http://www.rudset.com/.

CHAPTER 4

Staying Focused

Sehgal Foundation work was now being done primarily in four villages in Mewat. However, the range of activities in the Integrated Sustainable Village Development model kept expanding in each of the four program areas. Opportunities to make a difference in the lives of villagers seemed endless, but Sehgal Foundation resources—human and capital—were limited. For recognizable impact to be possible, the team had to stay focused within the parameters of the *Four, Four, Four* campaign and try to resist the impulse to do more and more and more.

Building on the positive outcomes of Family Life Education skill-training sessions, young girls were offered a similar opportunity to learn tailoring skills in sewing centers. Life Skills Education centers, teachers, and sewing machines were provided by Sehgal Foundation in a handful of locations. Each participant was required to pay for the raw materials for learning: thread, needles, and cloth. This program was the first Sehgal Foundation project to finally persuade villagers to readily agree to and actually make cash contributions for their participation. The fee was tiny, about five rupees (less than ten cents a month). But it was a start.

Training sessions on tailoring skills (measuring, cutting, and sewing) were held three days each week. The other three days covered family life topics. Girls were taught how to read and write at the same time that they were given opportunities for conversations about their identity, goals in life, emotions, values, gender stereotypes, reproductive health, and physiological changes in their bodies as they matured. An outdoor recreational component of the program (like badminton) aided in overall emotional and social development. As girls in the program increased their overall skills, their confidence was boosted, and their status in their families was gradually elevated.

To attract further involvement in Family Life Education, the field team spent time with groups of people to generate interest and obtain consent. Separate meetings and discussions were conducted with elders, adolescent boys, and parents, adapting the curriculum to each group. No cost was associated with this program because no materials were required.

The importance of preventive healthcare was generally agreed upon by everyone in the community. Girls were given permission to attend educational training sessions. During sessions on topics such as hand washing, hygiene, and sanitation, the foundation's physician extended the conversation to include facts and issues related to reproductive health.

In sessions with adolescent girls, any reference to delaying marriage or childbirth was framed in the context of empowerment and building self-confidence. The team watched these girls become more self-assured and expressive. They wanted to contribute in decision making at home, particularly with decisions to delay marriage. However, there was a wide communication gap between the young women and their parents.

To address this disparity, group leader Anjali Makhija[19] integrated dialogue with parents on those issues into several other topics presented in the Life Skills Education centers. A curriculum for parents was developed in the form of a series of six focus-group sessions in each of the four villages. Conversation covered gender roles, relationships with children and other personal feelings, along with the value of literacy. Mothers who participated remained fully engaged, but fathers were less interested. Many dropped out or gave work as their excuse for not attending. A few men admitted openly that such personal topics made them feel uncomfortable.

A Family Life Education course was offered to boys and girls in a cluster of sixteen villages including the original (*Four, Four, Four*) villages. Based on an interactive course developed by the Center for

---

19. Group leader was a senior management position at Sehgal Foundation with responsibility for supervising program leaders and other staff.

Development and Population Activities (CEDPA) in the United States, boys in the villages were presented for the first time with facts about gender inequality. The course content was reviewed by some school principals and approved by parents as well so it could be offered in a few schools within the cluster.

Engaging young boys in some form of gender sensitization, to lay the groundwork for their eventual involvement in village development, was no easy task. The foundation team launched a quarterly youth-oriented local newsletter called *Vikas Patrika* (translated literally as "development newsletter") to serve as a forum for communicating news and information and to celebrate local culture and feature role models for young people. At the event in Ghaghas to launch *Vikas Patrika*, the idea of a youth club was suggested. The boys present were enthusiastic about establishing a cricket club. Sehgal Foundation supported this idea by covering 50 percent of the costs involved in forming two clubs, one in Ghaghas and one in Goela. The Family Life Education classes that were a component of the club had the desired effect of inspiring boys to begin volunteering in village development.

Only seventeen primary health centers (PHCs), five community health centers (CHCs), and one district hospital existed to serve the one million residents of Mewat. Unfortunately, between bureaucratic procedures, insufficient infrastructure, and inadequate staff, the centers were not functioning properly. Trained medical staff was rarely on hand. Healthcare at the village level was limited to care from a public auxiliary nurse-midwife (ANM) and an *anganwadi* (childcare) worker in poorly maintained sub-centers.[20] Villagers more often resorted to a local untrained and unregistered practitioner called a *jhola chhap* doctor.

Sehgal Foundation staff kept track of any government-run health camps and mobile medical services to make sure the local people were aware of them. The foundation team held regular information sessions on health issues for the community. Topics included basic hygiene, sanitation practices, nutrition, communicable diseases, and the symptoms,

20. Anganwadi centers were established in rural areas as part of the Integrated Child Development Services (ICDS) government welfare program begun in 1975 for children under six and their mothers. Benefits include primary healthcare, preschool education, food, nutrition information, and referral services.

prevention, and treatment of fever, malaria, diarrhea, and tuberculosis. Local jholas were also invited to these trainings.

A project implementation team went door to door in all four of the *Four, Four, Four* villages to identify people in need of medical care and to assist in getting those individuals to appropriate public facilities. A good working relationship with the local auxiliary nurse-midwife was first established in Agon. She began visiting the local Family Life Education Center on a regular basis, administering immunizations and making referrals as needed to functioning healthcare facilities.

Sehgal Foundation took some basic but effective steps to address the high rate of infant mortality in Mewat. Most births in Mewat were attended by *dais* (traditional midwives) who, though usually illiterate and without formal training, had practical knowledge and were familiar with complications of childbirth. Young married men had little or no understanding or sense of responsibility for the reproductive health of their wives. Due to high neonatal morbidity, a key concern in the medical community related to basic hygiene. Home births exposed newborns and their mothers to increased risks. Certain practices, such as cutting the umbilical cord with any sharp instrument at hand, or the traditional practice of rubbing a newborn's navel with cow dung to protect the child from evil, added to the danger.

Sehgal Foundation conducted a series of training sessions for groups of dais (midwives) to promote cleanliness and the use of a low-cost dai kit. The kit included soap, a sterile safety razor, a polyethylene sheet, thread, and disinfectant. Simple actions such as hand washing before attending a birth helped to ensure safer childbirths. The foundation's dai training stressed the "Five Cleans": clean hands, clean delivery surface, clean cord cut, clean cord ties, and clean cord stump care.

Sessions with parents and community leaders illustrated the connection between large family size and poverty in a discussion about costs, risks, and benefits. In conversations with religious leaders, community mobilizer B. R. Poonia quoted the revered Indian Nobel Prize winner in economic sciences, Amartya Sen. His work on the economic theories of famine and the well-being of people in developing countries demonstrated that educated people and those with higher incomes had fewer children. The foundation team used this reasoning to help convince villagers that, when families have fewer children, it is easier to provide them with education, and they would be better prepared to earn higher wages. Women villagers in particular had no trouble seeing the connection between family size and shortages of food and water.

In the Income Enhancement program, crop-production practices were discussed with farmers in meetings and conversations about decreasing costs and increasing productivity. Most of the farmers in the villages with sweet water were vegetable growers who were not getting good prices for their produce. The majority of households had only one or two milk animals, usually buffaloes, certainly not a herd. The plan was to convince farmers that their farm productivity would improve with new cultivation practices, and their income would increase with direct connectivity to the market. Educating villagers about the available government agriculture and veterinary services and programs was an important component of the initiative.

The Income Enhancement program leader contacted Mother Dairy, the largest distributor of milk, fruits, and vegetables in Delhi, to see what could be done to get the Mewat villagers' produce for their market. Larger farmers in India had long been able to deal directly with Mother Dairy, bypassing third-party middlemen; but the small farmers in Mewat had never been included in the practice. Mother Dairy wanted a reliable supply chain that could deliver quality produce in bigger quantities. Mother Dairy representatives suggested that villagers form a cooperative to serve as a link with larger organizations interested in buying their products. If farmers in Mewat could join together, their milk and vegetable produce would be picked up directly by Mother Dairy without added cost from third-party middlemen.

The foundation team met with the farmers and explained, "If you pool your produce, you can create an organization that large distributors will do business with."

When forming a cooperative was first suggested to villagers, they were suspicious of the idea because the bank required an initial membership fee. Sehgal Foundation agreed to pay a portion of the initial fees, with the expectation that the farmers would pay back the money over time in small increments once their cooperative association had its own bank account.

The team explained that, as members of the Fruit and Vegetable Growers Association (FVGA), farmers would be able to bring their produce for pick up each day from FVGA by Mother Dairy. The farmers would receive payment for their goods within seven to fourteen days.

However, farmers were concerned about the time lag between giving up their produce and receiving payment. They asked, "How do we know the organization will not just keep our money?"

The foundation team agreed to guarantee the payment amounts in the beginning so the farmers could see how the program worked. Once this promise was made, the farmers agreed. They immediately raised the money required by the bank.

As promised, each participating farmer saw the results of this initiative in cash within two weeks. The creation of these cooperative linkages with the milk and produce market brought recognition to the Income Enhancement program in the eyes of the local farmers and within Sehgal Foundation.

Agriculture interventions from the foundation team in each of the *Four, Four, Four* villages involved training at every level from seed to market. Farmers were taught proper soil preparation, row spacing, plant-to-plant spacing, how to construct low-cost polyethylene plant nurseries, and the safe use of pesticides. Training was provided to farmers on crop diversification and to encourage the use of raised-bed vegetable cultivation as a way to use less water and increase yields. An interest-free loan provided to the Fruit and Vegetable Grower Association in Ghaghas made it possible for farmers to purchase a bed maker (tractor attachment for forming raised rows for planting) and chisel plow for soil cultivation.

The first secretary of the Fruit and Vegetable Grower Association in Goela was the son of a landless farmer from a lower caste.[21] His father, Puranchand, was one of the first farmers in his village to take a risk and try some of the progressive agronomic practices suggested by the Sehgal Foundation team. With assistance from the foundation, he constructed a low-cost polyethylene plantlet nursery and produced healthier and

21. Though the social stratification of the caste hierarchy in India is far less rigid than it once was, members of lower castes can experience social isolation and discrimination even in the poorest communities.

more robust seedlings than his neighboring farmers. His success with new methods, such as growing off-season seedlings on raised beds, was showcased during a "Farmers Day," which Sehgal Foundation held on his fields. By hosting 280 farmers from three neighboring districts, plus numerous scientists and agribusiness personnel, Puranchand gained respect in his community. Other farmers sought him out for his advice on new agronomic techniques and growing off-season vegetable crops.

Another farmer in Goela, Ayub Khan, tested methods promoted by Sehgal Foundation on a quarter acre of his five-acre farm before scaling up. He saw the most benefit from intercropping and began systematically mixing his crops to enhance their commercial value. He learned the best intercrop combinations for different seasons and which combinations helped prevent disease and pests in the main crop. Ayub was so impressed with his added production and income that he volunteered for every new crop-production initiative.

Ayub Khan was an early user of vermicompost to reduce chemical fertilizer usage and thus decrease his production costs. A handful of farmers were given a kilogram each of earthworms to establish vermicompost pilot units to produce vermicompost to sell other farmers. Vermicompost contains more nitrogen, phosphorus, and micronutrients than traditional compost. Two-thirds of the farmers in this project were women, and almost all vermicompost units in six villages were run by women farmers.

The breakthrough that finally came in the struggle to convince the village of Ghaghas to partner with Sehgal Foundation in a substantial check dam water-augmentation project can be attributed to a slow and steady grassroots approach on the part of a project implementation team. A goal in every village was to identify a group of citizens who were interested in the development projects. This way, any successful activities created during the partnership would be expected to thrive with or without the presence of the foundation. Sustainability was the hope and the measure of genuine accomplishment in any development undertaking.

In the absence of a fully empowered panchayat, the creation of a *gram vikas sanstha* (village-level institution or VLI) in Ghaghas turned out to be a useful mechanism for making decisions on behalf of the village. Village-level institutions sometimes served almost like "shadow" panchayats in villages where local government was not working well, which was the case in most villages in the early years of Sehgal Foundation's presence in Mewat.

To support the creation of a VLI in Ghaghas, the foundation team reached out to various demographic groups in the community, including those in different castes, different geographical areas, and even different *kutumbs* (ancestrally linked families). The team met with every identifiable subset of villagers in Ghaghas for focused conversations about working together for their own benefit. Each group was asked to choose representatives to serve together in a group to advocate for village needs, with the goal of ensuring sustainable development in their community. The villagers responded with interest to this very personal appeal.

The newly created group, which included dozens of villagers, was led by a sixteen-person executive team that included the sarpanch, members of current and past panchayats, several women, a youth member, and two people from Sehgal Foundation. From that point on, all foundation activities in Ghaghas went through this body. The group's first act was to create a five-person (including one woman) task force to manage the check dam project. The villagers were ready for action.

For a community to actively assume responsibility for its own development was the exact result the foundation team had hoped to achieve. Thrilled that the tide had finally turned in the direction of community involvement, the team suggested several ideas about how villagers could participate in different ways in the large water-augmentation project: the foundation would pay for diesel fuel if a farmer used his tractor as his contribution to help with trenches or digging for water storage structures; or one person in each of 300 households in the village could donate a day of labor; a farmer might donate part of a crop, such as mustard or wheat, when it was ready to harvest and put the money earned by selling it into the "check dam fund"; a villager with a job could contribute a portion of his daily wages. Any idea was worth considering.

The task force was responsible for all steps in the project, which included hiring the labor; procuring the construction materials, tools, and equipment; ensuring the participation of women; and resolving conflicts. As money was collected and used, the accounting process was tracked within the community. Wall-size balance sheets were hung in a central location in the village for all to see. By the end of the project, the village had raised even more money in different forms than their promised contribution!

For Ghaghas, the Water Management team suggested a comprehensive ridge-to-valley design for water flow into the storage pond (reservoir) at the bottom of the catchment area that would revitalize the local water table and water supply. In addition to the check dam itself, other water-harvesting structures were part of the overall water-augmentation system. For example, a series of small, loose-stone structures, called contour bunds, were placed high up in the catchment area. Loose stones covered with wire mesh, called gabions, were placed at intervals along the gulleys where the water flowed toward the valley floor. Gulley plugs, similar to gabions but without wire mesh, also acted to slow the speed of gushing water. Nallah bunds, created with bricks or stone masonry, were placed on slopes and in water catchment areas to slow or divert water. These structures worked together to interrupt the flow of water, improve soil moisture, and allow more water to percolate into the ground. The dry stone wall of the storage pond was layered with soil and covered with a polyethylene sheet to make the walls watertight.[22]

The storage pool structure was in place before the monsoons came in July. The groundwater level was raised by a full meter that first year.

By the end of 2003, the stone concrete masonry dam wall was constructed in Ghaghas. The fully completed project would include water guiding walls, a cushion chamber for protection from heavy water flow, spillways to direct excess water into adjacent pools, sluice gates to ensure desilting, and sand dune slopes cut at a stabilizing angle and covered with soil and vetiver grass. Those final parts would be carried out over the next year.

Any endeavors by Sehgal Foundation that were related to water produced the most visible and tangible results. Once a project was done

22. Though the check dam itself is only part of the overall water-augmentation system constructed in the watershed area, the term "check dam" was typically used by the team and villagers to describe the entire system, which had multiple components, such as nallah bunds, gulley plugs, contour bunds, gabions, reservoirs, etc.

and people could see a noticeable difference in their lives, villagers came forward with new ideas. Once they understood the potential value of a particular project, villagers came prepared not only to contribute but also to actively participate.

The community of Rangala Rajpur came through finally and contributed toward their earthen check dam project, so the containment pool was also finished in time for the monsoon in 2003. Each household contributed ten kilograms of wheat as well as cash and labor. When the monsoon came, the water level rose by six feet in the nearby village! With water percolating from the storage pool into the ground, previously dry wells began to fill again. Vetiver grass was planted on the banks of the storage pool to enhance stability, and a series of additional storage ponds were under construction. Water from the Rangala Rajpur check dam structures was also used to cultivate vegetation on ten acres of previously fallow common land.

Sehgal Foundation helped to rehabilitate underutilized common lands in each village. These heavily deforested wasteland areas were good places, depending on the soil, to plant fast-growing trees for wood fuel or vegetation that could be used for animal fodder. Villagers depended mostly on wood for cooking. Burning wood was not an ideal option due to all the unhealthy indoor smoke inhalation; but since few could afford propane gas or even acquire it in a village, wood was a common necessity.

Not all Sehgal Foundation water-augmentation projects that year were as successful as the first two check dam projects. For example, a new drip irrigation project did not work out as hoped. The foundation supported some environmentally sustainable crop irrigation technology developed by a nonprofit called International Development Enterprises. The technology was sound, but several complications quickly became evident. The system required a connection to a tube well, which only 30 percent of the farmers in the entire district had. Many farmers had no water source at all. In those situations, water would have to be purchased from elsewhere. In addition, the irrigation system itself had to be stored out in the open in the field, which left it vulnerable to theft or to damage from wild pigs or *nilgai* antelopes. These complications and the inequities in water distribution, combined with the high cost of the system, caused farmers to reject the technology.

Sehgal Foundation's water team was challenged to find creative solutions to capture, store, and fairly distribute freshwater to more villages in desperate need. A multifaceted approach was taken with water management in each *Four, Four, Four* village. In addition to plans for more large construction projects, such as check dams and ponds, the team encouraged the reintroduction of traditional methods for rooftop harvesting of rainwater being practiced in other water-scarce parts of the country, and introduced low-cost soak pits and soak wells for wastewater management. Education in water literacy was now an ongoing campaign in each village.

Without sewer systems in the villages, wastewater ran in the streets. An effective wastewater disposal model was needed to improve sanitation, hygiene, and overall health. Simple drainage structures were designed to facilitate the disposal, filtration, and percolation of wastewater into the ground.

A three-person project-implementation team conducted a door-to-door survey covering 618 households in the village of Agon to assess water availability and find out which homes had water taps or connections of any kind. Twenty-five homes were chosen to introduce the use of taps and soak pits. The first few dozen soak pits were about three-to-five feet in diameter and in depth. The below-ground pits were filled with layers of broken brick or stones followed by sand, which provided natural filtration of wastewater from bathing, cooking, or laundry. The sand acted as a fine filter, allowing clear water to percolate into the ground. To prevent clogs in the pit from the collected sediments, a trap designed to catch silt, grease, and soap residue was placed where the water entered the soak pit. The trap needed cleaning a couple of times each week. For areas with homes too small for soak pits, a much deeper soak well (up to fifty feet deep) was dug in the street, away from the houses. Each soak well was capable of handling the wastewater needs of twenty households.

Collecting rainwater from rooftops is a simple technology but, as mentioned, it was not practiced in Mewat. Some people could purchase freshwater from a private vendor, but poor people did not have that choice. The revival of traditional methods was imperative.

To illustrate one model, the Water Management team installed a rainwater-harvesting structure on the roof of the village mosque in Agon. The mosque rooftop could potentially, depending on the yearly rainfall, harvest as much as 205,000 liters of water. This water was channeled to a defunct well and, from there, into the groundwater table. Water from the well could now be used for watering animals.

Lalit had studied the water-scarce regions of Rajasthan and Gujarat in his search for sustainable solutions before designing a rooftop rainwater-harvesting system to be used in villages with saline groundwater. In his model, rainwater falling onto the roof was captured, directed to, and then stored in a concrete masonry tank. The team installed the system in some schools and held demonstrations to show how well it worked. Storing rainwater in concrete tanks for direct use also resulted in reduced runoff in saline groundwater areas, decreased recharge of saline groundwater, and less pressure on the limited sweet-water aquifers.

Villagers liked the model, but the construction of a storage tank with the capacity to meet the year-round water demand for a household was not financially feasible for most poor villagers. Lalit was challenged to find a cost-effective way to store water that did not rely on such a large, and expensive, concrete masonry tank. He approached the problem from a new angle to see if it was possible to eliminate or replace the tank in the system. As a result, he came up with an innovative concept for creating freshwater pockets *within* the saline aquifer.

In conventional recharging of groundwater with harvested rainwater, water infiltrates into the ground and forms a thin layer of freshwater that keeps spreading over a larger area of the existing saline groundwater as time goes by, maintaining hydraulic equilibrium. Left undisturbed, the two layers remain separate. To collect freshwater from the thin top layer, without mixing it with the saline water, was not possible. A mechanism was needed to relocate the freshwater to be below the saline groundwater table as a pool or pocket of freshwater that could be extracted.

After several more years of experimentation, and in collaboration with the Water Management team, Lalit's original design was modified to accomplish this. The recharge well was finally deep enough below the groundwater table, and at a height raised high enough above ground, to increase the hydrostatic pressure. Hydrostatic pressure created by the additional height and depth made it possible to push away the existing saline groundwater, allowing the harvested rainwater to form a pool of freshwater inside, within the saline aquifer. The pressure exerted by the surrounding saline groundwater held the pocket of freshwater together. A pre-filter inserted above the top of the recharge well prevented floating and suspended materials from entering the well. With this model, a sizable pocket of harvested rainwater was available for extraction with a hand pump. To make the water safe for drinking, a biosand filter was used as a cost-effective and natural method to remove disease-causing microogranisms and other contaminants. The pressurized recharge well model was one of several innovations by the Water Management team that garnered quite a bit of attention and resulted in a series of awards for Sehgal Foundation.[23]

The near absence of basic household sanitation in many villages was another challenge that required innovative thinking by Lalit and his team. The lack of privacy and the indignity of outdoor urination and defecation are deeply felt by women and elderly people when there are no latrines and the nearby fields serve as open-air toilets. The hardship and humiliation is even more profound for pregnant women and people with chronic health problems or physical disabilities. The Water Management team was determined to find a way to provide affordable latrines.

Lalit developed a low-cost latrine model, with very basic precast concrete walls and floor that could be installed within a few hours, even by an unskilled person. Many villagers agreed immediately that they wanted one in their homes. However, the people did not come back with their required portion of money or materials. Lalit kept a constructed latrine handy in the community center in Ghaghas; if a family agreed to provide their contribution in money or materials, the latrine

---

23. In 2009 hydrologist Salahuddin Saiphy joined Sehgal Foundation and was instrumental in the redesign. The pressurized recharge well model was ready for replication in 2014. The Government of India provided support to demonstrate the model in four areas. A request was made for funding for more demonstrations under various site conditions, such as where the saline aquifer was deeper, or other areas where saline water intruded. Sehgal Foundation was presented with the Millennium Alliance Award for this innovation in 2014, along with financial support to demonstrate it in more locations.

could be delivered the same day. The immediate delivery aspect worked in some cases. However, this project taught Lalit something more about the Mewati culture that was different from his own background. He explained, "If a villager in Mewat is asked to agree to something, the first response is always yes. In this culture, people don't refuse. They will agree to whatever you ask. If you ask a second time, and they say yes, then you know they are interested."

When villagers later requested a more attractive type of latrine instead of the precast model, Lalit developed a more appealing model and constructed about fifty for Ghaghas and other villages. However, shortly after this development, the government began subsidizing the building of latrines. The foundation's role shifted to creating awareness of the government programs, facilitating the process for villagers to acquire subsidies for latrines, and promoting more comprehensive water literacy programs.

As useful and significant as the check dam water-augmentation systems were, local women reported that sanitary latrines were the single most important development accomplished by the village-level institutions. An expanded campaign to build latrines and soak pits in the villages of Mewat had an immediate and valuable impact on public hygiene. Women no longer had to resort to going out into the field early in the morning or late at night and suffer the indignity of open-air defecation. The relatively simple low-cost intervention made a profound difference to everyday life that went beyond other improvements to the physical infrastructure of the village. This was an important step toward the empowerment of women in Mewat.

A glimpse into the life of a woman named Shahida, in the village of Ghaghas during that same year, provides insight into the relationship between the other main issues addressed by Sehgal Foundation's integrated approach to partnerships with villages in Mewat and the potential for women's empowerment.

Like most women in her village and other villages in Mewat, Shahida was acutely uncomfortable with the lack of privacy and the indignity of outdoor urination and defecation. She had to wake up at 4:00 a.m. to steal into the fields to relieve herself. A typical nineteen-hour day for this mother of six began with washing clothes, cleaning, feeding farm animals, and the first of five prayer sessions each day. By 6:00 a.m. Shahida had tea prepared for her family. Her husband, Aalabar, was home by then from his night job at the state Power and Water Department in Nagina village. Their four youngest children, two boys and two girls, were up by then. The two oldest daughters, ages eighteen and twenty-two, were already married and no longer living at home. Most girls in Ghaghas were married by age fifteen.

There was no time in Shahida's day for recreation, socialization, or contact with others in the community. In the gender-polarized social infrastructure of her village, most women had little contact with the world outside their home and the surrounding fields. Most families had no TV, radio, or telephone, including Shahida's. Socially isolated, most women in Mewat played no role in matters related to the village at large.

By 8:30 a.m. Shahida's two sons were off to school in Nagina. Any decisions related to the education of their children were made by Aalabar. The family sacrificed dearly to pay for the boys to attend a private school. The two young girls did not share such a privilege. They attended the free village government school where there was only one teacher for 115 students. The literacy rate among women in Ghaghas was about 29 percent. Shahida was determined that all her children would become literate and finish a full curriculum through twelfth grade. Her married daughters had only finished fifth grade.

Once the cooking and clean-up were done, and the kids had left for school, Shahida disposed of the household wastewater in the street, adding to the muddy mess from her neighbors, and headed for the field. She had to supplement her husband's income with whatever she could earn by raising crops. When she was not in the field, she collected fodder (plant leaves and stalks for the livestock) from the local forest area and common land. By the time she stopped for midday prayers at 1:30, she had already collected animal manure and patted it into cakes to be dried and used as cooking fuel. Her typical afternoon was spent cleaning up after and milking the animals. The kids came home by 4:00. The boys had private coaching at a tutor's home in the village. By the time dinner was prepared and cleaned up after, the children and remaining household chores were attended to, and all prayer times were completed, Shahida was able to go to bed around 11:00 p.m.

At the foundation team's first community meeting in Ghaghas, not a single *Meoni* (Meo woman) participated. Meonis rarely strayed from their prescribed roles within the male-centered power structure. Women were not free to speak; but Shahida attended the meeting. She sat in the corner, her face covered with the scarf that was required when in the presence of men.

Sociologist Anjali Makhija was a strong advocate for women, but she and other women on the team had worked cautiously in the Mewat communities to avoid any abrupt disruption in the villagers' way of life. Women field team members served initially as role models for the women in the village. They spoke up, expressed opinions, asked questions, and even questioned the wearing of the traditional head scarf.

Women from the foundation interacted with and supported Shahida from the beginning, engaging her in conversations about children, healthcare, and farming. By the fourth meeting, where the foundation team spoke about the Integrated Sustainable Village Development model, Shahida began to speak.

She kept her scarf on; that religious and cultural practice was unlikely to change. But she spoke. She asked questions. At one point a man "*shushed*" her. An elder told her to "settle down." But Shahida did not "settle down."

When Shahida became an active member of a village-level institution, she faced resistance from the entire community. She took on a difficult role for any woman in a strongly gender-biased culture. Even the male members of the foundation teams had been resigned to the presumption that women would not be allowed to take an active part in VLIs. This turned out to be another training opportunity for everyone involved, and served as a reminder of one of the foundation's important guiding principles—empowering women. The foundation team members were increasingly heartened by Shahida becoming vocal and expressing opinions.

Like most women in Mewat, Shahida was responsible for all tasks related to her family farm, in addition to her other numerous household duties. She was motivated to learn best agricultural practices introduced by Sehgal Foundation. She used raised beds for vegetable cultivation and operated a vermicompost unit on her land. Shahida was pleased with the results and encouraged others to adopt these methods as well.

She was active in the check dam project and made sure her family contributed their portion. Due to her persistence, Shahida's was one of the first few households in Ghaghas to have a latrine. She felt so strongly about the need for latrines that she lobbied Sehgal Foundation to help those who could not afford latrines. When the concept of soak pits was introduced to deal with household wastewater, she immediately wanted one.

When Aalabar found out that his wife was actively participating in the meetings against his wishes, and voicing her opinion in front of men, he strongly objected. He tried to forbid her from leaving the house at one point.

Observing the conflict between Shahida and Aalabar, the foundation team was keenly aware that the issue was not just inside the family. Aalabar faced pressure from other men who were not happy with women behaving assertively. Sensitive to issues raised by the changing roles of women, the foundation team knew they could not just attempt to empower women without addressing the situation from all sides. Men on the foundation team took great care to provide support and counsel to Aalabar as well.

Encouragement from the team included illustrating how Shahida's activism resulted in tangible benefits to her family and the community. Aalabar was able to appreciate the value of these improvements. He experienced a change of heart. Not only did he begin to support his wife in her association with the VLI, he began playing a larger role at home and in the field. Such surprising changes had a powerful effect on Shahida's self-confidence. No longer shamed for speaking out, she was proud to be offered a chair at VLI meetings and to share the forum with men. This type of transformation spread to other women and other families.

Observing the experiences of women like Shahida prompted the Sehgal Foundation team to strengthen their stand on women's issues. Sessions were held on gender sensitization for all team members. With the imperative to be more proactive in including women in all facets of their work, the team gradually witnessed more active participation by women in foundation projects. For the first time, two women's self-help groups were formed that year in Ghaghas. Progress in this direction was slow but steady. As with every strongly embedded cultural mind-set, the struggle for gender equity remained, and still remains, an ongoing challenge.

CHAPTER 5

Seeing Is Believing

Water literacy, mobilizing women to speak out, education in general, and good governance in particular were still in their infancy in Mewat as the Sehgal Foundation team met in the spring of 2004 to discuss the progress made in the first year of the *Four, Four, Four* campaign. Employing the Integrated Sustainable Village Development model was improving the quality of life in all four villages and positively influencing the satellite hamlets as well. The flexibility of the model allowed the four programs to have differing levels of application, depending upon the needs of each community. Individual team members were empowered to emphasize or adjust program components when necessary to make a greater impact.

About a third of the foundation's expenditures that year went to support income enhancement and best agricultural practices. The next largest chunk went to the water management projects and infrastructure development. The Rural Health and Family Life Education programs remained effective and low cost. Numerous small steps had been taken, and each small success made the next more possible. Good planning and a balance between short-term and long-term strategies were making a difference in subtle but substantial ways.

The *Four, Four, Four* campaign had begun with the intentional goal of "walking before running": developing successful models for each program, reviewing and improving models where possible, and then replicating the models that had larger impact. The reach of Sehgal Foundation programs would expand from four to eight villages, and high-impact programs would be initiated in satellite villages. Strategy sessions focused on identifying which villages should be chosen to replicate the models determined to have the greatest impact. This expansion would also be a test of the concept of replicating programs in village clusters.

A strategic alignment process was used to decide which programs, and which activities and interventions within each program, to "scale up" to make a more significant beneficial impact. Program leaders determined costs and timelines and evaluated the potential benefits, community psychology, and sustainability issues before the decision was made.

The foundation team's steady, holistic approach to integrating the issues within each community was laying the groundwork for sustainable development. The original catchphrase, *Small Interventions, Big Impact,* was revised slightly. Small fulcrum-like interventions were good, but the time had come to think big. The catchphrase was updated to *Small Is Beautiful, But Big Makes Impact.*

A new level of sophistication was evolving within the Sehgal Foundation team as the organization reaffirmed and crystallized its mission statements and participated in team-building exercises. As their roles shifted from initiating to facilitating in any given community, each person on the team—whether it was the core team, a field team, a project implementation team, or any other subset of the larger team—retained a shared organizational mind-set that remained fresh and unencumbered by dogma.

The foundation's position as an advocate for women, children, and the poor, was affirmed and further clarified as strictly "nonpolitical and nonreligious." This had always been the position of the organization, but it made good sense to formalize and publicize that commitment in light of deeply rooted fears—expressed from time to time by religious leaders within the more conservative Muslim communities—that the foundation had a hidden agenda to convert their youth to Christianity. These fears sometimes erupted when "outsiders" visited. Yet international visitors were coming frequently to see Sehgal Foundation's agriculture and water-augmentation projects.

Preserving credibility and mutual trust with the community remained a top priority. The foundation team had no intention of threatening the authority of village elders or religious leaders. Reminders from the Sehgal Foundation implementation team of the organization's goal to maintain respect for all religions were made whenever the concern was voiced in a community.

Foundation employees came from diverse backgrounds and represented a broad range of basic competencies. With social scientists at the core, access to topnotch internal and external experts, and valuable linkages with community organizations, the corporate sector, academic institutions, and government, Sehgal Foundation maintained the essential tools for transformative insight. Just as training opportunities were provided for villagers and community leaders, education sessions and advocacy workshops were also available to all foundation team members.

The organization's pool of talent was further enhanced by the expansion of the Sehgal Foundation Board of Trustees to include eminent experts in various fields of business, academia, and development. The new trustees brought fresh perspectives and were willing to help guide the program leaders and provide peer review of the work when needed. Board members served as Sehgal Foundation ambassadors and proactively engaged with their contact networks.

The business culture of the foundation had developed in a nonhierarchical environment of collaboration and mutual respect, which naturally extended to the communities. Sehgal Foundation team members served as powerful role models, working alongside villagers to accomplish their goals. The field team set a strong example of hard work, often showing up early and staying late into the evenings if needed for a project.

Strong role models inside the community were even more important to truly inspire the confidence required for people in such impoverished circumstances to take full advantage of opportunities for their own self-development. To help identify such individuals and provide them with the support they would need to take a more visible role in their communities' development, the team created a new training program. The people who agreed to be these "home-grown" advocates would be called "village champions." The qualities sought in these individuals included literacy, enthusiasm, compassion, and a commitment to social development.

The training curriculum, which was made available to other organizations as well, was designed to provide tools to help village champions inspire others within their communities to join in the quest for a better life. The program covered leadership development, project management, fundraising, program details, and processes for setting up village-level institutions and facilitating VLI activities. These energetic young people would be champions of the development models in their communities. The first six village champions would be ready to start training in early 2005 at the new community center Sehgal Foundation was building on the outskirts of Ghaghas.

The original idea was to create a community center on common property near a village cluster, build rainwater-harvesting structures for demonstration, and eventually give the community center back to the community. However, the Ghaghas panchayat was not able to provide Sehgal Foundation with a large enough piece of property, so the foundation purchased an acre of land by the road in 2003 that was large enough to be a demonstration center for water harvesting, solar energy, and agriculture practices. The well-equipped center, with a training hall, modest residential facilities, and a kitchen, was situated where people from nearby villages could also come for training sessions and Life Skills Education classes.

The leadership and training provided through the village-level institutions in each community gave people the skills and confidence to maintain the project infrastructures. As people in the villages began to see the results of some of the longer-term projects, trust in their partnerships with Sehgal Foundation grew. More often now, villagers knew what needed to be done, and only required some assistance to execute their own solutions. Each new achievement reinforced their momentum.

Tangible results were being seen in all four of the key programs.[24]

---

24. One initiative did not move forward as envisioned in 2004. Sehgal Foundation explored the idea of establishing a program to promote alternative energy sources as part of the Integrated Sustainable Village Development model. Solar streetlights sounded like a good idea in villages that were dark at night when women left their homes to relieve themselves in the fields. Batteries and solar options were attempted, but the community was unable to maintain the lights, and a viable end-to-end solution wasn't found at that time.

By spring 2005 the team observed a difference in the attitudes of villagers who had begun to take an active part in their own development, saying, "People have gone from watching things happen around them to making things happen."

The completion of the first two check dam projects in Rangala Rajpur and Ghaghas had further illustrated how "seeing is believing." The Ghaghas check dam and recharge well had reversed the depletion of groundwater in that area. In the Rangala Rajpur area, the water table rose by 1.5 meters. The villagers' open wells rose by seven feet after the first monsoon, and the once-dry wells began to fill. The large single dam structure was divided into three pools. One served as a recharge pool. The other two were storage pools, one of which was seeded with fish larvae.

Villagers were starting to grasp the enormity of the amount of water that had been wasted for so long. Seeing a large body of water in a landscape that had been arid for many decades had a profound effect on the mood of villagers. Bodies of water as part of scenic vistas instilled brand-new feelings of optimism. As Nabbi, an opinion leader in Rangala Rajpur, stood gazing at children playing in the water, he told a member of the foundation implementation team, "Just seeing this mass of water soothes us and gives us hope." He announced, "We are ready to work with you for further improvements in our village."

The moisture level in the soil adjacent to the water storage pools improved, and water was now available for irrigation of the nearby community land. As water awareness increased, villagers built more rainwater-harvesting structures and followed conservation methods. When a small leak developed in the dam structure, the villagers rushed to repair it themselves. And when the water-harvesting achievements were noted in the local newspapers, visitors came to see for themselves how water availability and quality had improved.

The entire community contributed money to dig a new well when the panchayat was unable to pay for it. In some villages, residents of particular streets agreed on their own to accomplish specific focused initiatives. These successes appeared to be a result of people being able to see immediate tangible results that benefited them directly.

Water literacy campaigns were held wherever possible as part of Family Life Education, Farmer Association meetings, and self-help-group gatherings in schools and healthcare venues. The local wisdom regarding the importance of percolating rainwater into the ground was explained simply: "Where water is running, make it walk; where it is walking, make it crawl; and where it is crawling, make it stop." Community water audits, facilitated by the village-level institutions, were effective communication tools for positively influencing the community to conserve water and make well-informed choices about wells, wastewater, and soak pits.

Besides promoting more recharge wells, the Water Management team promoted the construction of platforms around open wells, used for drinking, washing clothes, and watering animals, to prevent contamination from dirty water. Dirty water around the well was channeled into a soak pit. Open public water-pipe outlets were replaced by stand-post taps. Here again, wastewater was directed to a soak pit through an underground pipe. This simple intervention helped keep streets clean. The Public Health Department became a partner to promote this activity in Ghaghas. Dozens more were constructed in Goela and Agon.

Chisel plowing before the onset of monsoon resulted in rainwater percolation, which improved subsoil moisture. To promote chiseling, the foundation agreed to share the cost with farmers. Results varied from crop to crop, but all farmers reported higher production and better quality produce. The number of crop irrigations needed was significantly reduced, causing use of this intervention to spread to neighboring villages.

Appropriate management of the water supply in general led to better agriculture management, and better sanitation led to better health. In the process, participating rural communities became more empowered. Village-level institutions slowly became more responsive and started making positive changes in the community.

The village-level institution in Ghaghas was officially registered as a community-based organization under the Societies Registration Act, and began undertaking projects in partnership with Sehgal Foundation that extended beyond building and maintenance of water-related infrastructure. The foundation worked as a catalyst with School Management committees (school boards) to help fill gaps in government-mandated services.

As part of an initiative to improve the quality of schools, repairs were made to the Ghaghas school boundary wall. The Village Education Committee was revitalized. A shortage of teachers was a perpetual problem that Ghaghas tried to address. Sehgal Foundation assisted the village by providing funds for two teachers for one year. Parent-teacher meetings were introduced to increase parents' involvement in their children's education.

To make preventive health a priority for villagers, the foundation team worked on further strengthening the links between the community and available health services and helped to form a health committee in each village. The foundation team assisted the Ghaghas panchayat in applying to the State Health Department for funds to set up a sub-center in the village.

Goela, a small village of only 205 families, lacked amenities in every area. Its health center had been abandoned for years. The school building had a leaky roof and only one teacher for 200 students in different grades. Poor income on the part of Goela farmers was a result of their outdated agricultural practices. More community meetings were needed to mobilize villagers to join Sehgal Foundation in efforts to kick-start their development. An interest group was formed to work with the panchayat, and they were eventually able to complete a few small projects.

Over time, Goela's village-level institution, which had been dormant for months, became active. The community adopted vermicompost units and began raised-bed cultivation. They succeeded in reviving their Village Education Committee and hired an additional teacher. The community agreed to provide 50 percent of the teacher's salary. The vacant panchayat building was repaired and converted into a community center with a water storage tank.

The foundation team helped the Goela village-level institution register officially as a community-based organization. As a registered VLI, the community could more easily apply for government assistance programs, which Goela began doing. Village leaders mobilized to meet with government officials to address water access and electricity problems, and push for road improvements. As a result of the community's request for assistance with latrine construction, the District Rural Development Agency agreed to help subsidize each latrine constructed for *all* panchayats in Mewat. This was a celebrated achievement. Attempts to revive the Goela health sub-center, which was essentially defunct, were more difficult.

The Agon village-level institution eventually registered as a community-based organization and began repairs on their community meeting space. Agon's women's self-help group, comprised of mostly landless laborers, decided to start a group enterprise. With training from the foundation team, they set up a nursery for growing Gliricidia, a fast-growing tree that is a good source of green manure, among other uses. The women took turns guarding the nursery for three months until the saplings were ready for sale. As part of the promotional plan, Sehgal Foundation purchased their produce and marketed it at subsidized rates in several villages. The self-help group made a profit that was shared by ten women who used some of the money to rent land for another nursery enterprise.

Sehgal Foundation established a growing number of self-help groups in Mewat villages. The women in self-help groups were receptive to new ideas and proved to be reliable in paying back loans. By pooling their savings in order to access credit, poor women gained a voice with banks and other institutions and had the financial ability to create businesses.

A woman named Kavita joined a self-help group organized by Sehgal Foundation in Goela to get out from under a loan from the *dudhia* (milk collector or middleman). Similar to about a third of the population of Mewat, Kavita supplemented her family's income by selling milk. Families generally borrowed money from a dudhia to buy buffaloes to start a milk business. Imposing two unfair conditions on the loan, the dudhia required that he be the only buyer of Kavita's milk, and he also got to set the price. She was able to break this exploitive cycle by using her self-help group loan to pay off the dudhia and start selling her milk at a higher price to a new mini-dairy in her village. Within three months, she paid back her loan to the self-help group. Shortly thereafter, Kavita used another self-help group loan to buy a second buffalo. This allowed her to meet her family's milk needs and sell extra milk for cash. Kavita succeeded in increasing her income by 155 percent.

Self-help groups continued to empower women economically and to inspire their increased participation within the family and in the community. These women were keen to improve sanitation conditions in their villages and took part in trainings by the foundation on development issues and technical and business skills to strengthen their entrepreneurship. They spread positive messages among other women in the community as well.

Nasra, a thirty-five-year-old agricultural worker and mother of six from a self-help group in Agon, went on to become a *swasthya sakhi* (community health volunteer). Though she was illiterate, she was able to complete all of her Sehgal Foundation training assignments for community health volunteer, with occasional help from her children for the written parts. Training components included sanitation, cleanliness, immunizations, illness management, safe childbirth methods, and reproductive health issues.

When she first began in her new role, other women were jealous. But she soon won over the trust of the women in her village with her sincere interest in their healthcare. She gained the respect of the auxiliary midwife as well and was enlisted to help her distribute medications and birth certificates. When Nasra elected to undergo a tubectomy procedure, she became a willing resource to other women with questions about family planning methods.

Well-trained swasthya sakhis like Nasra perform a valuable service to their communities by helping to dispel myths and ill-informed practices, such as treating diarrhea by reducing fluid intake or thinking that immunizations cause impotency. Nasra clarified that misperception by explaining the relationship between immunization and reduced infant mortality. Though some people remained skeptical, most participated in getting the immunizations.

Many of Sehgal Foundation's swasthya sakhis went on to become government ASHA (accredited social health activist) workers.[25] As a

25. A key component of the National Rural Health Mission is to provide an ASHA worker to every village in India. This person serves as a liaison between the community and the public health system.

result, the foundation was asked by the government to provide ASHA training to government workers in Mewat.

Triumphs like this with self-help groups that were attributed to Sehgal Foundation pointed the team in more directions that were not originally envisioned. For example, Sehgal Foundation was invited by the United Nations Development Program through India's Ministry of Tourism to set up self-help groups and provide training in entrepreneurship in the town of Jyotisar in the Kurukshetra district in Haryana.

Jyotisar, a significant tourist attraction for Hindus, is believed to be where Lord Krishna recited the *Bhagavad Gita* to the warrior Arjuna. Hundreds of visitors travel to Jyotisar each day. However, the local residents were deriving no benefit to their livelihood from the many visitors. The proposed joint project had two goals: preserve India's cultural heritage by creating a richer tourism experience for visitors, and find a way to generate sustainable incomes for the local villagers, particularly women.

The second goal was key to the foundation's mission. Two-thirds of the women in Jyotisar were without marketable skills, and one-third were illiterate. A women's self-help group trained by Sehgal Foundation in Jyotisar succeeded over the next four years in creating several business ventures to attract tourists, such as clothing and crafts shops, eateries, lodges, and street entertainment. These persevering women became the instruments as well as the beneficiaries of the local tourism economy.

During the same four years, social issues such as sanitation and literacy were addressed in Jyotisar and its surrounding villages with the help of community health volunteers, a drawing contest for schoolchildren on the theme "Our Village, Clean Village," street theater (*nukkad natak*) by a youth group, and support work from the team that revitalized the panchayat.[26] Sehgal Foundation developed the village youth drama group, called *Abhinaya Samooh,* with help from an NGO theater group from Delhi called Deepalaya. Their street plays conveyed the benefits of basic hygiene and sanitation.

---

26. By 2009 the women's self-help group, called *Kriti Kendra* (Creativity Center), included about 200 women and was registered under the Societies Act. With this happy success, Sehgal Foundation phased out of Jyotisar.

The benefits of group ventures were already being appreciated by the farm cooperatives in Mewat. The accomplishments of the farmers' associations resulted in a decision by Safal, Mother Dairy's Fruit and Vegetable Division, to set up a local collection center in Goela. Instead of going through Safal's centralized facility, vegetables reached the retail market directly after quality screening at a local center. This change made it possible for farmers to use or sell their rejected produce in the local market while it was still relatively fresh.

Job market issues remained challenging in Mewat, but Sehgal Foundation continued to sponsor workshops on skill development and entrepreneurship for young people. Two young men from Agon, Ghanshyam Sharma and his brother, Amar Chand Sharma, participated in an orientation workshop for village youth. The brothers were both welders who had welding jobs in a shop in Ferozepur Jhirkha. After attending the workshop, they were encouraged to join RUDSET Institute to learn to set up their own business and attend a fifteen-day training in fabrication and welding. With help from RUDSET Institute and Sehgal Foundation, the brothers were able to submit a project proposal to the local bank. They procured a loan to open their own shop. Sharma Welding Workshop was a successful enterprise. With increased earnings, the Sharmas were able to pay back the loan and further expand their business.

While the direct service programs and projects in the Integrated Sustainable Village Development model continued in the villages, Sehgal Foundation maintained its ongoing outside efforts to promote sustainable agricultural practices, crop improvement research, biodiversity, and genetic conservation. Sehgal Foundation became a member of ICRISAT's newly created Hybrid Parent Research Consortia on Pearl Millet, Sorghum, and Pigeon Pea, and joined the United Nations Foundation's World Heritage Biodiversity Program for India (WHBPI) with the Ford Foundation, ATREE, and the Government of India. To strengthen maize research in India, Sehgal Foundation provided support to the International Maize and Wheat Improvement Center (CIMMYT) of Mexico for their corn research in India.

When an earthquake and tsunami killed 250,000 people in Indonesia, Sri Lanka, Thailand, India, and Malaysia, leaving millions without homes or livelihood, Sehgal Foundation gave financial support to nonprofit organizations responding to the disaster and worked diligently to raise resources to help the victims of the tragedy.

Sehgal Foundation's linkages in the public and private sectors expanded markedly throughout 2005 and brought recognitions that would help extend the organization's reach. The foundation was granted Consultative Status with the United Nations Economic and Social Council (ECOSOC) in recognition of its support of the ambitious UN Millennium Development Goals to reduce poverty around the world. As a partner in the Clinton Global Initiative, Sehgal Foundation made commitments to reduce poverty in rural India, and as a member of the newly formed consortium of voluntary organizations, Credibility Alliance, Sehgal Foundation endorsed the creation of an ethical code of conduct for NGOs in India.

Sehgal Foundation was recognized by the Centre for Development and Population Activities (CEDPA) for implementing the Better Life Options Program for adolescent girls in India. More than 200 girls across six villages completed the Family Life Education course. For more than 100 girls who could not attend the six-month course, intensive fourteen-day Life Skills Education curriculum camps were offered four times in four villages during summer vacation. The results of pre- and post-assessment questionnaires demonstrated that the girls started to adopt better hygiene habits and became actively involved in community projects. Significant improvements could be seen in the young women's attitudes toward gender equity and marriage age. Improvements were seen in self-confidence, communication skills, knowledge of reproductive and child health, legal rights, and the ability to set life goals.

A girl named Hayfa was a participant in the foundation's Family Life Education course in Ghaghas. Hayfa was the fourth child of a very poor family of eleven. She had never been to school. In the classes, she learned how to read and write, and how to sew garments. When she turned sixteen, her father arranged her marriage to a young man from a nearby village. However, within two weeks after the wedding, she became a target of her husband's violent temper. He was mentally ill and often physically abusive to Hayfa. When her father-in-law started behaving in sexually inappropriate ways toward her, she complained to her husband. As a result, Hayfa was sent back to live with her parents. Thanks to her new sewing skills and education, this was an acceptable, and highly preferable, alternative. She could earn extra income for the family and help her mother with her younger siblings. Hayfa made money tailoring clothes and working as a substitute instructor in the Family Life Education Center. The foundation assisted by buying her an embroidery machine. She filed for divorce from her abusive husband and decided to pursue a formal education. She started school for the first time in the fifth grade class at a government school. Hayfa's life changed for the better thereafter.

A range of new projects were extensions of the four programs in the Integrated Sustainable Village Development model that continued to be fine-tuned throughout 2005. Community libraries were opened in Agon, Ghaghas, and Goela. Sehgal Foundation held health camps and immunization drives. A partnership with All India Institute of Medical Sciences was instrumental in diagnosing villagers with cataracts, supporting their ability to travel to a hospital to have corrective surgery, and facilitating their follow-up care in the village. A camp was organized to immunize kids from polio. Work in partnership with the Delhi Council for Child Welfare helped kids who already had contracted polio to access disability aid, physiotherapy, and hospital care.

Health checkups were provided for girls in satellite villages, and more women's self-help groups were formed. Women in the groups were provided training in areas such as raising fruit trees.

Weather stations were installed in Ghaghas, Goela, and Agon to observe rainfall, humidity, and temperature for crop planning. Camps were held for soil and water testing.

The education implementation team joined schoolteachers and others going door to door to enroll more children in school. Many parents, illiterate themselves, were not convinced that literacy was necessary for their children, especially for girls. Girls were less likely to attend school if there were no latrines or if their mothers kept them home to work in the household.

Benches and rugs were supplied to refurbished schools. The foundation team submitted applications to the director of the General

Education Department and to the district education officer to fill vacant teacher positions in the model village schools.

The introduction of village champions into the communities was transformative. The newly trained young VCs spoke up boldly but respectfully in conversations with their elders. They took on their advocacy role with enthusiasm. The first six VCs were divided into three teams to compete in the coordination of a community mobilization project to construct water-harvesting systems in three schools in the *Four, Four, Four* villages. The VCs coordinated all aspects of the project, including community involvement, cost-benefit analysis, technical considerations, accounting, and finally presenting the final project to the community. The school in Ghaghas won the competition. All three teams felt a strong sense of pride in making such a visible contribution to their communities. Their involvement created additional goodwill in the communities as VCs began spontaneously taking on small projects. One VC conducted, on his own initiative, an information session for fifty people on the topic of HIV/AIDS. VCs helped out with library projects, agricultural practices, and a range of water projects, such as building hand pumps and digging wells.

The occasional suspicion and criticism from the villages for Sehgal Foundation's involvement in the community was dealt with head-on by VCs with thoughtful direct communication. Their team spirit of cooperation and good-heartedness made the difference in winning over their detractors. A second batch of VCs began training.

The positive influence of VCs could be seen in a number of areas. A drawing competition was held on Environment Day for school children in three villages. When asked to draw something about the environment, an eleven-year-old girl named Arsheeda surprised the team by writing on her drawing, "Water is important for our life, and we should save it."

The facilitator asked Arsheeda where she learned English. She explained that her parents took her out of an English-medium school (where English is the primary medium of instruction), deciding she was ready to be a woman and focus on household chores.

A village champion from the same community joined the foundation team for visits with Arsheeda's family on several occasions to try to convince them to let her go back to school. With the helpful influence of the village champion, her parents finally agreed. Arsheeda was very happy. Her family and others in her community were eventually uplifted by seeing a young girl empowered by education.

Suri and Edda Sehgal and other trustees and team members were pleased to see the programs making a difference. Everyone involved felt gratified by each achievement carried out in the Integrated Sustainable Village Development model. The model was clearly working. The programs were replicable, and some were proving to be sustainable. But Sehgal Foundation did not have the capacity to carry out all of the programs in a continually increasing number of villages. The team needed to find a different way to expand.

With lots of individual activities going on in eight villages plus the satellite locations, the team was again challenged to identify which programs were having the greatest impact. The most concrete and measurable results were associated with water and agriculture. Health and Life Skills Education were harder to quantify. The team could count participants in trainings or immunization programs, but measurement of qualities like self-confidence or the exact nature of a community's health could not be determined in a fixed way.

Suri Sehgal challenged the team to take a larger view of how to demonstrate the impact made by each project that was successfully completed. He asked them to consider how they could make the best use of Sehgal Foundation capital in those areas of greatest impact and with the most potential for sustainability. The team had learned a great deal from its mistakes as well as its successes. Was it possible to do more to share this information with others who had the same goal of helping the rural poor? Could Sehgal Foundation accelerate the development process in Mewat and other rural areas by pursuing partnerships with other NGOs, or by creating different types of linkages? Could the foundation expand geographically with fewer programs?

More sharp minds would eventually be invited to join the conversation. Scientists, economists, anthropologists, sociologists, and experts in agricultural development and water resources would gather together with foundation staff and community leaders from the villages of Mewat during the next eighteen months to answer these questions.

As 2005 came to a close, Sehgal Foundation broke ground on a major three-year construction project in Gurgaon that would play an important role in the expansion strategy.

CHAPTER 6

A Rude Awakening

The Sehgal Foundation team was still small enough that everyone on the team was actively involved in the ongoing group strategy meetings. Conversations were lively, and each person was invested in the possibilities for growth of the organization. Scalability and sustainability of programs were discussed in every session. Three ingredients were needed for scaling up program operations: expertise, trained people, and funds. Without question, Sehgal Foundation had accumulated and developed the expertise. The essentials in short supply were the numbers of trained people and more funding.

Additional skilled individuals were needed to take the Integrated Sustainable Village Development model to more villages. The team hoped to expand their work to forty villages. To have enough village champions for that many communities, a larger interactive facility was needed where they could be trained quickly. Training had been the first identified purpose for the new foundation office building then under construction, along with rural research, governance, and other programs.

The first name proposed for the new facility was Academy of Rural Research and Development (ARRAD). "Academy" was soon changed to "Institute" to be more inclusive of the potential uses for the building that went beyond training and teaching. Now named the Institute of Rural Research and Development (IRRAD), the space would also be an ideal place to showcase models of programs Sehgal Foundation was using in Mewat. Examples of the technology and innovations created by the foundation team could be displayed in the building alongside photographs and other media presentations.

Financial realities brought a sharp focus to foundation goals with the reminder that, although the needs of the poor in rural India were overwhelming, Sehgal Foundation funds had a ceiling. The Sehgal family could not continue indefinitely to finance all projects, as it had from the start. Paying for the replication of the Integrated Sustainable Village Development model in more and more communities was not possible with the limited funds of a single NGO. Raising capital from other sources would eventually be necessary.

Finding out how that process might be handled required further research. Experts pointed out that fundraising was usually more difficult when a family name is associated with a philanthropic enterprise. Words in a name that provided some idea of the intent of the organization would be more effective in attracting interest.

The idea of changing the name of the entire organization, from S M Sehgal Foundation to Institute of Rural Research and Development, appealed to the founders. That name better reflected the foundation goals. Suri and Edda Sehgal preferred that the organization have its own identity or "personality," and not be dependent upon the personalities of the founders. In addition, the possibility of IRRAD someday becoming an independent, self-sustaining entity that could survive and move forward whether or not the Sehgals were a part of it was, for Suri and Edda Sehgal, a somewhat exhilarating thought, similar to imagining an infant learning to walk.

While the Sehgals looked into the course of action for changing the foundation's legal name, the foundation's Communications team began creating a new branding identity for the organization. Due to technicalities in India's Foreign Contribution Regulation Act, the formal name change was never actually made. However, while the name-change effort remained in play, the foundation was branded as "IRRAD (an initiative of the S M Sehgal Foundation)." Several awards received by the foundation over the next several years were in this name.

The concept for the use of the building facility in Gurgaon, called Phase 1, evolved over the next year as construction continued. The land was a little more than three kilometers from Sehgal Foundation headquarters. When the property was first purchased in 2002, with enough land for two large buildings, the Sehgals made the decision to ensure that any building constructed on that land would be ecofriendly. Suri and Edda insisted the buildings meet the highest level of efficiency and sustainability set by the U.S. Green Building Council (USGBC). The goal for the Phase 1 building was to meet all requirements for achieving the platinum rating LEED (Leadership in Energy and Environmental Design) certification. A search was conducted for an architect with experience designing "green" buildings.

Not only would the facility be used to demonstrate the foundation's program innovations and technology, the green building itself would be a demonstration model. Suri Sehgal reaffirmed, "We must practice what we preach. We can't tell villagers to harvest rainwater if we don't do the same."

Modern office towers, residential complexes, malls, hotels, and other large buildings were popping up all over Gurgaon, as they were in some other cities in India. The metropolis was referred to as the "Millennium City" due to its rapid expansion and leadership in finance, information technology, and other industries. Gurgaon became a popular home for young professionals, the upwardly mobile middle class, and the wealthy. One glaring flaw, however, was the lack of planning. Urban development was allowed to take place quickly, with inadequate infrastructure and little oversight or enforcement of building codes. Every new building seemed to have its own generator to deal with the frequent power outages. The resulting diesel fumes had a negative impact on air quality. Few buildings complied with water-harvesting directives, leading to rampant overextraction of groundwater. Sehgal Foundation had an opportunity to demonstrate a better alternative.

Suri and Edda Sehgal said, "Our building will be a model for others to see and consider emulating as their buildings are constructed. The IRRAD campus will lead by example, combining simplicity of design with the latest knowledge and environment-friendly technologies."

All uses of energy, materials, and water had to meet international standards for recycling, environmental preservation, energy efficiency, and conservation. The structure would be equipped with solar power to meet its energy needs along with a complete rainwater-harvesting system, groundwater recharge, and wastewater recycling to reduce off-site pollution. The building would be a zero-water-runoff site with total gray and black wastewater recycling. A 400,000-liter-capacity tank would collect rainwater for reuse and excess would flow to groundwater recharge.

Ramesh Kapahi, the foundation's director of finance and administration, was involved in each aspect of the Phase 1 construction: government documents and approvals, water and electrical connectivity, and building-completion certificates. He joined Jay in meetings with architects and other experts. He explained how hard it was for some people to imagine the unique vision for this building, saying, "The only other platinum LEED certified building in Gurgaon was commissioned by a huge multimillion dollar conglomerate. For a small NGO to take on this type of project was a significant challenge. But Dr. Sehgal told us, 'Nothing less than the highest standards are acceptable.'"

Finding an architect who had the appropriate experience, shared a passion for environmental issues, and understood the green building concept was a challenge. The architect chosen, Ashok B. Lall, had the interest and passion, but this was his first green building. He was fully committed to the task at hand. He said later, "It is every architect's dream to work with a client who not only shares his values and dreams but also inspires and challenges him to excel. The challenge was straightforward: make a campus that reflects the ethos of the foundation, build it well but without ostentation, make it environmentally and socially responsible, take full responsibility, and we will support your efforts!"

Another complication was the lack of available skilled manpower to do the work. Ramesh explained, "We had to hire and train the workers on-site ourselves, and our choices of material and equipment were dependent on what was available locally. We always emphasized and followed safety measures to avoid any accidents on the construction site."

Ashok B. Lall and/or his assistants were available on-site daily, selecting materials and guiding the workers. The general perception was that buildings of this sort are very expensive, but the cost of construction was on par with any other building "because we kept things simple. There is beauty in simplicity," as Ramesh pointed out.

The team did not use expensive materials, such as glass paneling or carvings. The design was modest and uncomplicated. The goal was to capture and use maximum sunlight, reduce the burden on energy, and recycle the waste materials on-site. Construction materials were chosen for low energy consumption. The building used very few traditional burned bricks and was virtually free of aluminum. Bricks were made on-site using extra earth from excavating the basement. Wood came from Indian certified and controlled teak forests. Rapidly renewable bamboo was used for the plywood wall panels. Some internal walls were paneled with leftover wooden shutter materials. Even wood pallets were recycled and used for flooring in the atrium.

According to Ramesh, obtaining the approvals for various stages in the construction process was sometimes slow. "Such processes are tough in an environment where corruption is common, even rampant. But guidance from Dr. Sehgal was helpful." Having worked with the Sehgals previously for many years at Proagro, Ramesh was comfortable and familiar with the Sehgals' approach: tight on principles, loose on most other aspects of work. Treating people with respect and transparency kept the team working at peak creativity.

Ramesh said, "Dr. Sehgal always told us, 'Be patient even if it takes longer.' We were very diligent on every aspect of the construction process. We always presented a complete plan. We never succumbed to pressure from dishonest officials and never indulged in unethical practices, bribes, or kickbacks. On the contrary, we told them that if there was any deviation or anything found to be wrong, we were willing to pay the related taxes and fines and fix the problems as per the government policy and procedures. We'd rather pay a penalty than a bribe."

According to Jay Sehgal, "The architect was entirely cooperative with the intent, and particularly conscientious about the goal of perfection in all aspects of the building process."

From day one of construction, Jay opened the Phase 1 work site for tours. There were no restrictions on who might come to watch the project unfold at every stage. Students, architects, civil engineers, and anyone else interested in learning more about environmentally sustainable building design were invited to walk through the site and watch how each system and feature was being assembled.

Visitors could watch how bricks were made on location from the excavated soil, or watch the installation of the 57.75 kW photovoltaic solar panels on the roof that provided energy-efficient heating, cooling, and lighting. Landscaping around the atrium and courtyard of the building consisted of indigenous plants supplied by Dharma Vana Arboretum of Hyderabad.

Though the hope was for this "smart" facility to inspire similar efforts, there was no way to know for sure who might be influenced to take similar steps. The team took time to share information at every opportunity in the hope that visitors might be inspired to adopt their own resource-efficient environmental practices as a result of seeing the Phase 1 demonstration model. The construction was covered extensively by the media in magazines, newspapers, and dailies, sparking various debates about the need to "go green."

Suri Sehgal had frequently used the metaphor of a pyramid for the foundation team's approach to program development. The base of the pyramid was wide, to include many pilot projects. Staff had been given a lot of freedom in choosing ideas to try. The team was tasked to select whatever worked and was cost-effective; if an idea was good, they were free to run with it. Over time, the intention was still to reduce the number of activities to those with the most impact and greatest potential for sustainability within the communities. Those programs at the top of the pyramid would be chosen to scale up. Other programs, even if successful, would be phased out if they were not sustainable.

The cultivation of jatropha, sweet sorghum, and a few other biomass-producing plants was being promoted in the country for biofuel. The foundation shied away from recommending their cultivation because of the strong belief that biomass production for fuels was not the right thing to do on land that could be used for food or fodder production. However, the foundation experimented with the cultivation of daincha (*Sesbania bispinosa*) in saline soils and low-lying areas to improve the soil quality and make biomass briquettes for fuel. The briquettes project had business potential but needed further experimentation to make it cost-effective.

In an effort to stop the deforestation in the Aravalli hills, the foundation helped the community establish a pilot reforestation project on two acres of forest land, from rootstocks still standing there. Though the project was successful, the foundation decided not to pursue it further because reforestation was an identified responsibility of the government. The foundation remained in a support-only role in this type of endeavor.

In most villages, when wood was not available, women used cow-dung cakes or agricultural waste for cooking fuel. Either way, the smoke was a known health hazard. A safer and more efficient alternative cooking fuel, biogas derived from animal manure, was made with a simple process whereby bacteria decomposed the manure anaerobically. The team set up a model biogas plant in Goela to demonstrate its benefits. However, Sehgal Foundation remained in a support-only role with this initiative as well.

The slow process of constructing the new building to house IRRAD gave the foundation team more time to think about how the organization might scale up. They were still feeling enthusiastic about taking the Integrated Sustainable Village Development model to forty villages, if they could only find a way to identify sources for the needed funds.

The staff engaged in a comprehensive evaluation of the *Four, Four, Four* campaign that had expanded by this time to cover seventeen villages and satellite communities and hamlets in the Mewat and Kurukshetra districts of Haryana. As the team reviewed the work accomplished during this period, they experienced what Suri Sehgal described as a "rude awakening" concerning the nature of development.

"Although progress was being made in the communities, we had little to show for it, even in the first four villages," Suri explained. "There was no hard data. Our people were so busy doing the work; we hadn't done much to document our successes. We realized that our goal of expanding the Integrated Sustainable Village Development model to forty villages was wishful thinking. In the business world, we were used to seeing exponential growth rates, but here we were stuck. Development was a painfully slow and complex process. Sustainability was a mirage that was hard to accomplish in even four villages."

Though the comprehensive changes the team had hoped for in the first four villages had not occurred as dramatically as originally envisioned, there had been many successes. Better farming practices were being tried and proven productive; several communities had more access to potable water and conservation technologies; and literally hundreds of incremental changes had been made in the areas of healthcare, education, skill development, and agriculture.

More girls were back in school in many villages. Anjali Makhija observed the changes she saw in women's confidence. "The veil is removed; there is openness in body language. Women are learning about reproductive health, and marrying a bit later. Members of the field team have evolved as well. These social aspects, however intangible, change whole lives and will affect future generations as well."

There was no doubt that the programs were working. But something had to be done to show concrete, measurable results that would demonstrate impact in a more visible and sustainable way. In light of the slow, lengthy, and capital-intensive nature of development, Sehgal Foundation had to find a "magic bullet" for sustainability to be able to scale up.

Concluding that the scaling up process would be just as slow as every other aspect of development, the team realized that they might not need all the space that was being created in the new building under construction. The large three-story building, with a basement level as well, had far more space than the foundation needed. The offices, exhibition galleries, auditorium, cafeteria, classrooms, interactive training rooms, library, and program areas could all be accommodated on the ground floor. Village champion training and job skills training would continue at the community center near Ghaghas where there were ample workshop areas and classrooms. The community center was a more appropriate and comfortable venue anyway for small training sessions. The unused offices in the new Phase 1 building would be made available for rental to tenants who preferred upscale, modern, and ecofriendly venues. Sehgal Foundation could use the rental income to help sustain ongoing field operations.

Following the team's well-established practice of concentrating on finding solutions, Suri shared an idea he had been considering for some time: "We may not have the capital or the time to convert lots of villages fast, but what we can do is synthesize our expertise."

He explained his vision for expanding Sehgal Foundation into a research-based knowledge institute. Since expertise at the grassroots level was Sehgal Foundation's greatest strength, the team could assemble, synthesize, and document knowledge and information they gathered from the ground level about what it takes to fully develop a village, while also acknowledging the conflicts and barriers they confronted along the way. They would share all steps in their learning processes, the proud achievements as well as every mistake, no matter how minor.

The ability to learn from any experience was the team's added advantage. As research was done and knowledge was generated, it would now be made accessible to others. The overarching goal in establishing the foundation in the first place was to promote more and more sustainable development in India. Considering the magnitude of the need, lots of partners would be needed to further this goal. Documentation would also demonstrate to the team and others what Sehgal Foundation had been working so hard to accomplish in Mewat.

The team had already been creating stronger linkages and partnerships in the public and private sectors to accelerate the development process. Now the group's enthusiasm grew as they embraced the idea of sharing their knowledge, proven interventions, and sustainable skills in a larger context.

Research findings and other information would now be submitted to and promoted in academic journals and technical and nontechnical publications. Documentation of the foundation's baseline surveys, agricultural development, needs-based studies and assessments, and field research would be shared in training workshops and local, national, and international conferences. The foundation would provide evidence of programs and initiatives that had shown the greatest potential for impact. Others interested in development would be able to take the ideas, modify as needed, and replicate them elsewhere.

By strengthening and utilizing relationships with state government bodies, Sehgal Foundation could become a leading resource organization with access to both government and nongovernment funds. With information about poverty and livelihood dynamics, and the ability to discern poverty indicators not already being addressed, Sehgal Foundation could become a globally recognized think tank. The foundation could play a role in advocating policy at higher levels of government and in the private sector. As a premier knowledge institution and learning platform for rural development and poverty reduction in India, impact would be assured.

The team had lofty aspirations to discuss at a forum hosted by Sehgal Foundation in April 2007 that brought together a group of inside and outside experts to examine whether Sehgal Foundation was on the right track. The group discussed in depth the efficacy of the practical solutions proposed for the foundation's future work.

Participants supported and affirmed the team's ideas for the new direction. Academicians, economists, and scientists shared their views on the challenges and opportunities for replicating the Integrated Sustainable Village Development model across India. The experts agreed that linkages were crucial ingredients. More robust documentation was a necessity for reaching any of the goals being discussed, particularly if any research findings were to be converted to policy papers.

The structure, vision, and mission of the organization were reviewed and reconfirmed in a discussion of the synergy between Sehgal Foundation's main centers. In addition to implementing programs and experimenting with rural technologies, a new Rural Research Center would undertake research, analysis, and synthesis of information on rural development for dissemination. More research staff would be hired to assist in conducting baseline assessments and surveys, evaluating the impact of specific programs, and identifying those that had the greatest impact. Programs such as the Life Skills Education program, which by this time had graduated 387 girls from seventeen villages, definitely had impact; but the question bothering the team was whether the impact could be quantified. Skill-building programs also needed to be quantified for their impact. The idea was to prune those programs with limited impact or where impact could not be quantified.

A Capacity Building Center would provide training to village champions and people in each program development area so they would help support and build the capacity of village-level institutions to better meet their communities' needs. A Policy, Governance, and Advocacy Center would endeavor to promote good governance in the villages and influence national policies on rural development. The decision was made to hire new people in research and governance so each center had a leader.

The work done in each of the centers was conceived as interactive and interdependent. The scope of the Capacity Building Center expanded in collaboration with other training institutes and government agencies. Hosting and attending conferences and trainings were now regular events. Rural Research Center activities further expanded linkages with academia and other research institutes and organizations. Impact assessments were conducted to evaluate the direct effects of Sehgal Foundation models. Overall research emphasized uncovering needs not already being addressed.

Linkages with state government occurred with specific projects throughout 2007. For example, the Public Health Department contributed to a water tap campaign in three villages and assisted with a rainwater-harvesting project for a hospital. The Water Supply and Sanitation Department took part in public water supply, storage, and disposal works in Rangala Rajpur. Sehgal Foundation partnered with the Department of Health and Family Welfares for the prevention, diagnosis, and treatment of polio and tuberculosis. Eye-care camps were organized with a government hospital to help people with vision impairments receive needed treatment interventions. The Department of Education referred government teachers for field training provided by Sehgal Foundation on the composition, responsibilities, and importance of School Management committees.

The state government Horticulture Department provided vegetable-washing machines to farmers at a 75 percent subsidy and provided thousands of fruit trees for commercial cultivation. The department subsidized vermicompost units and seed storage tanks; supplied free seeds, sprays, and fertilizers; and provided training in water and soil testing, and improved horticulture practices. The Animal Husbandry Department organized training on dairy development in the village of Taoru. The District Rural Development Agency provided solar lamps in Taoru at a 65 percent subsidy.

Each of these projects led step by step to more opportunities for villagers to receive the help they needed. But for citizens to access their full benefits and assistance from programs intended for the poor and to take advantage of publicly sponsored development opportunities, everyone involved needed more training and information. The Indian constitution guaranteed citizens many rights, but the wide disconnect between policies and their implementation through a stifling bureaucracy often prevented the intentions written on paper from reaching the proposed beneficiaries.

The foundation created a task force in 2007 to provide information to panchayat members and village interest groups about the mechanisms for obtaining entitlements and exercising their rights. The Sehgal Foundation team was poised to capture the advantages of two specific major new laws designed to help those in poverty: The Right to Information Act, 2005 (RTI), and National Rural Employment Guarantee Act of 2005 (NREGA). Each had the potential for large benefits to the poor and their communities. With the assistance of an outside legal consultant, panchayat training programs were held in Goela and in Ghaghas to explain the two major laws and to train the trainers. The entire foundation team participated in the forums.

RTI was a powerful piece of legislation that gave villagers the ability to obtain answers from bureaucrats. For example, they had the right to request information about the basic government-authorized services they were entitled to receive. Citizens could now get answers from bureaucrats about why they were not receiving their food rations through the Public Distribution System (PDS), which was barely functioning in many villages. The government ration shop in each village was supposed to distribute basic foods and fuel at highly subsidized prices to the poor. Corrupt and unscrupulous administrators had kept many people from receiving their mandated services. Misappropriation and embezzlement were commonplace. In the absence of oversight, the people in charge used bureaucracy as a barrier to enshroud information and intimidate illiterate people. They directed the goods elsewhere, sold them at higher prices, and kept the money. The poor were left with low-quality items and no recourse, until now. Any citizen could now request information from a government authority, and follow their requests through to completion.

The twofold goal of NREGA, later renamed the Mahatma Gandhi National Rural Employment Guarantee Act (MGNREGA),[27] was to provide an income to the poor while improving the area's durable infrastructure. A a minimum of 100 days of employment was guaranteed to each household whose adult members were willing to perform

27. The name change was made in an amendment in November 2009. The association with Mahatma Gandhi's name was intended to reinforce the legislation's focus on equity and inclusiveness of marginalized communities, affirm the dignity of labor, and serve as a concrete expression of the development vision of the Father of the Nation.

unskilled labor, such as building roads and digging wells. The program was funded by the government though panchayats and started in 200 districts in 2006, with the aim to reach all districts by 2008.

Guaranteed income for 100 days each year could change many lives for the better. However, similar to other entitlement programs, the people first had to know about the programs, learn how to access the benefits, and be confident enough to pursue their entitlements as citizens.

A Sehgal Foundation village champion trained in the new law went to his community's Block Development Office[28] to ask for information and financial details about development tasks that had been carried out by the panchayat. By citing the Right to Information Act, he gained full access to the information as well as new respect from the sub-district magistrate. A few small successes like this one provided more hope that once officials realized people knew their rights, those in authority would have to become more diligent about their obligations to serve the people appropriately.

During strategy meetings with the team in the fall of 2007, Suri Sehgal was feeling increased urgency about achieving some concrete "breakthrough results" in the villages. He pointed out that there was no single village in Mewat that one could walk into and *see* the changes that had been made. The environment around the homes and schools in each community was still filthy. Roads were in poor shape, and trash still covered the landscape.

Reminding the team, "Seeing is believing!" Suri said, "Seeing a clean developed village—that would inspire people in more villages to get on board!" His voice betrayed a little frustration when he asked, "Will I ever see such a village in my lifetime?"

The group directed its attention to an examination of what characteristics would be present in a "developed" village. What would a truly developed village look like?

Staff talked at length about what they had accomplished and what they had learned so far in the many types of work in different villages.

28. A block in India is a district subdivision that typically includes from twenty to sixty villages. The Block Development Office administrative responsibility falls between the village panchayats and district-level officials.

As they imagined the best physical features of a clean "developed" community, innovations with water had to come first. Every building would have water collection and storage structures, and wastewater disposal. Every home would have a toilet. The school would be clean, with intact or rebuilt boundary walls, appropriate furnishings, available water for drinking and meal preparation, and separate toilets for boys and girls. At least one teacher would be female. A developed village would have a clean and staffed primary healthcare clinic and a well-equipped, sanitary delivery hut for childbirths. The streets would be paved with brick and lit at night with solar streetlamps. Shade trees would be planted along the streets to offer relief from the blazing summer sun, with guard rails to keep the animals from eating the saplings before they were fully established. A clean and furnished community center nearby with a library would be in use frequently for events, trainings, and meetings of village-level institutions and panchayats. An all-important ingredient would be an income-generating enterprise, such as a fruit orchard, that would create a continuing source of income for the sarpanch's use to assure the sustainable maintenance of the village infrastructure. This component would depend on the village leadership and, in particular, the honesty of the elected sarpanch.

The conversation in the group moved quickly to the possibility of creating a single demonstration village that met all the criteria they described. His enthusiasm mounting, Suri proposed, "Let's choose one village as a demonstration model on every level, a model that others can learn from, a model that can be replicated elsewhere. We will make it as self-sufficient as possible. We can see for ourselves if this is the goal we are shooting for, and we can create ambition in the minds of people from other villages who have only experienced dirt and filth. We will bring them to the demonstration village so they can see what is possible. That will motivate them to want to achieve more, too. These people have seldom, if ever, seen a city; they have no easy access to public transportation; they are not aware of anything else. Let's get them out of their shell. Let's choose a village and get it done!"

Edda Sehgal was present, as she was in all meetings, providing her perspective and speaking up for the issues dearest to her, especially advocacy for women and any project focused on sanitation and cleanliness. She understood the complexity of India and served as a motivating force to the foundation team in general. Her presence and caring, kind nature always added harmony to the team. She was in full support of Suri's idea, as she was with each of the foundation goals and objectives. She loved the idea of a clean village and shared her husband's enthusiasm. She agreed that seeing the final result would inspire other villagers to want the same level of development in their communities.

A few on the team were a bit hesitant about the idea at first, unsure that doing so much *for* a village would have the desired result from the community. The team in general had learned, and sometimes relearned, that sustainability could only be assured if the community was convinced that any project was their own and not a project of a foundation or any other outside group. The people had to have a vested interest in the solutions. With this in mind, the choice of village was critical, just as it had been when the first four villages were chosen in 2002. Such a demonstration village must have an active panchayat with a sarpanch who was a strong and inspiring leader.

The team agreed that the 160-household village of Notki was a viable option for proposing the idea. The village-level institution and panchayat were active. The sarpanch was a dynamic and honest woman, but her son spoke for her in public.

To turn Notki into a demonstration village in record time, the foundation would fund 90 percent of the costs. In essence, the Notki conversion was another pilot project, another experiment.

When the idea of being a demonstration village was proposed to the people of Notki, they were interested and willing to participate in the work, though they did not share the team's sense of urgency. They no doubt found it hard to fully imagine the outcome that was possible in their community.

Sanitation was an immediate and pressing concern in Notki. The foundation team took villagers on a collective visit to one of the dirtiest areas in their community to introduce the idea of making Notki an open-defecation-free village. The group stood near the local school where the abundance of human excrement was vivid. After discussing concerns about children's health, and hearing about the advantages of sanitation, the people agreed to adopt a community-led total sanitation approach to making Notki an open-defecation-free village.

Throughout the village, men, women, young people, and even children soon began digging latrines. Within two days of their decision, thirty-five households already had latrine pits dug near their homes, more than doubling the current number in the village.

An official from the Mewat district commissioner's office observed all the people digging and asked the village sarpanch if there was a new government program that inspired this activity. The sarpanch, also busy digging, looked up from her work and said, "*Hum bana rahe hain!*" (*We* are constructing them!).

The sanitation drive was so successful that the program was extended to all seventeen intervention villages, increasing the number of latrines in every village by at least 50 percent from the previous year for a total of 1,813 new latrines. As the word spread, sarpanches from the region, villagers from neighboring communities, government officials, and private-sector entrepreneurs began visiting Notki to see the transformation taking place.

CHAPTER 7

The Magic Bullet

The Notki experiment was still in its early stages in February 2008 when a director was hired for the Policy, Governance, and Advocacy Center. Attorney and human rights activist Ajay Pandey joined Sehgal Foundation after fourteen years of human rights work and a master's degree in clinical legal education he earned as a Fulbright scholar at Vanderbilt University in the United States. Clinical legal education is an experience-based (learn-by-doing) teaching method with two primary objectives: to develop skills in the learners and, most important, to promote social justice. This method turned out to be an important feature of the new perspective Ajay brought to the foundation's quest for good governance in rural India.

The foundation team had envisioned the center as a vibrant platform for discussion and advocacy of good village governance. The main objective was to help rural villagers learn about policy and governance and voice their concerns in appropriate forums. The team grappled with the operational concept for meeting this objective. Staff already understood the importance of good governance as an aspect of every project and initiative, but their dilemma was how to most effectively engage the people of Mewat.

In team discussions of how to best move forward, Ajay framed their challenge in terms of the law and good governance—the essence of the democratic process. Good governance could only be achieved through *effective citizen participation*. India, the largest democracy in the world, was home to millions of disempowered and illiterate poor people who had no idea how to participate or represent themselves in the democratic process. Their difficulty was exacerbated by widespread corruption that could be found at every level of government. In light of such realities, Ajay was sure that providing people with information about their rights and entitlements as citizens would not be enough.

He described the predicament the team knew well. People who reside at the bottom of the social hierarchy feel entirely powerless. Many villagers, especially women, were afraid to speak out. Traditionally discouraged from education and prevented from acquiring influence, many of these poor people were focused on basic survival from one day to the next. These people needed support for raising their voices to anyone "in authority," particularly when those in authority were entirely unaccustomed to answering in any way to poor people.

Knowing that villagers could not fully comprehend how laws would actually make any difference to their lives, the Policy, Governance, and Advocacy team had to demonstrate how change *could* happen, and sometimes happened quickly. The team's mission was to empower citizens to use their voices in spite of the challenges, so people could see for themselves that they had the ability to influence and change the shape of their government. Shifting a culture of resigned hopelessness to one of empowered self-advocacy would illustrate how citizen participation is an effective path to achieving the life of dignity envisioned by India's constitution for all people.

Earlier trainings about the Right to Information Act and the National Rural Employment Guarantee Act had been offered to panchayats and others in community leadership by the Capacity Building team. Training members of the panchayats was necessary but, in addition, each individual member of the community—each citizen—needed the information and the know-how to take action. All villagers had to be *participants* in reaching the larger purpose of law in the first place: justice.

Ajay insisted that no matter how fervent the team felt about their objectives in this regard, any decision or plan had to come from the villagers themselves. Sehgal Foundation had to remain a catalyst for change, a medium only, not the change-maker. The team's role was pure and simple advocacy that would be driven by wishes and needs identified by members of the community.

Two more people were hired for the Policy, Governance, and Advocacy team, and more experts were consulted. Over the next couple of months, enthusiastic discussions continued about these concepts within the team and with small groups of villagers in Mewat. By summer, a one-year training program was conceived.

Drawing from his work in legal aid and human rights, his study of clinical legal education, and his years of training paralegals, Ajay proposed a hands-on clinical legal education approach. Trainees from villages would start right away and "learn by doing." The team would not wait for the entire program design to be fully completed before jumping into action.

Not surprisingly, Suri Sehgal was pleased with this idea and enthusiastic about the approach. "Learn by doing" was the exact approach the Sehgal Foundation team had been using with regard to development in general from the beginning.

Six villages known to have active village-level institutions were chosen to hold meetings about good governance. Through these meetings, trainees were recruited to participate in a program that would teach them how to make a real difference in their communities by practicing effective citizen participation in governance. Foundation staff and village champions helped spread the word and invited villagers to a central location, generally a primary school in each community.

Ajay welcomed each group of villagers and opened the discussions by acknowledging the sordid state of affairs affecting their communities—poverty, illiteracy, corruption, feelings of helplessness, and so on. Though the people nodded in agreement that these were generally their experiences, they appeared to be resigned to this fate.

Many villagers openly admitted feeling helpless and expressed doubt that they could do anything to change their circumstances. "*Kuch nahin hoga, eisa hi rahega*" (Nothing will happen and everything will remain the same.)

Ajay spoke of India's long and difficult struggle for independence from British rule and the hard-won guarantee in India's constitution of a dignified life for all citizens. At the same time, he acknowledged the obvious "disconnect" between that guarantee and the reality in the poor villages of Mewat. He then told three stories.

For the first, he asked his listeners to focus on the message, saying he could not verify the facts since the story came from his childhood memory. He spoke of a woman who put a lamp outside her house every evening after sunset. Her neighbors found this behavior peculiar. They ridiculed her for being more concerned about lighting the street than lighting her own home. They even trampled the flame and doused the light. Nevertheless, the woman continued to put a lamp outside her house every evening. Over time, neighbors started noticing the convenience of having light on the street. One by one, they began putting lighted lamps outside their own homes each evening. Once every neighbor on the street followed this practice, the ongoing use of streetlights was adopted by the entire community.

Ajay's next story illustrated what prompted him to become a lawyer. He began, "While on summer break from university, my mother asked me to get the cooking-gas cylinder refilled. During those days, we had just one gas cylinder, which was replaced each time it emptied. As I was paying for the refill at the gas agency, I was asked for ten extra rupees."

Ajay did not think the man's feeble explanation for the extra fee was legitimate. He reasoned that such a mandatory collection of money without the consumer's consent was not right. As he argued with the agency man, people in line behind Ajay became very interested. Some of them could see right away that the excuse given for the fee was questionable. Seeing that others felt the way he did, Ajay decided to challenge the matter further through appropriate channels. In order to take home the gas refill, he paid the extra amount, but he also told the man and his colleagues that such a fee was unwarranted and illegal. He warned that they would have to pay everyone back eventually. The gas agency men scoffed at Ajay and dared him to try getting his money back.

Ajay admitted at this point in his story that he had no real understanding of the legal system at that time, but he had recently read something about consumer rights in the newspaper. He knew that if no one took on the gas agency for its unfair trade practice, consumers would continue to suffer the added expense and be subjected to injustice. Armed with very little information, but lots of conviction, he sued the gas agency. The case went on in the district consumer forum of his hometown, Etawah, for four years. The media supported the cause, the law supported his action, and Ajay won the case.

He explained, "This was a huge learning and empowering experience despite the hurdles. As soon as the case was accepted by the consumer forum, the practice of collecting extra money from consumers by all gas agencies in my hometown stopped forever."

With each group of villagers Ajay spoke with, he shared different aspects of his experience during those four years that motivated him to become a lawyer and to use law as an instrument of justice, equality, and empowerment.

His third story was about the organization of a community luncheon. Villagers were to assemble in a common place to help with the preparation of the meal. An announcement was made the night before, asking each household to add one glass of milk to the large common pot for the meal. However, when the villagers gathered the next day for the big meal, the common pot was filled only with water. Every person assumed that others would put in their fair share of milk and that no one would know the difference if some water was added instead.

Ajay explained, "This is the story of our democracy. We all pour in water, thinking everyone else will pour in milk. That is how we ended up in this situation with so many disconnects. The message is—we *all* need to participate effectively in democracy to strengthen it. We must each think, *If I don't participate effectively, nobody else will!* Good governance has the power to effectively address citizens' helplessness, poverty, illiteracy, and everything else that is ailing our democracy!"

He stressed again and again that "We have the power" to be responsive and supportive—and that effective citizen participation is the true key to addressing "the disconnects we all know so well."

Listening to Ajay, the people in the group began to see what he was describing. Their eyes revealed glimmers of understanding as they finally agreed that, as citizens, they all needed to participate effectively in the system to make it better.

Ajay told each group that he was seeking the participation of thirty-five trainees to learn about good governance. However, he explained, the training group would actually be thirty-six members, because he included himself as one who would be trained and "learn by doing" along with the others. Ready to move ahead with a willing team of trainees, he said, "I will wear your shoes and work with you."

Ajay made it clear that the Sehgal Foundation was not "in charge" and not leading this training program. This would be a citizen-led initiative in the villagers' hands. Participants would decide which issues to confront. Villagers would choose the time and place for trainings, their own level of involvement, and so on. People listened attentively as he said the teaching aspect would be more of a dialogue than formal training.

Ajay had approached the villagers with his own strong and passionate conviction that there was no other choice but to participate effectively in democracy to bring about good governance and achieve the objectives of the Constitution of India. In addition, he stressed that the initiative could not succeed without equal participation by women. He likened effective participation to serving a greater cause. He asserted that, together, this group was about to achieve something "truly great." He repeatedly declared, "We will serve the cause of truth and justice, and achieve the dignified life that everyone deserves." He asked people to stand together and work for that cause.

Ajay observed a growing enthusiasm among the villagers as he described the results-based, "learn by doing" approach he proposed. In each of the six meetings, Ajay could feel relationships being forged with them. He felt a resonance and power in these connections. He encouraged people from every sector to consider being trainees: farmers and landless people, elected leaders and laborers, the illiterate and teachers. Any willing adult who agreed to participate for a full year of training was welcome. As an incentive for participating in the training, each participant would be paid a modest amount, Rs. 100, and provided transportation to the training center and lunch each day the trainees met.

The nominees came together for a group discussion and were asked questions to determine the sincerity of their commitment and their availability. Evaluators, including representatives from the villages, assisted in the final selections.

Inclusion of all kinds of citizens in governance training was unique. Ordinary citizens had been left out of the democratic process for far too long. These "ordinary" citizens would be the people to sustain the values of democracy. With effective citizen participation, change was possible. In fact, Ajay asserted, "The sky is the limit!"

The team had originally found it particularly challenging to convince women to participate in good governance training. But Ajay was adamant about equal participation. Though he was not sure he would attract 50 percent participation by women in the first year, he said, "We must try."

Ajay explained more about why the involvement of women was vital to their quest for justice. In a culture dominated by men, a corrupt status quo was more difficult for men to even recognize, let alone try to change. Their reality was "business as usual," which meant bribes and other illegal but common practices. Women, on the other hand, who had been isolated at home for the most part, were less likely to be familiar with, and thereby accepting of, the existing economic and political power structures and mind-sets. His explanation was not easily grasped by the villagers; their further understanding of the concept would come in time during the "learn by doing" process. The initial group of trainees included only nine women.

The training program began with fifty days of classroom instruction, held three days a week in combination with two days in the field. This format was designed to provide a broad perspective on rural governance; an understanding of the roles of panchayats and other functionaries, institutions, and mechanisms of rural government; and a basic review of the most important government programs to benefit poor people in rural India. This training helped illustrate to villagers how shortcomings with many of the programs designed for their benefit were the result of corruption and a lack of transparency and accountability.

Sehgal Foundation sponsored a series of panel discussions in the fall of 2008 to complement the training and create more community interest in good governance. Speakers came from various levels of government, business, academia, and the media. The village trainees, community leaders, and the foundation staff, trustees, and board members all attended and participated.

One of the panel discussions about the current status of the Public Distribution System spurred trainees to gather information from ration-card holders in their villages. They collected a list of all citizens with yellow cards, which indicated that they lived below the poverty line, and a list of pink-card holders, the poorest of the poor who were entitled to food grains. Interviewing these people about the quantity of rations they received, what rates they were being forced to pay, and the behavior of depot holders toward them highlighted numerous specific shortcomings in the system. One example: the quantity of rations distributed to every family was the same regardless of the number of people in the family. And the amount was insufficient for any size family. The rations were poor quality, old, and sometimes mixed with sand! In some villages there was no ration depot at all.

The trainees' report documented more inequities in the system that resulted in poor people being unable to access much-needed food rations and/or kerosene oil for cooking fuel. Once people could see how they as citizens could shine a light on these issues, they understood that they could play a role in bringing about transparency and accountability in the programs they cared about and needed most.

When a meeting was held in the Ghaghas Community Center to discuss how to address these inequities, two of the corrupt depot holders from the surrounding region showed up, pretending to represent below-poverty-level households. They were disruptive and tried to sabotage the gathering with threats. But the villagers who organized the meeting stood strong, firmly demanding reasonable improvements from the depot holders.

The Notki depot distributed rations to eligible villagers that same evening. Seeing genuine results occur so quickly impressed the villagers and inspired them to stay active.

Similar successes could soon be seen in all six communities where village trainees were working. Ration depot managers cooperated in eliminating the corruption and other problems in the Public Distribution System in each of the six villages. Some depot managers asked governance trainees to guide them in setting prices and quantities. In cases where only partial improvements occurred, villagers kept track of the progress and continued to make appropriate demands. When people could see more results, they began to feel empowered to take more and more actions.

Trainees gained a positive reputation in their respective villages for their work. Meetings were held with stakeholders, such as licensed depot holders, school lunch program cooks, and ICDS (Integrated Child

Development Services) workers and helpers in the six villages. Each trainee took some action to improve rural governance. Some inspected depots to evaluate their functioning. Some went to schools, inspected the meals, and made lists of the number of children being fed. Women trainees visited and inspected anganwadi (childcare) centers to determine if and how childcare was being conducted.

Trainees used the Right to Information Act to find out why certain poor people in the village of Agon were denied their 100-square-yard plots under *Mahatma Gandhi Grameen Basti Yojana*, a rural housing program instituted in 2008. As a result of villager inquiries, the district administration canceled the entire allotment of plots in the village and required redistribution of the plots to include any eligible people who had previously been excluded.

These types of victories helped to convince residents of the six villages that they were indeed the rightful owners of the democratic process. Village trainees went beyond their districts to express their views about the implementation of the Right to Information Act in Haryana. As people in all parts of village life began to take action, panchayat members were better able to appreciate their power, roles, and responsibilities.

During this same period, Sehgal Foundation achieved a number of milestones within the Integrated Sustainable Village Development model. Water literacy education was furthered with the help of children and young people. Schoolchildren began calling adults' attention to situations where water was being wasted. Parents were often influenced by their children to change their behaviors in favor of more sanitary practices and better disposal of wastewater.

By measuring the impact of children's street theater performances promoting "Our Village, Clean Village" in Jyotisar, Kurukshetra, the Rural Research team saw the effectiveness of this novel approach in creating increased awareness among schoolchildren as well as members of the panchayat. Water literacy plays were taken to more villages where people were entertained, and more minds were changed. Each water management innovation spread as well. Two new check dam water-augmentation systems were constructed, and more were planned.

Farmers resource centers in five Mewat villages were now active as information dissemination hubs, providing monthly training events for farmers. Inter-village group visits showcased field demonstrations of new and improved practices, such as the balanced use of micronutrient fertilizers, intercropping, pulse (bean) cultivation, crop diversification, and better livestock practices.

The Fruit and Vegetable Growers Association in Mewat was strengthened by agricultural workshops, trainings, and "exposure" visits.[29] The foundation team helped village volunteers, called *kisan mitras* (farmers' friends), build farmers' capacities (aptitude and capability). They went from village to village, and walked from farm to farm, to provide information about sustainable agriculture. They invited farmers to training events and meetings, called *kisan gosthees*, to demonstrate agricultural techniques and also to teach marketable skills to village youth. Skill centers trained students in computers, typing, apparel design, electrical work, and plumbing.

Rural Health program support included more eye clinics and cataract surgeries, immunizations, disability rehabilitation, and nutritional studies of children. Random-sample surveys gauged the continuing positive impact of the Life Skills Education programs. Despite the strongly patriarchal culture of Mewat, noticeable gains in female empowerment were achieved in every area.

Meanwhile, the foundation's crop improvement work in Hyderabad continued to enhance the diversity of the maize germplasm and identify inbred lines that combined well with other lines to develop high-yielding corn hybrids tolerant of biotic and abiotic stresses. In light of recent intellectual property laws in India, the Sehgal Foundation team took steps, in keeping with their policy and strong commitment, to make sure that elite germplasm did not become the exclusive property of the private sector. The foundation continued to make germplasm freely available to anyone as long as they did not seek intellectual property protection on the seed.

With so many changes going on in the villages, the foundation team organized interdisciplinary workshops that included government, religious leaders, local professionals, and panchayat members. The idea

29. These "exposure" visits were intended to expose farmers to the larger world outside their own, sometimes isolated, communities.

was to make sure that anyone who might feel threatened by, or resistant to, changes would hear all sides of discussions about development activities. Guest speakers were invited from Muslim universities and other institutions to speak to foundation staff and engage in brainstorming about religiously acceptable ways for Muslim women to engage in personal and village advancement.

Sehgal Foundation's Communications team shared knowledge in person, in print, online, and on television. Community interactions escalated as more events, meetings, and brainstorming sessions were held. A few academic papers were published in professional journals on the topics of water, health, and life skills. Popular articles were submitted to newspapers and magazines, included in annual reports, and posted on the Sehgal Foundation website.

Vikas Patrika, Sehgal Foundation's quarterly Hindi newsletter, steadily gained popularity, providing villagers with a platform to voice opinions. Field team members wrote many of the articles about Sehgal Foundation work in the villages. The communication team assisted with interviews of villagers and field team writers. The newsletter covered information about water literacy and the new check dam water-augmentation systems, two recently completed childbirth delivery huts, conversations about laws and entitlements, announcements about trainings, and notification about awards received by Sehgal Foundation for its successful initiatives. A series of "leadership case studies" showcased profiles of outstanding villagers who served as inspiring examples for others.

By the end of 2008, the Phase 1 building of the Sehgal Foundation campus in Gurgaon[30] was complete. The demonstration village of Notki was three-quarters finished, and the time had come to celebrate. The new Sehgal Foundation headquarters was inaugurated by the Honorable Governor of Haryana, Dr. A. R. Kidwai, on December 2, 2008. A choir of village girls opened the program by singing the national anthem. The festive event was covered by a few dozen national newspapers in Hindi and in English, seven television stations, and numerous media

30. Sehgal Foundation and its Gurgaon campus were still being referred to as Institute of Rural Research and Development or as IRRAD, an initiative of S M Sehgal Foundation.

websites. The daylong celebration was attended by staff from Gurgaon and Hyderabad, dignitaries and funding partners, villagers and friends, and the Sehgal family.

In the auditorium, Suri Sehgal's welcome included a description of the history of the foundation as a learning journey from its inception. He emphasized that poverty in rural India *could* be alleviated if the development funds allocated by the government reached the villagers, and if there was transparency and accountability for the funds in the public sector. He invited people from every sector—public, private, and other NGOs—to work together as partners in progress to empower rural India. After a few words from Jay Sehgal, an enlightening speech by the governor, and a luncheon, everyone was invited to wander around and explore the dynamic new space.

Though the LEED certificate itself from the U.S. Green Building Council would not be presented officially for another thirteen months, the final Phase 1 building met all the requirements to attain the platinum (highest) LEED rating envisioned by the founders. It was only the second building in Gurgaon to achieve this distinction, the fifth building in all of India, and the seventy-fifth building in the entire world. Guests were able to see all aspects of the ecofriendly building while learning more about the range of Sehgal Foundation's work in the villages.

More workshop tours and demonstrations were held over the next few days. At the community center in Ghaghas, visitors saw training workshops with equipment and tools for cellphone repair and computer training. Villagers greeted Suri and Edda Sehgal affectionately, putting a colorful turban on Suri and a shawl around Edda's shoulders.

The tour included a look at demonstration fields that showed crop diversification, experimental rows of crops in raised wooden beds with drip irrigation, and a vermicompost display. Near a large check dam basin in the Aravalli foothills, a description of the water-augmentation system included explanations about water collection and storage, and groundwater replenishment.

A visit to the demonstration village of Notki included a tour of a new two-room childbirth delivery hut with privacy screens, modern equipment, and supplies that included dai delivery kits. Diagrams on the walls illustrated preventive health procedures. The space was clean and hygienic. Thanks to solar panels, continuous electricity was available for lights and a fan. The communities in eight surrounding villages now had a safe alternative to home births.

In a classroom at the nearby school, bright-eyed little girls wearing headscarves sat in rows. Suri spoke to the children in Hindi and asked them questions. The children were eager and expressive in their replies.

Large wall paintings and signs hung in prominent places, illustrating projects the villagers had undertaken to turn Notki into a clean village. Members of the education team spoke, acknowledging the participation of the villagers in their cash and in-kind contributions. Men and children of the village gathered close to hear what was being said. Women more often watched from a distance. The people appeared pleased with the difference in their community and proud of their part in the conversion process.

Many households in Notki now had latrines. New recharge/soak wells had been dug and new pipes, storage tanks, and soak pits had been installed. The main streets were paved with cement. Solar streetlamps were in strategic locations throughout the village. An orchard had been planted on 4.3 acres with 897 plants of thirteen species.

The final stages in the conversion of Notki to a clean demonstration village would occur over the next year and include a nearby hamlet. Promotional materials and articles about Notki invited others, including corporations and philanthropists, to adopt a village like Notki to help foster this type of change all across rural India.

The Integrated Sustainable Village Development model continued to have a lot of moving parts. No other single NGO was working on an integrated model for development in India. The Sehgal Foundation team was convinced from its successes that this elegant approach was absolutely needed in every poor village in the country.

Scaling up was still considered to be the only way to reach more communities in need. However, when the team began to solicit donors for the ISVD model, they realized right away that no other single donor would want to become involved in funding so many complex interconnected components. As Suri and Edda Sehgal had learned years before, when they first created their foundation, other NGOs focused on single programs. Donors in general preferred to choose one project at a time that could demonstrate specific observable objectives, even if the initiative stretched over several years.

Despite this reality, the foundation team recognized the essential nature of keeping their own development projects integrated. They saw clearly, year after year, how no one problem in any village existed in a vacuum. With so many complex and interrelated problems, each element naturally led to the next—poor nutrition, a sick child, no access to healthcare, no water, girls unable to go to school—whatever the issue, each was linked to the other.

Suri Sehgal observed, "For anyone who feels compassion in the face of such difficult circumstances, continuing to move from tackling one solution to the next is as natural as breathing. Without more and more money, we couldn't keep doing it all. But we would not give up either."

He explained, "The solution in this case was to limit the Integrated Sustainable Village Development model to our twenty-village cluster, and not scale up further unless money came from other sources."

The team could continue to experiment with what worked in those villages, refine the models, test and adapt new technologies, and continue to gather and report their findings. The team had expertise in each area of development, which would be shared in the form of education, training, interactive dialogue, advocacy, and support where needed.

Relocation to the United States by Jay Sehgal fit well with these plans. By working in the Des Moines office of Sehgal Foundation, Jay would be able to pursue linkages there with other research and donor organizations, and with development institutions. His goal was to solicit funds and to attract volunteers, students, and postdoctoral candidates from the United States to visit Sehgal Foundation in India and consider internships there. By seeing rural India, young people would hopefully continue to be interested in development work when they returned home.

Until the right person could be found to become the new CEO in India, Jay would continue in his leadership role and travel back and forth to India every few months. When in the United States, he would stay in regular contact with his team by phone, email, and Skype. He was confident that, with discipline and good planning, this arrangement would work for the interim.

The Sehgal Foundation team was an "empowered" group. The dozen or so members of the core team functioned almost like a tight-knit family. With Jay at a distance, program leaders stepped up and took on added responsibilities. Staff maintained smart access to information and each other through an intranet, which helped with transparency and coordination. Though they missed Jay Sehgal's supportive day-to-day attention to operations and his presence in the villages, program leaders were able to carry on independently.

Grassroots activism was emerging little by little in the six communities where good governance trainees worked, but formidable barriers remained. Generating greater civic awareness and responsibility was a slow process. Many of the local bureaucrats resisted the change and were often hostile and dismissive of newly empowered poor people, refusing to answer to those at the bottom of the social hierarchy. This dynamic inspired the foundation team to refine its strategic approach to development in 2009.

Empowerment had always been the key ingredient in the Integrated Sustainable Village Development model. With a stronger understanding that overcoming poverty was a matter of human rights, the Sehgal Foundation approach to development underwent a shift from "needs based" to "rights based." For good governance advocacy, the foundation team recognized this as an effective tool for putting more power into the empowerment of villagers in Mewat.

By putting an overarching focus on human rights, the foundation finally had the "magic bullet" Suri Sehgal had long been looking for to ensure sustainability of program interventions on the grassroots level. A rights-based approach emphasized the empowerment and accountability that would mobilize more people in the villages to break free from their entrenched mind-sets and be inspired to jump-start their own development through effective citizen participation. Advocating for good governance had already demonstrated a strong potential for meaningful transformation in the communities of Mewat.

While the new rights-based strategy was being refined and tested, Ajay Pandey and the governance trainees continued their efforts to empower communities to demand honest implementation of government programs. They hung posters and created wall paintings throughout the villages with illustrations that showed the correct allotments and benefits of various entitlement programs.

Governance trainees found that the Mid Day Meal Scheme, a program intended to provide free lunches to schoolchildren, was so poorly administered that the food was often inedible. This school lunch program, the largest in the world, was tasked to provide one free meal a day to approximately 120 million students ages six to fourteen in government-funded primary and upper primary schools. In some cases, corrupt school administrators and principals had been keeping the government money allocated for Mid Day Meals and education facilities.

The foundation team created wall paintings to illustrate what was supposed to be included in the meal plan. The paintings had the desired effect of visually highlighting the profound discrepancy between the intent of the program and the outcome in the community.

The images on posters and walls in public places created greater awareness and inspired villagers to demand from their school committees that services be delivered properly. As villagers spoke up, with support when needed from field team members and governance trainees, and asked for the correct quality and quantities of goods, administrators began delivering more of the appropriate items.

Change was happening, but it was slow. The grievance redressal system was completely dysfunctional in almost all government offices. Foundation teams and the governance trainees faced opposition from various stakeholders in the programs, including some of the workers, licensed depot holders, teachers, sarpanches, and panches (council members) of gram panchayats.

One day in March 2009, Ajay was having a conversation with trainees and other villagers about the critical need for good governance in their communities. He was trying to emphasize the urgency of the situation as he described the tremendous power people had—if they only knew it. His impassioned discourse was motivated by something he had just read in a book by Dipankar Gupta, called *The Caged Phoenix: Can India Fly?* Gupta's book described the backwardness in so much of India despite all the hopes and promises of independence. The growth that had occurred in some parts of India had never reached millions of rural poor people. In his book, Gupta lamented, ". . . we have the vote, we should all be in a hurry."

Ajay's voice rose a bit as he said to the group in frustration, "It has been sixty-two years since India's independence! We are voters in a democracy! We have the *ultimate* power to bring about desired changes! *When* are we going to effect good governance?"

Aroused and inspired by Ajay's words, the villagers responded, "Yes! Yes! We need good governance *NOW!*"

The phrase instantly became a new Sehgal Foundation catchphrase: "*Sushasan Abhi!*" or "Good Governance Now!" The group erupted spontaneously into brainstorming mode as villagers imagined the features of their new *Good Governance Now!* (GGN) campaign.

They discussed a wider, holistic view of good governance, not just with respect to a few segments of rural life. They talked about something greater—the idea of creating such a powerful culture of good governance that corruption would be inconceivable, a culture wherein the welfare of citizens would be a true priority. The people became increasingly excited as they imagined the possibilities and agreed, "We have already waited sixty-two years—we want good governance now!"

Chief components of the new campaign, the tenets of good governance, were the basic characteristics in the training program design. The program integrated community participation, women's leadership, supportive governance, better coordination of actions, and zero tolerance for corruption, with a goal of obtaining the most needed, basic services as a starting point. People from the community could see that these tenets held the promise for raising their standard of living and enabling them to make better use of resources and opportunities, and would ultimately lead to a more just society. *Good Governance Now!* trainees made posters that depicted those six key components of the campaign. They placed them in each of their six villages.

As the first *Good Governance Now!* training module was nearing its conclusion before the summer of 2009, villagers who participated were asked to cite one good thing and one bad thing about their training. They each stated that there was nothing bad about the training. The good points were primarily about the personal changes they felt. Trainees described experiencing a new sense of empowerment. They appreciated being aware not only of their rights but also of their duties.

They now felt that if the system did not work properly, it was their personal duty as citizens to take measures to correct the problem—and that government officials were answerable to them. This new feeling induced life-changing self-confidence in the participants.

Of the thirty-five people from six villages who took part in the first *Good Governance Now!* training, nine went on to become "master" trainers, five of whom were women. The nine were provided with additional training so they could train others.

After successfully completing the two-month training of trainers, called TOT, each master trainer earned the title "governance guide" and was presented with a copy of the Constitution of India in Hindi. This gesture was intended to remind them that, in their work for the *Good Governance Now!* campaign, they were equipped to uphold the Constitution and effectively realize its provisions for the common citizen. By this, Ajay wanted to convey the somewhat elevated role of those who served as governance guides and to keep them aware of the high hopes their communities had for them with regard to this work. He stressed this concept in ongoing mentoring sessions he organized for them.

Ajay had originally said, after the first good governance training module was done, that if there were not enough women participants for the next training, he would not do it again. But by year two, close to 60 percent of the 100 trainees in the *Good Governance Now!* program were women. For each subsequent year, women continued to comprise at least 50 percent of the group being trained.

Momentum was building.

CHAPTER 8

New Heroes Emerge

Governance guides and trainees made slow and steady headway in their villages. One victory that was a long time coming was accomplished by a village woman named Kamlesh Sherawat, who was one of the first trainees to become a governance guide. While still in training in March 2009, she had taken direct action to resolve a dilemma for thirty-three villagers in Dingerhedi, in the Taoru block of Mewat. More than a year prior, villagers had applied to receive household electricity connections and paid a deposit, but nothing was provided. Having learned about the Right to Information Act, as part of her governance training, Kamlesh filed an RTI application with the District Electricity Department on behalf of the Dingerhedi villagers. Within a month, meters were distributed to the villagers, and a future date was given for installing them. However, the date passed, and again nothing happened. Kamlesh took the matter to the State Information Commission in Chandigarh.

She was pleased to learn that an inquiry had been initiated, to be followed by disciplinary action against the sub-divisional officer guilty of ignoring her RTI petition. But Kamlesh knew enough not to celebrate until she saw tangible results. Her persistent slogging footwork resumed when she learned that villagers were now receiving bills for their uninstalled electricity meters. Exasperated but determined, Kamlesh filed a complaint.

This time the office of the sub-divisional officer responded to her. Immediate installation of the meters was ordered and carried out, and the erroneous bills were cancelled. Each similar success depended on steadfast perseverance to overcome the enormous hurdles created by an encumbered bureaucracy. Dogged determination was emerging as the hallmark of the governance trainees and others joining in the *Good Governance Now!* campaign.

In Agon, an unacceptable situation was turned around by the resolve of a villager who learned about good governance from his wife, a trainee. Three anganwadi centers had basically been abandoned. The assigned childcare workers did not even visit the centers, let alone provide childcare services. A group of training participants joined with the villager to submit a complaint to the child development project officer. Receiving no response, the trainees held a meeting that brought workers and helpers together with intended Integrated Child Development Services beneficiaries in order to assess the situation collectively. Their findings were unsettling. The child development workers told the group that the Mid Day Meal beneficiaries were not even registered for the services included in the program. Many villagers were unaware of their beneficiary status.

In the face of such irregularities, villagers felt prompted, with back-up support from the Policy, Governance, and Advocacy team, to make sure that errors in the system were corrected so that the village children would receive their rightful services. A complaint letter was sent on behalf of the beneficiaries to the National Commission for Protection of Child Rights (NCPCR) and the Supreme Court Commission for the Right to Food. Acting on the complaint, the NCPCR asked the District Administration to inquire into the matter and prepare a report, also to be signed by the complainants. This sparked quick action by district-level officials. The project officer delivered rations the same day to the three anganwadi centers in Agon. The *tehsildar* (block-level official) visited Agon and spoke directly with the villagers, who made him aware of the deplorable state of the anganwadi centers and the need for staff to be present.

Similar nonconfrontational, yet effective, activism was carried out on a very personal level by a trainee with a relative who worked in an anganwadi center. The young trainee threatened to register a complaint against the worker if she didn't do her work efficiently. When another trainee filed an RTI application about the poor conditions in the schools in Ferozepur Jhirka block, school officials and staff, and even his own family, pressured him to withdraw his application. But the trainee held firm. Fearful that their own corrupt practices might be exposed, school officials resumed work on the long-neglected projects in the schools.

Changing the status quo was not easy or quick. At legal literacy camps held in the community, villagers learned more about government programs and citizen entitlements. Separate stalls were set up so individuals could receive help with specific issues, filling out application forms, or writing complaint letters. Facilitators provided follow-up with individual concerns.

The emerging awareness by citizens of their rights rattled some officials. During a legal literacy camp held by Sehgal Foundation in 2009, a district-level officer, who was a key guest, said to a field team member, "Why does your organization engage in such activities? Activities like awareness camps will only cause unrest in society."

Officials were startled by the proactive responses and behavior of the villagers, which were unlike the more prevalent passivity they were accustomed to from the community. The people in authority were eager to know how the villagers learned about the National Commission for Protection of Child Rights in the first place. Officials from the Department of Education and the Department of Women and Child Development regularly asked the governance trainees, "Why are you encouraging villagers to file Right to Information applications and complaints?"

Such questions were typically accompanied by "advice" suggesting that filing RTI applications would only slow down the delivery of public services. Governance trainees could not be sure whether the officials' remarks were intended as subtle threats, or if certain officials might deliberately hold up work for villagers who filed applications and complaints. No hard evidence was ever found either way.

Because much of Sehgal Foundation's work in certain areas, such as water management and capacity building, was done in cooperation with various government officers, brainstorming sessions were held to discuss how to respond to disgruntled or angry government officials. Regardless of any potential pushback, Sehgal Foundation zealously championed the *Good Governance Now!* campaign and the governance training programs. The tangible results were truly empowering the rural communities.

As additional valuable information conveyed to villagers inspired grassroots actions, social inclusion, and further empowerment, the foundation's Communications team explored media options to spread the messages more widely. Community radio as a medium for inspiring change was an exciting idea that would give voices to people in rural Mewat. The Communications team did feasibility studies and surveys in fifty-one villages, and visits were made to community radio stations in other parts of India. After further research and discussion, Communications team leader Pooja O. Murada began the application process for obtaining a broadcasting license so the foundation could launch a community radio station.

The station would be located within the Ghaghas Community Center and staffed with local people from the villages. The license and approval from the government to broadcast would take almost three years to obtain. Each step in the process directly involved the citizens in the communities of Mewat.

Throughout 2009, as the Integrated Sustainable Village Development model was implemented in a cluster of twenty villages and the rights-based approach was further refined, research continued to identify the most sustainable and replicable models for rural development. New staff included field researchers who conducted surveys, baselines, and periodic evaluations. The team conducted impact studies on local, state, and national government policies intended to benefit the poor, which served as valuable preparation for advocating policy reforms. Research studies mapped progress in various models and projects to determine where the most impact was being made and where there was potential for scaling up. The studies in water management, education, income, life skills, agriculture, demographics, and vulnerability had the added benefit of being helpful to the team in creating a deeper understanding of village dynamics.

Due to the crucial need for water in every village, Water Management was still thought of as Sehgal Foundation's flagship program. Water augmentation project successes reported in the annual report for 2009 included thirty check dams and related structures,[31] seven new ponds, 650 soak pits, forty-five recharge wells, forty-four roof-water-harvesting systems, six revived traditional ponds, numerous stand posts with taps and hand pumps, and latrines.

Two check dam and recharge well projects completed in Kotla successfully reversed the village's water depletion and well salinity. The surface water storage ponds assisted with crop irrigation and domestic purposes. More girls were in school instead of having to fetch water every day.

Another water project in Kotla sparked efforts to preserve India's cultural heritage. The village had a dilapidated *baoli* (step-well), an elaborate fourteenth-century structure for storing water that measured sixty- by twenty-five feet. At one time, India was peppered with thousands of baolis, which were used for relaxation bathing, rituals, and as rest stops for shepherds and herders. In an inspiring display of *shramdaan* (voluntary manual labor), villagers, grass-pickers, university and grade school students, and field staff wielded spades and pickaxes to revive the long-neglected well. Together these people contributed a total of 440 days of free labor to the effort. Once the baoli was cleaned up, district authorities stepped in to fully restore the structure.

In Rangala Rajpur, the Integrated Watershed Development Program was implemented by Sehgal Foundation with financial support from Mewat Development Agency. Water collected in five ponds connected to the check dam opened fifty acres of fallow land to cultivation, saved forty acres from flooding and topsoil erosion, and supported a micro-irrigation system over 300 acres. This replicable project could now be used to help solve water problems in other villages.

As a result of long deliberations on water management with community groups, the foundation team organized a three-day water awareness march as part of the Jal Chetna Yatra national water awareness campaign. The march, which covered sixty villages and reached

31. This number included check dams, nallah bunds, contour bunds, and gabions.

150,000 people, culminated in a large public meeting where villagers spoke to government representatives about their water concerns.

Group leader Lalit Mohan Sharma and the Water Management team were participating in a community meeting about building a water augmentation system in the village of Bhond in mid-2009, when a villager told them about an old man named Bhure Khan who had taken some extraordinary measures to conserve water. Many years before, he had singlehandedly created a pond in the Aravalli hills to provide drinking water for animals. Intrigued, the foundation team did further research to find out more about this man. Members of the field team went up in the hills to see the pond. They discovered that Bhure Khan had done far more than build one pond. His conservation efforts were nothing less than remarkable.

Eighty-five-year-old Bhure Khan was only fourteen when he relocated with his mother from Rajasthan to the village of Bhond in Mewat to find a better life closer to their relatives. To earn a living, he plowed other people's fields and raised grazing animals. When taking animals up into the Aravalli hills to graze, he witnessed the drudgery of women carrying heavy loads of firewood and water pots to the bordering villages in Haryana and Rajasthan. Sympathetic to their hardship, he wanted to find a way to solve the scarcity of water. He scouted for areas that could be used to store surface water. When he found a promising spot, he began digging. He kept digging for three years. Bhure was twenty-five years old when he completed his first reservoir.

Inspired by his determination, other local herdsmen helped him build a second reservoir. Bhure continued digging to create two more reservoirs to help the community. Seeing that the village women had no proper footpath, he then took several more years to single-handedly forge a walkable path that connected Haryana and Rajasthan. His path was shorter and easier for the women to navigate uphill.

Bhure Khan never married and never had a house of his own. Well known throughout the village of Bhond, he was appreciated, cared for, and regarded with affection by the people in his community who readily opened their homes to him for a meal or a place to sleep. Because of his unbiased loyalty to everyone in the village, he was often approached to resolve differences between individuals or families. Bhure Khan was a binding force within the community.

The Water Management team members were happily surprised and greatly impressed to find that the sites Bhure Khan had selected to locate ponds perfectly matched the characteristics that Lalit and the team looked for when choosing a site for pond construction. The ponds constructed by Bhure Khan were ideally situated. The ground gradient was gentle, which helped to avoid erosion and silting. The soil type was impermeable, minimizing percolation loss. The inflow was greater than the runoff. There was tree cover on the southwestern side of each pond, casting shadows on the water. Either a tree line or protruding rocks diverted winds to minimize the evaporation loss. A natural rock formation at the appropriate level allowed the overflow of surplus water without causing any erosion, and the ponds were easily approachable by the users. Lalit wanted to find a way to honor this unsung hero who had worked so hard to provide water for his community.

The Sehgal Foundation team organized a special celebratory event on the evening of November 19, 2009, and invited members of the press. At the large community gathering, a film screening on water management was presented, and Bhure Khan was honored and thanked publicly. People of all ages were inspired to hear about his lifelong water conservation achievements.

His story soon appeared in four Hindi daily newspapers and was covered by three television stations, garnering the attention of the deputy commissioner. As a result, Bhure Khan was honored as part of Indian Republic Day celebrations on January 26, 2010,[32] in front of dignitaries and thousands of people at district headquarters in Nuh, Mewat. He was presented with a commendation certificate and a wrapped gift by Aftab Alam, special secretary, Government of Haryana, and member of the Legislative Assembly.

When asked by the media what inspired him to do this work, Bhure Khan answered, "I have done this for my family. I don't have my own family, but the whole village is like a family to me. Water is the existence of life and is needed in all areas. Without water, trees can't grow, humans can't live."

After the event, Bhure unwrapped his gift to find that it was a

32. Republic Day honors the anniversary of India's constitution, which was adopted on January 26, 1950.

lovely wall clock. Villagers gathered around him in a spirited discussion about where to put the clock. Some suggested he put it in the *chaupal*, a community gathering place where elderly men of the neighborhood spent their days telling stories or reciting epics. Others suggested that putting the clock in the local mosque would benefit more people. Bhure Khan allowed his community to make the decision.

Bhure Khan lived several more months after receiving recognition for his lifelong work on behalf of his village family, leaving behind the ponds and paths, a clock of appreciation, and an example of a life lived in service of his community. His legacy continues to inspire others.

Agriculture in Mewat during this period became more competitive as more farmers used the tools and methods Sehgal Foundation introduced to increase yields, and they took advantage of the improved extension services and market linkages to increase their income. Soil health and the application of balanced crop nutrition were now recognized as key to increasing crop productivity. With support from the Haryana Agriculture Department, the Sehgal Foundation team developed a soil fertility map of the entire district of Mewat. As in other parts of India, the soils in Mewat were degraded due to continuous cropping over many years. The revised strategy of the foundation's agriculture program focused on soil health management through the application of organic manure and essential micronutrients, and stopping the overuse of subsidized fertilizers, particularly urea and diammonium phosphate (DAP). Field demonstrations showed the benefits of balanced and need-based fertilizer application.

Farming practices such as raised-bed planting, deep chiseling, mulching, and drip and sprinkler irrigation continued to spread as farmers' groups were trained in each village. A field team, consisting of kisan mitras (farmers' friends), agricultural specialists, and village champions, worked closely with farmers at each stage in the process, from preparing the land to selling the produce. Linkages with Haryana Agriculture University, Indian Agricultural Research Institute (IARI), the state agriculture department, and an agricultural extension center provided added information resources to farmers' groups.

While looking for ways to enhance farmers' incomes, the foundation team looked into the potential of *daincha*—which had been tried earlier in a pilot project as a source of biofuel—to increase crop productivity. Because this versatile plant could grow in saline areas and, at the same time, add organic content and balanced nutrition to the soil, it was promoted as a cost-effective and natural method to improve soil health. The foundation also worked in collaboration with India's National Institute of Research on Jute and Allied Fiber Technology to explore possibilities for using daincha fiber in handicrafts to generate employment for rural women. The fiber, seeds, and charcoal made from the plant were marketable and had the potential to be developed as cottage industries. However, the foundation continued to promote daincha primarily as a green manure crop.

The team used soil analysis to explain to farmers how soil health would improve with the addition of organic matter, and how crop yields would improve with the use of balanced fertilizer with micronutrients, irrigation, and high-yielding quality seed. Farmers willing to try new methods were encouraged to plant half of their field the new way. The foundation held regular field days on a demonstration plot. Even farmers less willing to experiment could see the difference in the side of the field where the newer methods were used.

Due to what became an ongoing partnership with a leading fertilizer company, The Mosaic Company, India, the crop productivity model was able to spread rapidly in Mewat. As a result, more demonstration plots were planted in more villages. The visible benefits had a ripple effect, causing more farmers to attempt and adopt new agricultural practices. The impressive results attracted new visitors to Mewat, which made a difference in reaching more potential partners and taking the methodology to more of rural India. Donors who visited the plots could see successes firsthand in the villages.

A nine-month pilot program in 2009 was carried out in partnership with an NGO, One World South Asia (OWSA). The program, *Soochna Se Samadhan* (Life Line Agriculture), was launched in ten villages in Mewat using OWSA's mobile voice-recording system to provide agricultural advice to farmers within twenty-four hours of receiving calls. Farmers sent pictures or short video clips of symptoms of diseases or insect pests observed in plants or animals. Issues with the technology and local dialect kept the program from expanding at that time, and some solutions provided by the experts were not applicable in the local context. However, several beneficial results occurred during the pilot program: information in treating animal ailments was used to save animals' lives, farmers' incomes increased due to cost savings in controlling the seed rate, excess use of pesticides was eliminated, and plant and animal diseases and termite damage were controlled in a timely fashion. Advice on using optimum plant populations in vegetables and using good quality seeds resulted in increased crop yields. The largest impact of the project was in improving soil health by adding organic matter and using balanced fertilizers with micronutrients. Apart from quantitative benefits, farmers' knowledge improved in the areas of integrated nutrient use, pest management, soil testing, and better farming practices.

Small interventions by Sehgal Foundation in education and healthcare continued to work wonders, such as building girls' toilets in schools, and organizing immunization drives. In addition to the delivery hut in Notki, a delivery hut was revived in the village of Raniyala. The two huts now served a combined twenty-seven villages. The presence of the huts prompted greater prenatal and postnatal care and was credited with ensuring 98 percent of child immunizations. In its first year, the delivery hut in Notki hosted seventy-six deliveries and provided services to 1,670 outpatients. The foundation team pushed to have the Notki delivery hut integrated into the government database and upgraded to a sub-center clinic for maternity and general healthcare.

A disability camp was held in collaboration with the Delhi Council of Child Welfare for children up to age sixteen, in fifty-six villages. Experts identified forty-six patients needing mobility aids and forty patients who needed corrective surgeries. Additional camps addressed breastfeeding, sanitation, HIV/AIDS awareness, and other health issues.

Sehgal Foundation sponsored a sixteen-day "International Campaign on Violence Against Women" to spawn conversations in the villages about topics not usually discussed openly: domestic violence, participation of women in politics, and the subject of dowry. Visual media and input from attorneys were designed to teach women about their rights related to violence and law enforcement. The event ended with a shared group vow opposing any form of violence toward women.

By the end of 2009 the rural governance training program that Ajay Pandey and the Policy, Governance, and Advocacy team had begun in six villages was now on course to expand to all twenty villages in the cluster with the help of governance guides. Every member of the Sehgal Foundation field staff participated in the governance training. The Policy, Governance, and Advocacy team now included another attorney, Navneet Narwal, with skills in policy training at the grassroots level. Field staff now included two governance guides from each of the cluster villages. These master trainers conducted two training sessions each month in each village. More trainees learned the proper function of a democratic state and the rights and entitlements of citizens in programs benefiting the most vulnerable—the poor, women, and children.

To share the success of the program and train law students in this methodology, Ajay accepted a position as associate professor at Jindal Global Law School. His role at Sehgal Foundation shifted to part-time. Suri Sehgal was in full agreement that partnering with a law school had the potential for accelerating the expansion of the good governance programs and bringing about more rapid transformation in rural India. Ajay continued the trainings and visiting villages to keep the momentum growing.

Good Governance Now! action groups continued to be successful in prodding officials to deliver promised services and benefits. Awareness had spread concerning the important government programs and related policies meant to support the constitutional rights of people in India. The goal was to make sure these programs were implemented openly and honestly in the core villages where the team was working and to make sure the benefits were spread widely and fairly.

In the beginning, the *Good Governance Now!* program had inspired a few dozen villagers to speak up; now hundreds of people were speaking up! With the engagement of villagers, the Public Distribution System and the programs in Integrated Child Development and Mid Day Meals were now functioning in the core villages. The new rights-based approach to achieving good governance was turning passive recipients into empowered citizens who stood up to improve the delivery of core public services in all areas: education, food and water, employment, information, and healthcare.

The Policy, Governance, and Advocacy team was prepared to help people access the potential benefit, for girls especially, of the new Right of Children to Free and Compulsory Education Act (commonly abbreviated as Right to Education or RTE) that was signed into law in 2009 and would go into effect in April 2010. The new act mandated up to eight years of free and compulsory education for all children ages six to fourteen, including children with disabilities, in their own neighborhood. The Act addressed other aspects of education, such as appropriate school infrastructure and teacher-to-student ratio. The team saw that this act had the potential to send many more girls to school in all the villages.

As 2010 began, Sehgal Foundation operations were running smoothly. The Phase 1 building on the Sehgal Foundation campus received its official LEED platinum rating from the U.S. Green Building Council. A gala was held in January to celebrate Sehgal Foundation's ten years in Mewat and the LEED certification.

Construction now commenced on Sehgal Foundation's Phase 2 building. The decision to expand into another building was prompted by the need for adding rooms, or "flatlets," for visiting student interns, faculty, and volunteers from the United States and other countries. The employee-friendly facility would be 30 percent residential; the rest would be rental property as a source of income to further sustain the organization's work. The Phase 1 building was considered a great success and the tenants were satisfied.

Just as the Phase 1 building was constructed to reflect Sehgal Foundation's commitment to resource conservation and leading by example, the Phase 2 building would also meet the highest standards required for LEED platinum certification.[33] With Jay in the United States, Ramesh Kapahi took the primary role in coordinating the project and the construction. The same architect and the same building crew were hired again. The entire process went more smoothly this time, largely because the workers were no longer "unskilled."

33. The certification by the Indian Green Building Council (IGBC) would be officially awarded in 2013 for Phase 2. The IGBC licensed the LEED Green Building Standard from the U.S. Green Building Council. Both facilities remain among very few such buildings in India.

The building design was similar to the Phase 1 building. Another 400,000-liter storage tank, similar to the one in the Phase I building, was built to collect rainwater. The same quality standards and simple modern design elements were used. The interior was slightly different. Instead of an atrium and courtyard, the Phase 2 building had a terrace and open courtyards. Just as with the Phase 1 building, there were no accidents during construction.

Suri and Edda Sehgal continued their regular visits and kept in close touch with the foundation team. The enormous needs in the core villages kept the staff compelled to do more and more. Though there was a tremendous buzz of activity in the cluster of twenty villages, Suri was once again feeling that too little was being accomplished in the larger picture. Successfully implementing programs in a cluster of twenty villages out of 640,000+ amounted to a mere drop in the ocean of need. He wanted to find more powerful ways to make a bigger difference to more people and achieve strategic depth in more villages.

The dilemma was familiar. Sehgal Foundation did not have unlimited financial resources. To provide all the implemented services that were running smoothly in a cluster of twenty villages to more and more villages was not possible. Yet scaling up was necessary for greater impact beyond those twenty villages.

Suri again challenged the team. How could Sehgal Foundation expand with limited resources? How could the vast experience and positive changes already accomplished reach more people? A decision was made for Sehgal Foundation to start raising funds from other sources. Jay Sehgal was in a good position to do this in the United States. The search for a new CEO to be on-site in India was ramped up.

CHAPTER 9

Critical Learning

A strange and unexpected occurrence affected Sehgal Foundation on a variety of levels starting in the spring of 2010. Suri Sehgal, in Florida, and Jay Sehgal, in Iowa, received an email from group leader Anjali Makhija on April 27 with the news that a *fatwa* had been issued against Sehgal Foundation. She wrote, "As you are aware, a fatwa is a decree by a Muslim religious body."[34]

Posters had been pasted onto a few walls in Ghaghas and other communities in Mewat. Each poster had three seals that represented the three *madrasas* (Muslim educational institutions) that issued the fatwa. One was local, in Nuh, the district headquarters of Mewat. The other two were prominent madrasas in Deoband and Saharanpur, in Uttar Pradesh.

The printed fatwa, as roughly translated from Urdu into English, prescribed four things: (1) all Muslims must stop Sehgal Foundation work, (2) all Muslims must get together to "finish" Sehgal Foundation, (3) men and women becoming members or employees of Sehgal Foundation are wrong and *haram* (forbidden by Islamic law), and (4) if Muslims are lazy/slow in stopping this activity, they will face the anger of Allah.

34. A fatwa is a religious decision, legal opinion, or ruling by an Islamic scholar, leader, or recognized authority. These rulings or decrees are not binding, and it is possible to seek a second opinion. Note: Western media have incorrectly associated the term with a death sentence or declaration of war. See http://www.islamicsupremecouncil.org/understanding-islam/legal-rulings/44-what-is-a-fatwa.html.

Flyers denouncing the foundation were strewn along streets. The complaints listed in the flyers and posters, phrased in somewhat inflammatory language, said that Sehgal Foundation took photographs and posted pictures of young girls online and in printed publications, took women out of their villages, promoted Western culture, encouraged women to do away with the *purdah* system (veiling and seclusion), and promoted family planning.

Anjali's email described a proposed course of action, some of which she had already begun to implement. She had notified Pooniaji, program leader for Community Mobilization and the most senior staff member on the core team, who was on leave in Rajasthan and already on his way back to Gurgaon. She had immediately called together the Sehgal Foundation field team, most of whom were Muslims and residents of these same village communities.

The field team responded to the news with incredulity and a sense of calm. They knew from their own experience that Sehgal Foundation was fully supportive of women and girls. The goal was always to empower them with knowledge and build their self-confidence. In addition, the foundation's core values and principles, in writing and as expressed by the teams in words and deeds, were altogether respectful of cultural and religious differences. Neither religion nor politics were ever part of foundation efforts to bring development to Mewat.

The field staff took the initiative to address the issue collectively. Four long-time field team members stepped forward to take immediate action. Three young men, Nasir Hussain, Zafar Hussain, and Saheed Ahmad, joined the more senior Jaan Mohammad to form a representative task force to find out why this fatwa was issued and whether there were any real issues for the foundation to address among the accusations of wrongdoing. With determination in his voice, Nasir Hussain said to the members of the core team, "Don't worry. We will take care of this thing."

Work in the villages would be scaled down until the situation could be fully assessed. The receipt of a few anonymous phone threats to demolish the foundation-owned Ghaghas Community Center prompted a call to the local police. They were on alert in case any violence erupted.

The foundation's chief operating officer, Sanjiv Chatrath, was instrumental in maintaining a calm atmosphere during this period.

Though he had only recently joined Sehgal Foundation, he was a steady force on the team. Not entirely familiar with the sensitive cultural and religious issues related to a fatwa, he had called Jay Sehgal in the US for guidance. Jay suggested consulting with B. R. Poonia, who was also in charge of field team activities. With Poonia on leave, Sanjiv wisely gave full authority to the second-most senior staff member, Anjali Makhija, for handling the situation.

In her email, Anjali summarized the next steps the team had decided to take: visit with the Muslim religious leaders (moulvies) at the three madrasas and invite them to see the foundation's work firsthand; request a meeting with the individuals who applied for the fatwa to find out their concerns and interests; and initiate a face-to-face dialogue (*rubaru*) with religious leaders, as the team had been doing from time to time anyway.

The task force members suggested that the foundation wait a couple of days to gauge community reaction before taking *any* specific action. They weren't sure how villagers would respond to swirling gossip about the foundation. For villagers to openly protest anything declared by their religious leaders would be considered highly disrespectful. The low literacy rate in the villages of Mewat also included poor religious literacy. Unquestioned obedience to religious leaders was foremost. Conservative elements in communities with such a strong patriarchal cultural tradition were especially quick to condemn any perceived attempt to change the role of women. With Sehgal Foundation's ongoing intention of empowering women, the teams had been dealing respectfully and carefully with this reality from day one.

The team knew it was possible for anyone to request a fatwa from their religious leaders, and they had already learned that some of the dozen or so individuals listed on the fatwa request were not even aware of the decree. However, somebody, somewhere, was not happy with Sehgal Foundation, and the true extent of the threat or the potential danger was not yet clear.

When Jay Sehgal consulted with Suri Sehgal, he found his uncle fairly unconcerned about the news. Suri's comment was matter-of-fact: "We're spending our own money to put these villages on the path to development. We are working very hard, honestly and correctly. If the community does not appreciate what we are doing, there are at least 640,000 other villages in India that need help. We will move on."

Suri was convinced that the source of the fatwa was the work of a few individual instigators trying to stir up trouble. He knew the communities in Mewat appreciated the progress being made in partnership with Sehgal Foundation. He also knew that in any valuable endeavor, there would always be occasional malcontents and troublemakers. Suri told Jay that he trusted the community and the foundation team to handle the situation appropriately.

Jay responded to Anjali's email with his support for each of the steps she was already taking. He suggested meeting with groups of villagers to let them know that Sehgal Foundation was willing to leave Mewat if that was the wish of the people. The foundation's work with the community was a partnership that would not exist without the villagers' full support and participation. He offered reassurances and urged the team to stay focused on the good work they were doing, adding his personal certainty: "The villagers will stand beside us."

In the ten-plus years that Sehgal Foundation had been working in Mewat, only one village had ever been unwilling to go along with a proposed partnership project. When no agreement was possible, the team had stepped back completely and walked away, working instead with other communities. Decision-makers from the "unwilling" village had quickly realized their mistake and invited the foundation back. Their work together resumed.

When Pooniaji returned the following day, he met with Anjali and the field team and consulted with Salahuddin Saiphy, a Muslim member of the core team, to gain a better understanding of the situation from his perspective.[35] Together they considered how to appropriately address the fatwa with the three groups that issued it. Outside events unfolded quickly as the field team task force took the lead. They started by examining the pamphlets more closely. The language used in the

35. Salahuddin Saiphy, a well-trained expert in geology and hydrogeology, had been working as program leader in the foundation's Water Management Program since the previous September. Lalit Mohan Sharma's role changed at that time to group leader (a senior management position).

flyers and posters sounded so distorted that the team sought out the original language of the fatwa to discern what it actually said.

The field team split up to meet with each of the three religious institutions and to find out the reactions of people visiting the madrasas in Nuh and Nagina. They hoped to stop further distribution of the inflammatory flyers before *juma*, the Friday sermon at the mosques in two days. The moulvies of Mewat would no doubt discuss the matter in their weekly meeting at the mosque in Nuh, and then in the cluster meeting in Nagina the following Sunday. The subject would of course be noted by the *namazees* (attendees and readers of the prayers).

That same evening, the team met with the *mufti*[36] who headed the Nuh madrasa's fatwa department. He explained that the department's role was merely to endorse the written fatwa request as issued at Darul Uloom Deoband, a highly respected Islamic seminary in Uttar Pradesh that was revered by the majority of the population of Mewat. The mufti advised the group to meet with the leaders at Deoband to resolve the issue. They would be the ones with the influence to convince the other two parties in the fatwa to stop the flyer distribution.

With advice and support of two sympathetic moulvies who accompanied them, the field team task force consulted with Deoband leaders face to face and discussed the authenticity of the fatwa. During the meeting, one moulvi recalled having a meeting with a few complainants a couple of months earlier. However, upon seeing the written material about the foundation's work, he found no evidence of wrongdoing and had considered the matter closed. Again the team was advised to go back to resolve the issues with the complainants.

Some field team members reported back that they had been asked by a few people in their communities whether they planned to continue their employment with the foundation, since working there was declared "against Islam" in the fatwa. Bothered by the queries about it from their friends and relatives, many field staff members had spoken with their families and others to refute the allegations.

Salahuddin Saiphy met with field team members individually and in group sessions, reminding them as often as needed that the decree was based on false accusations. He assured them, "I am also an educated

36. Islamic scholar who gives legal opinions.

Muslim, and I would be the first person to quit from Sehgal Foundation if it were doing anything wrong."

Almost everyone on the field team readily joined the efforts to counter the baseless fatwa. But one field team member who said he felt the pressure did resign. However, he started another job so quickly that some on the team assumed he planned to leave anyway.

When anyone on the staff expressed concern about losing their jobs in light of the controversy, Jay provided assurances to everyone that none of their jobs were in jeopardy. Sehgal Foundation would continue working, elsewhere if not in Mewat. He reminded them that the Ghaghas Community Center was only fifty kilometers from the Rajasthan border, in close proximity to many more villages that needed help. The foundation's work would continue no matter what. He still believed the communities would stand by the foundation.

However, obtaining open support from the communities took time. The majority of villagers knew that the foundation had done nothing wrong, but they were reluctant to say so publicly. When a group of people from nearby villages gathered outside the Ghaghas Community Center, a few raised voices tried to incite the crowd, accusing Sehgal Foundation of teaching against Islam. They shouted for villagers to attack the center. But the rabblerousers were unsuccessful in garnering any support from the local people. The community center was never harmed.

Over the next few days, individual community members in each village came forward one by one to say they objected to the fatwa. They knew the decree was based on false allegations; the foundation had always worked as a partner in their communities, and the work being done was good. Jay was right; people in the villages of Mewat did not want their partnerships with Sehgal Foundation to end or their work together to stop.

Though the initial disruption died down after several days, and the teams went back to work, there was much more to be done to resolve the situation. Anjali, Pooniaji, and Salahuddin traveled together to Jamia Millia Islamia University in New Delhi to consult with a professor in the Department of Islamic Studies. The professor examined the fatwa and the foundation's brochure and concluded that the sort of dispute described was actually within the jurisdiction of a different type of court called *Darul Qaja*, where both parties present their case, and a judgment is rendered. He suggested that a letter be written from Sehgal Foundation questioning the justification of the fatwa from an Islamic point of view. The professor agreed to review the letter for accuracy before it was sent.

A meeting with the forty-two members of the field team and the eight members of the core team was held one week after the fatwa was issued to talk through the issues involved, separate facts from misconceptions, and make decisions about their next steps. Field team members shared concerns they now had about the possible validity of some allegations noted in the fatwa. Reviewing the text and pictures used in two of the health session modules in the Family Life Education classes, the group agreed that some material could be interpreted as unacceptable from an Islamic viewpoint; the classes were also teaching family planning to girls.

Carefully examining each point in the fatwa, the group made several proactive decisions. The two health modules on anatomy would be removed from use in the Family Life Education classes. The remaining class content would be revised to do away with any aspect that could be construed as objectionable. Moulvies would be invited to address and discuss any issues of concern. Written materials about Sehgal Foundation work would be translated into Hindi and Urdu and provided to individuals in the community. Taking photos of female subjects would be curtailed in Mewat, and no current photos showing the faces of women or girls in Mewat would be placed in foundation publications. All photos of women and adolescent girls were removed from the website for the time being. No printed foundation materials that pictured women or girls, even if they were of women or girls from Rajasthan or elsewhere, would be distributed to the villages. Family planning issues would be directed to the auxiliary nurse-midwife. No foundation staff members would take girls or women to other villages to engage in sports competitions or any activities, events, or trainings offered to women farmers, self-help groups, and so on. Women on the foundation team would consistently wear more conservative attire, such as "ladies suits," when in the villages. Hiring unmarried girls on the field team would be avoided.

With these modifications to programming and operations, the field team task force continued to meet with moulvies, sarpanches, and local community leaders to clarify the foundation's work and intentions. A letter given to religious leaders explained that the most critical activities cited in the fatwa were actually not true, and that some activities had now been discontinued due to concerns cited. Pointing out that Sehgal Foundation had not been informed about any of these complaints before the decree was issued, the letter requested a review of the fatwa.

Pooniaji and Salahuddin accompanied field team member Nasir Hussain back to Deoband and Saharanpur in Uttar Pradesh to meet the muftis who signed the fatwa. Scholars explained that they had no system or process for verifying allegations made by complainants. Fatwas issued were based solely on written complaints they received. The Deoband muftis acknowledged that the positions held by the complainants and Sehgal Foundation were poles apart. The group was again told to sort out the problem directly with the complainants. They were encouraged to meet with the local religious leaders at the madrasa in Nuh (the third party that signed the Fatwa).

On a hopeful note, Salahuddin received a response from a senior Islamic scholar in New Delhi whom he had contacted earlier. An emissary had been sent to look into the facts. Satisfied that there was no wrongdoing by Sehgal Foundation, the Islamic scholar produced a written opinion that was forwarded to the villages, along with the directive that "All good activities of Sehgal Foundation should be supported by all good Muslims," and vice versa. He suggested to Salahuddin that the foundation team consult with Islamic Fiqh Academy in New Delhi, another prestigious and highly respected center with the authority to issue fatwas. It was possible to seek a different ruling on the subjects described in the fatwa.

Meanwhile, Sehgal Foundation hosted a community gathering with elders and opinion leaders to present a summary of the foundation's work done in partnership with the communities over the previous ten-plus years. Seeing the concrete ways in which communities benefited from the Integrated Sustainable Village Development model, the demonstration village, the employment generated, and other programs and projects, convinced a group of *ulemas* (Muslim religious scholars) to visit Sehgal Foundation's training center in Ghaghas to see if they could find any objectionable evidence "from an Islamic point of view." While there, the men even inspected the women's toilet facilities to be sure there were no hidden cameras placed there.

Field team members spoke with the scholars and discussed the activities of the foundation in contrast to the allegations cited in the fatwa. Personal interactions helped to dissolve many misunderstandings, some of which were a matter of semantics. For example, one of the complaints raised was in regard to the word *ling* used on some of the foundation's printed materials. Ling, the Hindi word for "gender" and used in that context in the brochures, was also slang for penis (derived from the Sanskrit), which was how the complainant saw the word.

Another misunderstanding had to do with "exposure" visits organized by the Federation of Self Help Groups. Women and girls were taken to other communities, and cities such as New Delhi, to introduce them to the larger world outside their small villages. This idea did not sit well with some people.

A public endorsement of Sehgal Foundation came from villagers in a passive form when a series of large public gatherings, called *jalsas,* were held in several villages. The first was in the village of Karheda, a few kilometers from the foundation's community center at Ghaghas. Religious leaders had intended to discuss the Sehgal Foundation fatwa and hold a religious discourse. The field team task force attended the meeting and reported back to Pooniaji that as soon as the foundation was spoken of "unfairly," a number of the villagers in attendance stood and left. Those who left said they had been misinformed about the purpose of the gathering. They said that if they had known it was a meeting to criticize Sehgal Foundation, they would not have attended. As with the attempt to cause trouble at the Ghaghas Community Center, any perceived criticism toward Sehgal Foundation was met with passive nonparticipation by the villagers.

Such expressions of non-support for the fatwa from community members caught the attention of religious leaders, who then decided to relook at the issue and visit the foundation to see firsthand what Sehgal Foundation was doing in the villages. Pooniaji served as the coordinator of their visits.

As these religious leaders actually saw the work being done, they admitted finding nothing offensive. Any criticisms from individuals outside the villages did not stand long, because the visitors could see that citizens in communities working in partnership with the foundation were firmly in favor of the work. A beneficial outcome of this round of visits was the formation of a *salahkar* council (advisory group) that included religious leaders and Sehgal Foundation representatives. Quarterly meetings were launched to apprise the group of foundation activities and receive counsel on any activities that might be construed as against Islam.

With sincere and helpful input from the field team, the core team also became more sensitized to issues that could be seen as disrespectful of Islam. The team's intentions had always been respectful and responsive to Islamic religious practices, not just for the villagers, but also for Muslim staff members. Plans were already in place to construct a *wudukhana*, a washing station for use before formal prayers, in the Ghaghas Community Center, since so many people from the villages spent so much time there. Needed modifications were made, and the construction was completed.

Following up on the advice provided by the Islamic scholar consulted in New Delhi, Salahuddin contacted the Islamic Fiqh Academy to request that the center issue a new (counter) fatwa supporting Sehgal Foundation activities. A mufti who had accompanied Salahuddin and the team in making the request again vouched for the foundation's work. By granting the request, an additional vote of confidence came from a senior mufti at Islamic Fiqh Academy. He endorsed the foundation's work to help the poor in Mewat and encouraged the team to continue their good work. The original fatwa was effectively countered.

Once Islamic Fiqh Academy's supportive fatwa was issued in writing, further negative intervention from the original fatwa complainants ceased. Hoopla surrounding the controversy died down almost as fast as it had erupted. The morale of Muslim members of the field team quickly rose. Only in retrospect did they realize and admit how stressful the fatwa had been for them.

The salahkar council met regularly for a couple of years. Field team members continued to meet informally at regular intervals with religious leaders and others with influence.

Minor rumblings from a few troublemakers occurred occasionally, such as when the foundation hired an agency to produce a video to illustrate Sehgal Foundation activities and a concluding scene showed colorful balloons being released and floating up in the air. Village onlookers in the area were surprised and awed by the vibrant sight. When a religious leader from Ghaghas made an outlandish suggestion that women and girls should go inside to avoid being photographed by cameras hidden in Sehgal Foundation balloons, no one responded. People in the community no longer took such remarks seriously. Villagers retrieved a balloon and demonstrated that there was no camera inside.

Over time, taking photographs of women and girls in Mewat was acceptable again, but only with their verbal approval. The Communications team avoided using photos of Meo women in the foundation's annual report for the next couple of years. Foundation visitors were now instructed to refrain from taking photographs of people in the villages, particularly of women and/or children, unless the visitor asked permission from the subjects. The issues related to photographs eventually disappeared almost completely. The Sehgal Foundation team continued to honor the practice of asking permission before taking or using any villager's photograph.

Observing the faded effects of the first fatwa within the community, a few religious leaders, feeling threatened by their diminishing influence, organized smaller village-level gatherings to try to influence public opinion against the foundation. Participating actively in these meetings, the field team task force diffused any attempts to cause further problems by bringing together religious leaders with key people within the community who now stood up openly and supported the foundation and strongly and convincingly refuted the allegations made in the original fatwa.

One particularly loud-mouthed critic of the foundation was apprehended much later by local police for alleged anti-national activities. Though his legal troubles were unrelated to the foundation, all rumblings associated with the controversy evaporated completely after his arrest.

The foundation team eventually learned that some supporters of the original fatwa were a few local individuals who held personal grudges against Sehgal Foundation. They had not been selected for jobs or their jobs were terminated for cause. Job opportunities of any sort were so few in Mewat. Any positions at the foundation were highly desirable. When any job opened up that could be filled by someone from the community, there was huge response and interest. Many more people wanted the jobs, even volunteer jobs that paid a small stipend, than there were available opportunities. Criteria for the volunteer jobs included many factors, such as education, experience, and personal rapport with people. Sometimes the criteria for selection were hard for applicants to understand. Inevitable conflicts erupted when a sarpanch or a village elder tried to influence the selection process, recommending a nephew, son, or brother. The team was aware that this sort of thing was part of the culture. They made sure the process was always carried out fairly in order to maintain the organization's strong reputation as credible, ethical, and as a desirable employer. However, in an act of angry vengeance for their hurt feelings, these men, who were not chosen for jobs or were fired, had tried to incite discord against the foundation.

As Suri Sehgal had rightly observed, there would always be occasional troublemakers, and Salahuddin Saiphy reflected, "It's a big world, you can't please everyone. Let's continue our good efforts to achieve the vision and mission of the foundation by serving the underprivileged. That is what constantly motivates us and brings us to this work every day."

Although distracting and difficult in some ways, the entire fatwa experience, which transpired over a few months in 2010, actually served to further the credibility of the foundation's work in the region. Both fatwas (the original and counter decrees) served to shine a light on the impact of the foundation's work with communities, and resulted in many other villages inviting Sehgal Foundation to partner with them. Sehgal Foundation work continued to expand in partnership with the communities, with a goal of reaching all the villages of Mewat.

Though a few changes were made in the Family Life Education program as a result of the field team's recommendations after their careful examination of program components, a much larger, very positive change came around that same time that brought an end to the program. When the Right of Children to Free and Compulsory

Education Act went into effect in April of 2010, enrollment of girls in school promptly increased. Participants in the popular and successful Family Life Education program had mostly been young girls who had never before been to school. Any who had attended school in the past had either dropped out or been forced by their families to quit. Now the same girls who would have taken part in the Family Life Education classes could all be in school instead. Before the end of 2010, the Family Life Education program was discontinued with the provision that it would be revived again in the future if needed.

According to Suri, it had been a "powerful" program that helped girls gain confidence, learn useful skills, and develop independence. But the team had not found a way to demonstrate sustained impact of the program. Once girls finished the program they were back in the realm of a patriarchal family structure and culture, where they had to be subservient.

The team's attention to this empowerment area now evolved naturally toward good governance initiatives to make sure girls in the villages were not prevented from attending school. The foundation then directed support toward the creation of centers within the schools where tailoring and other skills could be taught. The empowerment of girls and women would continue to be woven into every Sehgal Foundation initiative.

© J.D. Geertsema

Indoor cooking

Hauling cluster beans for fodder

Suri Sehgal with villagers

Washing clothes

Making dung cakes for fuel

Jay Sehgal and team with village youth

Villager with field team member Jaan Mohammad

Life Skills Education

Life Skills Education

Lalit Mohan Sharma and B. R. Poonia discussing water situation in Agon, 2003

Field team and villagers praying before community meeting

First group of village champions with B. R. Poonia

©J.D. Geertsema

Mothers meeting on health

©Mick Minard/REEF Reports

Bringing water home

Bhure Khan, water activist

Check dam, a water harvesting structure in Kotla village

Side view of water harvesting structure in Kotla

Carrot harvest

Drip irrigation

Women farmers event in Alwar, Rajasthan

Millet demo plot in Rajasthan

Delivery hut room, Notki

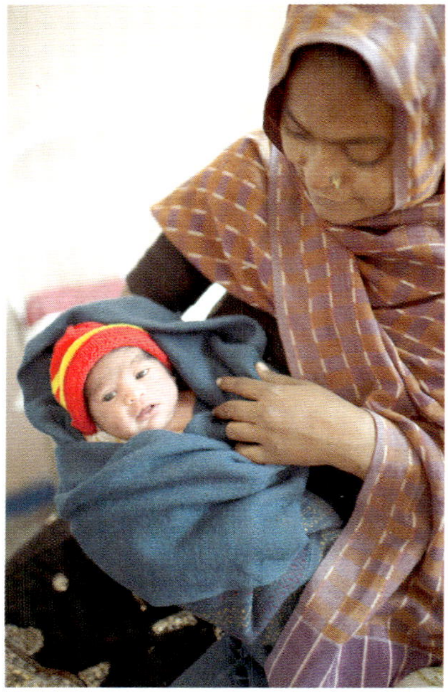

Mother and child

© J.D. Geertsema

Suri and Edda Sehgal honored

Trees for Notki

Ajay Pandey discussing Good Governance Now!

Notki School

Mid Day Meal at school

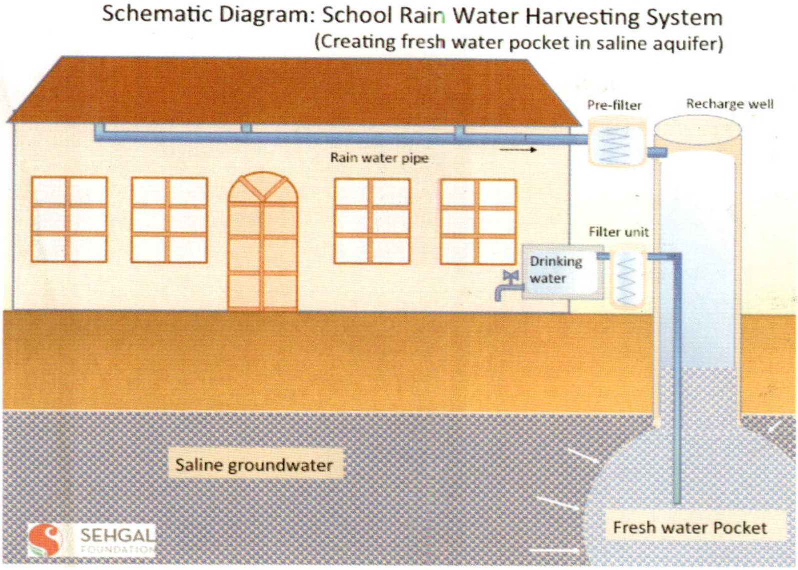

Award-winning concept presented at United Nations Solutions Summit in 2014

Rainwater harvesting in a school

On air at Alfaz-e-Mewat

Radio Alfaz-e-Mewat FM 107.8

Radio interview in mustard field in Ghaghas

Public Distribution System depot

Mahila Gram Sabha creating village development plan

Mahila Sangathan (women's collective)

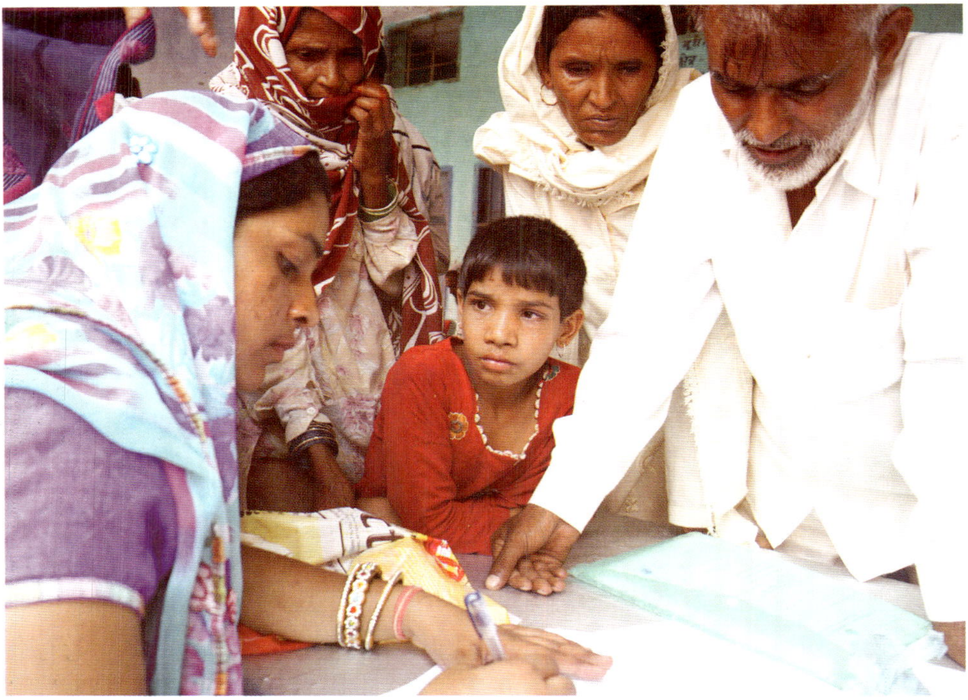

Governance guide assisting villagers

Legal literacy camp (Vikas Jha with mic, and District Legal Services Authority official)

Jane Schukoske and Anjali Makhija in community meeting

Kamlesh Sherawat conducting a survey

Sehgal Foundation Platinum LEED-certified Phase 1 Building

Sehgal Foundation women, 2014

Sehgal Foundation Team, 2014

Sehgal Foundation trustees, advisors, and CEO, 2014

Jay Sehgal and scientists, P. Vani Sekhar and Dr. Murali Dhar Gupta, in Sehgal Foundation corn research plots at ICRISAT

Suri and Edda Sehgal

Suri Sehgal and Ben Sehgal

©Marcie Woodward

Jane Schukoske

Some Sehgal Foundation awards

Suri Sehgal speaking at Seeds for Change *book launch in Hyderabad, India, 2015*

CHAPTER 10

Good Rural Governance

Myriad events throughout 2010 helped crystallize Sehgal Foundation's strategy for how to proceed in light of limited resources. The Integrated Sustainable Village Development (ISVD) model was excellent and badly needed by every village, but the associated costs were well beyond the scope of a single NGO. The foundation's work in India was still primarily being financed, as it had been from the beginning, by the founders' parent organization in the United States. Scaling up ISVD required funding from additional values-driven external donors. However, the reality was that most donors expressed interest only in individual components or modules of ISVD, and not the model in its entirety. To go beyond a limited number of villages would require a wider range of stakeholders and partners to lend greater visibility and credibility to the work and make sustainable growth and development possible.

This decision to partner with other organizations to scale up ISVD coincided with a formal rollout of the now-refined rights-based approach to good rural governance. *Good Governance Now!* and capacity-building of village-level institutions were people-intensive (rather than being capital-intensive) initiatives propelled by individuals and teams, including lots of volunteers and trainees. Not only were these two initiatives cost-effective, villagers were able to see that they benefited from both directly. The combination constituted a good rural governance model—an elegant, solid, and replicable model that promised the kind of impact the Sehgal Foundation team had been seeking.

Good rural governance initiatives had the largest potential impact in the long term and the greatest chance of creating Sehgal Foundation's intended legacy—to make a positive and enduring difference in rural India. However, a critical mass of motivated citizens demanding change was necessary to force the bureaucracy to function properly. When enough citizens were able and willing to participate, they could demand an effective culture of good governance. The team was enthusiastic about pushing forward to achieve that critical mass.

Suri Sehgal described the two-pronged approach the foundation would now take moving forward: "First, we will continue to build and refine models in water and agriculture within our cluster of villages in Mewat, using Sehgal Foundation funds. That will be the organization's experimental living laboratory of fieldwork. Any scaling up of those models will be dependent upon support from our donor partners. Funds for those projects will be proactively sought, and we will work in whichever geographic area is chosen by partners providing the funds. We will solicit financial support to develop the in-house capacity to implement projects ourselves and, if necessary, outsource parts of the work to other NGOs. For any venture undertaken, Sehgal Foundation will hire temporary staff from the local area, working under the leadership of a trusted foundation team coordinator. To provide employment opportunities to those on the field staff for upward mobility, project leader selections will include members of implementation teams, village champions, and others."

About the second part of the two-pronged approach, Suri explained, "Our experience has already shown that donors and partners interested in development are most attracted to tangible 'brick and mortar' projects. For as long as our rights-based initiatives (good rural governance) appear intangible, a large portion of funds for those will, by necessity, continue to come from Sehgal Foundation so as not to slow the momentum we are seeing now. The continuing growth of good rural governance will be organic and systematic. External funding will always be welcome, but the good governance movement will not depend exclusively on external resources."

Good rural governance programs advanced to a starring role within Sehgal Foundation. Simultaneously, the team sought more partnerships in each area of ISVD for scaling up. The fertilizer company, The Mosaic Company in India, had already been a valued partner since 2008. The relationship had brought knowledge, training, and resources to several agricultural intervention areas. In 2010 a new training module called *Krishi Jyoti* (krishi meaning agriculture, and jyoti meaning light) was rolled out to farmers in twenty villages in Mewat. With the application of balanced fertilizer based on soil health analysis, using less Urea and DAP and increased use of essential micronutrients, at least 4,500 farmers saw the benefit and adopted more effective and sustainable methods that improved their crop productivity and income.

Other productive relationships like this were pursued with the help of Sehgal Foundation's director of Resource Mobilization and Partnerships, Aparna Mahajan. With support from the trustees, she attempted to motivate the entire Sehgal Foundation team to appreciate the need to focus on securing external funds and grants. In an environment where so many NGOs competed for the same limited sources of funds in the market, this was a significant challenge for a team that never before had to consider these issues.

The low-visibility profile Sehgal Foundation had always maintained had to change quickly. Good work by itself would not attract partners and donors. The foundation had to become more visible and active in seeking outside funds. Publicizing the organization's successes would help attract those funds.

Pooja O. Murada, Communications team leader, said that when she began working at Sehgal Foundation in 2007, a huge amount of work was being done in the field, but very little had been documented. Her first tasks back then included assembling success stories for documentation and publication, and putting a plan in place for developing internal and external communications.

The Communications team ramped up their production of newsletters, articles, and videos that demonstrated how the various technologies and programs functioned in the villages. International contacts continued to bring visitors to Sehgal Foundation and help spread the information. More students, interns, volunteers, and researchers took part in foundation activities.

No singular strategy was used in proposing or building collaborations. Aparna and her team knew that every potential donor was unique and that understanding the values and priorities of the people involved was essential in enduring relationships that involved faith and trust. For the foundation's potential partners in rural progress, the resource mobilization team was tasked with demonstrating credibility, impact, work quality, and value, so donors could be assured of good returns on their investments. Goodwill meetings were held with potential partners.

An engagement letter was signed with Coca-Cola India Foundation. Sehgal Foundation would conduct a feasibility study prior to launching community water conservation and watershed projects in Mewat villages in April 2011. Within nine months of signing the first agreement, another public-private partnership agreement was made with Coca-Cola and the Mewat Development Agency for integrated check dam projects. Harmonious donor relationships resulted with a host of new organizations and quickly advanced partnerships to higher levels. New and continuing partnerships were formed with government departments at district, state, and central levels; foreign government bodies and trusts; academic institutions, corporations, foundations, other nonprofits, and national and international donor agencies.[37]

Changes in some roles and programs helped to solidify the new direction. Lalit Mohan Sharma's role expanded to include agricultural development initiatives in addition to water management. Healthcare and education initiatives were made the responsibility of the Capacity Building Center team. In keeping with the goal of helping villagers assume direct responsibility for their own development, the team was no longer directly involved in creating healthcare or school infrastructure, but rather served as a catalyst, assuming a supportive role in strengthening gram panchayats, School Management committees, and Village Health, Sanitation, and Nutrition committees.

The Sehgal Foundation's four program centers (Natural Resource Management; Capacity Building; Policy, Governance and Advocacy; and Rural Research) each had its own team and its own block facilitators in the villages. The responsibilities of village champions evolved into more specialized areas within each center. Their new titles included field assistant, community capacity builder, or research assistant. A few became governance guides.

---

37. See appendix: Sehgal Foundation Partnerships.

Anjali Makhija helped to define the Capacity Building team initiative that served as a complementary arm to *Good Governance Now!* Just as empowering individuals to demand rights and entitlements from bureaucrats included training and learning on the part of citizens to know their rights, village leaders (sarpanches and panchayat members) and members of village-level institutions required training. The foundation team had assisted in activating village-level institutions all along in order to sustain specific programs or projects. But now the goal was to build and strengthen the capacities of village councils and other village-level institutions by providing them with the knowledge and skills to interact effectively and honestly with government officials on behalf of their communities, access funds to maintain and improve village infrastructures, and hold government departments accountable to the communities they represented.

The pace of the two good rural governance initiatives was not the same. Inspiring individual citizens with *Good Governance Now!* involved large groups of volunteers, many of whom jumped into action immediately once they had the information and training. But making changes in long-entrenched practices by representatives from panchayats and other village-level institutions was a slower and more complicated process due to corruption, ignorance, and cultural factors.

Panchayats had the ability to obtain funds for village development, but some unscrupulous sarpanches made quick money by bribing government officials and taking the money for themselves. Other sarpanches and panchayat members were without the skills or knowledge to even try to access the funds they were entitled to receive for their communities. When women were elected as panchayat members, their husbands, sons, or other men in their families commonly spoke for them and carried out their panchayat work. The governance teams continued to encourage women to become panchayat members and supported them to become more active, use their voices, and gain more influence.

In many states of India, responsibility for training panchayats lies with the State Institutes of Rural Development (SIRDs). The Haryana Institute of Rural Development (HIRD) posted an ad on its website in 2010 seeking NGOs to provide training to panchayats. The Haryana Development and Panchayats Department, which oversees HIRD, had allocated funds for this purpose. The Capacity Building team responded to the ad and was invited to make a presentation. Sehgal Foundation was awarded funding for the panchayat training project. The training, held in the first quarter of 2011, emphasized budgetary and accounting procedures, financial audits, the Haryana Panchayati Raj Act,[38] activity mapping, and decentralized planning.

In a strategy meeting the team agreed to a plan to train leaders in at least 10 percent of the 431 villages in Mewat. Anjali and her team collaborated with the Haryana Development and Panchayats Department on a project to train the 308 panchayats in Mewat. Though the foundation was only working in seventeen villages at the time, this project was useful in identifying more panchayats with the willingness and drive for development in their communities. The method for training was the already-familiar "learn by doing." Training topics included panchayat roles, the 73rd Amendment (about the powers and responsibilities of panchayats), gram sabhas, and revenue generation for village administration and rural development programs.

After two months of training panchayats, the Capacity Building team selected thirty-five panchayats with oversight of fifty-three villages (including the original seventeen) to work more intensively to streamline the training model. HIRD funded the second phase of the training to include 231 panchayat members, of which 200 were sarpanches. The team helped train panchayats with curriculum provided by HIRD, which showed how to maintain records for financial accounting and legal issues, how to maintain data on specific government programs, and how to administer and implement the programs. Since panchayats did not have access to computers, they maintained records by hand and submitted them to the district office.

A Panchayat Advisory Group (PAG) was created early in 2012, consisting of people with experience working with panchayats—NGOs, government officials, development experts, and panchayat members. The PAG was helpful in providing direction and assisting with future action plans. Work with the thirty-five panchayats spanned the next four

38. The Panchayati Raj Act provided for the constitution of gram panchayats. See http://www.panchayat.gov.in/documents/10198/350801/The%20Haryana%20Panchayati%20%20Raj%20Act%201994.pdf.

years and was instrumental in the eventual creation of five more model villages.

Specific characteristics of a "model village" were not generally agreed upon. There were many definitions. The Association for India's Development (AID) had not identified a set of guidelines for its vision of a model village, stating that such a definition would be self-defeating because imposing outside opinions on the people of a region would discourage local participation. The AID view, consistent with the Sehgal Foundation view, was that the vision of a model village must be developed by interacting with a local community and be fully dependent on community inputs.

While all this was going on, Policy, Governance, and Advocacy program leader Navneet Narwal and the governance guides on the team conducted *Good Governance Now!* trainings in collaboration with Jindal Global Law School, where Ajay Pandey was teaching. Law students were becoming familiar with the issues faced by citizens in rural areas and witnessing the power of effective citizen participation. More and more villagers experienced successes for themselves, expanding the scale of good governance one step at a time.

One well-documented example was a man who attended informational meetings and said that his sick buffalo had been wrongly treated by a veterinarian. During an informal discussion, he learned that he could approach a consumer forum and discuss his situation. He learned how to file a complaint against the veterinarian and subsequently won the case. For one illiterate person to have the power to move the court and achieve justice became an example to others. Newly empowered villagers became actively involved in the development of their communities.

The most dramatic shift in the good governance training occurred with the greater participation of women, according to Anjali Godyal. She had come to Sehgal Foundation as a rural management intern in 2005, working with village women on the indigenous tourism project in Jyotisar. She was soon hired to the core team to work in the Life Skills Education program and eventually became program leader. Now working in Capacity Building, she was able to observe the differences she saw firsthand when women felt empowered.

Godyal described witnessing the transformative power that emerges when women take leadership roles: "Male governance trainees who went to the Public Distribution System depots recognized the rampant corruption and saw it as normal. Women trainees were not willing to accept business-as-usual." When male depot holders became angry that their work was challenged, women trainees calmly explained exactly what happened when depot holders didn't follow the law—sharing both the legal ramifications and the hardship they caused families. The explanations put their actions into context, diffused the depot holders' defensiveness, and often resulted in win-win solutions.

The team was primed to continue expanding the good governance programs as fast and as far as possible. To bring further support to the initiative from the global legal community, the foundation's first annual International Conference on Good Governance and Citizen Participation was presented in partnership with the University of Baltimore School of Law and Jindal Global Law School in March 2011. Invited participants included an array of accomplished people in the area of democracy and human rights. Commenting on the ideal represented by good rural governance and effective citizen participation, Vanderbilt Law School Professor Frank S. Bloch—a global figure in the field of clinical legal education (CLE) and executive secretary of the Global Alliance for Justice Education[39]—observed that the framers of the CLE model of learning may have perhaps never imagined such an innovative method for addressing the disconnect between the law and the lay person and, at the same time, strengthening legal education, as did *Good Governance Now!*, which "has taken clinical methodology beyond professional training of law students to use in the field with community members."

Among the other dignitaries who participated in the conference was an American law professor with significant experience in India, Jane Schukoske. In 1995, while a tenured faculty member at the University of Baltimore and a senior Fulbright scholar in Sri Lanka, Jane became acquainted with Indian legal educators at the National Law School of India University, Bangalore. Professor N. R. Madhava Menon,

39. See http://www.gaje.org/.

considered the father of modern legal education in India, had invited her there to serve as a resource person at a month-long teachers' training on clinical legal education. Thereafter, Jane maintained ties with Indian professors interested in clinical legal education, and her writings emphasized the potential of greater Indo-US collaboration. During an eight-year period that Jane directed the Fulbright Program in India, she and Professor Frank Bloch obtained approval for a Fulbright-Vanderbilt master's fellowship program in clinical legal education. Ajay Pandey was one of six Fulbrighters from India who earned a Vanderbilt master's degree.

Overall, Jane's career had centered on legal aid to the disadvantaged and on clinical legal education. A community development clinic she established in 1996 at the University of Baltimore was still going strong. She was naturally attracted to the foundation's social justice focus in rural India and had visited Sehgal Foundation in 2008 at Ajay's invitation. Intrigued by the mission of the foundation, she expressed interest in the open CEO position.

She met with Suri and Edda in Captiva, Florida, in January 2011. Jay Sehgal was also present for the meeting. They discussed the mission of Sehgal Foundation, and the good governance programs in particular.

Jane was immediately recognized as an ideal candidate to be Sehgal Foundation's new CEO. Her expertise and her contacts with law schools in India made her a perfect fit for the further development and refinement of the foundation's rights-based strategies. A keen understanding of the good governance programs was essential to provide needed support, and Jane was the one who could carry it forward. In keeping with the high standards expected of work by the foundation, the Sehgals asked Jane to map out her vision of short-term, midterm, and long-term goals.

Suri said to her, "Good governance is our strategy, our future. Your job will be to make sure it becomes an all-India movement."

Jane accepted the challenge. She joined Sehgal Foundation officially as the new CEO in July 2011 and brought a new level of vitality to the organization along with credibility, visibility, strong links with law schools, and her committed interest in good governance. Jane immediately began placing more of the organization's emphasis on the empowerment of women and creating programs that were led by women and responsive to the needs of women. Under her direction, the foundation's long-avowed gender equality policies were articulated in print for the first time. Though an American "white lady" who spoke very little Hindi or the Mewati dialect, Jane was able to establish relationships of mutual comfort and rapport with people she met in the villages. She felt at home within Indian culture. Sarees had been her preferred attire since the mid-1990s, and her warm and respectful manner put others at ease quickly.

When Jane started at the foundation, the good governance initiatives had reached seventeen villages in Mewat. By the end of 2011, the program had spread to fifty-three villages—meeting the goal of reaching 10 percent of the villages in Mewat in a matter of months. Achieving that number with only nine trainers boosted everyone's confidence. The team expanded to thirty trainers when the next group of well-qualified governance guides completed the training of trainers course on *Good Governance Now!*

Attorney and program leader Navneet Narwal was the chief architect of a series of four legal literacy camps in 2011. The training camps, which he organized at the block level, attracted participants from fifty-three villages. As part of the foundation's legal literacy initiative, the training camps continued to offer fairly large-scale guidance on the expression of individual claims and rights. Within a year, legal literacy camps would span more than 400 villages. Navneet began reaching out to the District Legal Services Authority in an attempt to create linkages that would benefit the citizens of Mewat, but this effort would take more time to nurture.

Good Governance Now! made an impact from community to community. In the village of Papda, as soon as its community leaders became aware of the appropriate nutritional meals their children were meant to receive at school, they insisted on the correct distribution and allotment. Similar action in several villages in Mewat resulted in improved access to Mid Day Meals in more schools every year.[40]

The ideal of good governance attained recognition even beyond the communities of Mewat. *Good Governance Now!* was declared a

---

40. Ninety-two schools in 2011, and 120 schools in 2012.

2010 finalist for the Japanese Award for Most Innovative Development Project, sponsored by the Global Development Network (GDN). A consultant for GDN, Dr. William Carmichael, an economist and former vice president of the Developing Country Programs for the Ford Foundation, had conducted an evaluation of *Good Governance Now!* and visited several Meo communities in the Mewat District. Months later, he commented in an email to Jane Schukoske that he "came away from that visit with an immensely positive view of the project and of the effectiveness of its strategies for empowering members of the communities that it serves. Indeed, on the basis of my experience (over a forty-year period!) in developing and assessing projects focusing on 'better governance,' I regard the IRRAD[41] project as an exceedingly instructive (and regrettably rare) model for effective action in that field."

As a third place winner, Sehgal Foundation received Global Development Network grant money that was used to fund a series of four regional workshops on Good Rural Governance and Citizen Participation during 2011 and 2012. Interactive and participatory workshops were held at law schools in Silchar, Assam; Mysore, Karnataka; Patna, Bihar; and Jodhpur, Rajasthan.

In November 2011, Vikas Jha joined the Policy, Governance, and Advocacy Center as group leader, bringing years of global experience in social accountability and decentralized governance. With a PhD in international relations from Jawaharlal Nehru University, Vikas had a strong interest in, and knowledge of, democracy in all its dimensions. Under his leadership, the *Good Governance Now!* program training grew from 278 trained villagers in fifty-three communities to 1,130 villagers in 400 communities in 2012. The team was approaching its objective of reaching all the villages in Mewat.

The Rural Research Center's role had expanded in 2010 when Suri Sehgal and the trustees asked the team to collate documentation of all Sehgal Foundation work to date as part of a comprehensive impact assessment of the organization's development activities. Dr. Pradeep Mehta, a development specialist with a PhD in economics, had joined the foundation staff in February 2010 as a research scientist

41. Sehgal Foundation was still being called IRRAD until 2014.

and within a year was made head of the Rural Research Center team, which also included field team researchers, data entry experts, and other researchers. Pradeep and associate scientist Niti Saxena guided the project, which was to examine the impact of interventions in key areas: rural health, water management, income enhancement, education, and community mobilization (which was considered part of every initiative), and draw conclusions about what was working and what wasn't working.[42] The goal was to be able to make informed decisions about which initiatives could be merged, eliminated, or scaled up.

The Rural Research Center team involved external experts to review the report. This process yielded important learnings about trying to do too many things, tracking too many interventions, making frequent shifts in strategies, and the need for consistency in recordkeeping. These results assisted in better internal coordination of work among the teams.

From that point forward, the foundation teams conducted baseline surveys before starting work in a new region. In adjusting to this valuable preparation, team members had to get used to creating written goals with needed inputs before taking direct action to solve problems. Knowing the needs of a particular community in a given situation, and then comparing those needs with available resources, made it more likely to reach a successful outcome and measure the impact of the intervention. The extra step also served to check the impulse to jump in quickly to take steps *for* communities rather than *with* them.

A key finding in the impact assessment report was that many of the "brick and mortar" infrastructure projects that had been done in partnership with communities were not actually being adequately maintained, including soak pits and check dam structures. This disturbing information supported the need for greater advocacy work and ownership of the project by the community. Strengthening community engagement and mobilization would be crucial for village development and the sustainability of foundation interventions.

A process was identified for evaluating the potential for longer-term community involvement. Work in any village had always depended

42. Since baseline studies had not been done before 2011, the team used experiment-control design to minimize the effects of the variables, and a logical framework approach for each program.

on interested and willing villagers. Results of a subsequent report confirmed that the criteria for community partnerships worked, to some extent, but were not a guarantee of sustainability—in community interest or responsibility. Infrastructure projects were expensive and not necessarily sustainable. However, Sehgal Foundation was not about to abandon this important work.

What was still happening in Notki, the first demonstration village attempted by Sehgal Foundation, illustrated the dilemma. The foundation team never fully left Notki after all the work was done to create a model village. However, the method of working with the community changed to a supportive role once the responsibility for maintenance of the infrastructure and the direction of any ongoing interventions were taken on by the Notki panchayat. At least that was the plan.

Sehgal Foundation had made a huge capital investment in Notki. Visitors from far and wide had seen the demonstration village and learned about the interventions done there. However, the newly elected sarpanch in Notki was less active than his predecessor and lacked a shared commitment to development. He took no action to initiate repairs or maintain improvements. He presumed that Sehgal Foundation would take care of any maintenance needs of their community. Villagers did not even bother to make requests to the government for repairs or services typically provided by the government. Due to the large scale of the work done in Notki with foundation assistance, some members of the community actually thought Sehgal Foundation "owned" the village. They had come to expect a fast clean-up of any problems, just as they saw happen at times when high-profile guests visited Notki during the period when the infrastructure work was still being done.

The foundation team had a hard time watching the deterioration in Notki and not being able to fix each thing that was going wrong. But they knew they could not foster continued dependence or intervene to do repairs *for* the village. The team had learned a valuable lesson about the importance of strengthening village-level institutions. There had to be continuous pressure on each elected sarpanch to be honest and motivated. Peer pressure was a powerful tool in the battle against corruption in the political system, in general, in each panchayat, and with each sarpanch.

The foundation team was already replicating the initiatives carried out in Notki in other villages, and using a more effective approach to citizen empowerment and capacity building work with village-level institutions. Community members constructed toilets and cleaned villages with the help of the panchayats' funds and facilitated by the Village Health, Sanitation, and Nutrition committees; School Management Committee members prepared development plans; and community members implemented water infrastructure projects, including rainwater-harvesting systems, soak pits, and soak wells. Five more model villages (Jatka, Mundaka, Sarai, Untaka, and Khedli Khurd) were developed using government funds, with sustained results.

Even in a village where a sarpanch was dynamic, the foundation team and field-level committees continued their work with villagers to underscore the power of good governance so that the sarpanch and the panchayat remained accountable to the citizens. The more the villagers learned about good governance, the more empowered they became in keeping their leadership honest, and the more they became involved in interactive management of their own villages. This had been the goal in Notki as well, and the Capacity Building team was working hard to try to engage the village leaders, but progress there was much slower under the current panchayat leadership. Successes were easier to sustain in the other demonstration villages because the foundation's approach was made clearer from the start.

As Suri asserted, "A model village is only possible if the panchayat is active, and the community is empowered and demanding. The panchayat serves as a peer group watchdog to keep the sarpanch honest. This is why it is so important to work simultaneously with the community and build the capacity of the panchayat and the village-level institutions."

In an effort to generate more ideas for successful solutions and share the important lessons from the team's grassroots experiences, Sehgal Foundation facilitated regular seminars, consultations, discourses, and external trainings for other NGOs in rural development. Organizing and participating in more conferences and speaking engagements gave the team the chance to share cutting-edge knowledge with a greater number of current and potential partners, provide useful insights to others involved in similar work, and learn from others. At the same time, collaborative initiatives at various levels resulted in more recognitions and honors from esteemed organizations in the areas of water, agriculture, global development, social justice, and good rural governance.[43]

Every Sehgal Foundation program would eventually benefit from the Communications team's three-year effort to launch a community radio station. An accessible and dedicated medium of communication *by* the community and *for* the community, the radio station was envisioned as an effective means for people to learn about issues and voice opinions. Community radio promised to be an effective tool for bringing about social inclusion, empowerment, and change at the grassroots level, while also being a source of entertainment. Pooja O. Murada, who had spearheaded the project from the start, asked two members of the field team, Jaan Mohammad and Susheel Bama, to participate in the required presentation that was part of the process of receiving a license from the Ministry of Information and Broadcasting. Once again field team members made a great impression, and the screening judges were convinced that Sehgal Foundation had the skills and reach to work directly with the grassroots community. The foundation received a three-year grant agreement for close to Rs. 5,000,000 from the Ministry of Agriculture to set up the radio station in the Ghaghas Community Center and provide it with all necessary equipment and broadcasting support.

To select a team to manage local day-to-day operations of the radio station, Sehgal Foundation had offered a six-month broadcast training program. Thirty-four young people from all over Mewat participated in the training. The Communications team worked hard to enlist women in the training. Women-friendly policies were adopted during the training and maintained thereafter. Women would be provided with shared transportation, and no women would be required to do evening broadcast work. The foundation's gender and sexual harassment policies would be strictly adhered to in all situations.

Community members and local talent came forward well before the launch and at every step along the way to help shape the broadcast programming. Villagers said that since the radio station was going to be

43. See appendix: Awards and Recognitions.

the "mouthpiece" of Mewat, they wanted it called *Alfaz-e-Mewat* (Rural Voices of Mewat). However, some local villagers were entirely unfamiliar with radio towers or transmissions. Fewer than half of the residents of Mewat owned radios.

At dusk on the evening after the radio tower was installed outside the Ghaghas Community Center, the team was testing the tower connection and the radio antenna. The small red light bulb on the top of the tower became a subject of curiosity and unease. A rumor that it might be a camera for taking pictures of women spread fast, and a group of curious villagers gathered outside the center, some looking fairly concerned. To squelch the unrest, Pooja called members of the team who lived nearby and told them to open the gates and invite people inside to see the radio operation.

Senior field staff member Sayeed Ahmed turned off the red light and explained to the people how radio waves reached them. A few folks went into the recording studio and the team turned on the radio so those outside could listen to the conversation inside. That was the very first "broadcast" from Alfaz-e-Mewat! Sayeed invited the people who had gathered to listen to the radio each day to "please advise us for improvements." All concerns were gone as villagers left with smiles. The first test broadcast of Alfaz-e-Mewat FM 107.8 MHz was on January 10, 2012.

The first station manager was a well-qualified young Meo woman who was one of two women who had completed the training. Razia[44] had a natural style in public speaking. She was an ideal role model for other Meo girls who were not confident or allowed to go to school or work.

Razia came from the villages of Mewat with a burning desire for education and to serve her community. Most of her family had discouraged her from attending school and actively tried to stop her studies, but her mother was supportive. As Razia continued to win prizes for academic excellence, her family finally acknowledged their pride. She

44. Razia was one of the three women associated with Sehgal Foundation featured in the book *Poetry of Purpose: A Portrait of Women Leaders of India* by Dr. Shashi Gogate and Mick Minard, Purpose Press Books LLC, 2015. See http://www.poetryofpurpose.org/. Razia did not use a second name.

was permitted to stay in school, despite disapproving taunts from the conservative community.

Razia went on to college, something quite rare for a woman from her circumstances, and graduated first in her class. Her academic achievements were acknowledged in 1998 when she won the Mewat Development Agency's Best Woman Award. She completed a master's degree in sociology and worked for the Society for Promotion of Youth and Masses as part of a project funded by Sehgal Foundation. When the project ended, Sehgal Foundation recruited Razia to a full-time position on the field team. As a community mobilizer, Razia was instrumental in convincing Meo women to step out of their homes to receive healthcare, seek vocational and life-skills training, and participate in community work. She stood up and spoke to the men in the villages and inspired male youth to take part in community work by posing questions about particular problems and engaging them in dialogue.

To support girls' education, Razia was appointed project leader for the TARA Akshar literacy program, a learning program for adults created by an NGO called Development Alternatives. Among her other work for Sehgal Foundation before accepting the management position at the radio station, Razia had been block coordinator for a cluster of villages, assisting in implementing the Mahatma Gandhi National Rural Employment Guarantee Act. She had supervised Life Skills Education and the Rural Health program.

In Razia's position as a facilitator on the Sehgal Foundation field team, several Meo men had reported to her, which was quite uncommon. She met new challenges with determination, confidence, a positive attitude, and occasional coaching from the Sehgal Foundation team. Her primary motivation was to help empower girls and women in Mewat, and her new position at Alfaz-e-Mewat FM 107.8 provided her with a broad-range opportunity.

The announcement that the station would be "Bringing Airwaves of Change" went out in the local language to more than 183 villages within a twenty-kilometer radius of Ghaghas, reaching up to 200,000 people. After seven weeks of test runs, the formal broadcasting launch was on February 28, 2012. Starting with four hours a day, programming increased to nine hours a day before the end of the first year. Outside of Mewat, people with Internet access could listen online.

The station offered a blend of program formats and topics that addressed issues in agriculture, water, soil health, local culture, education, governance, and village-based institutions. While a variety of programs were presented, care was taken to feature those geared specifically toward women, highlighting issues such as reproductive health, women-oriented government programs, the importance of educating girls, and so on. These fit well with the key interests of the station manager and the entire radio team. Early programs that focused on women included *Saaf, Safai, aur Sehat* (Cleanliness, Sanitation, and Health) and *Waqt Hamara Hai* (Our Time Has Come).

Razia faced some friction at first as a Meo woman working in an untraditional role at the radio station. Villagers with patriarchal mindsets were particularly concerned when they heard her speak on the air. She attracted the attention of religious leaders in the region who kept a close watch on her broadcasts. One day a few moulvis arrived at the radio station during one of her programs to inquire about her. The young woman, wearing her *hizaab* (head covering), faced the moulvis directly and spoke to them about her work for the welfare of the people of Mewat and her desire to promote positive change in their lives.

Though the moulvis found Razia to be a faithful Muslim, they continued over the next few months to monitor and screen her radio work. Razia eventually won over her critics, who began to express appreciation for her program delivery and offer advice on how to improve her Urdu diction. When she went out on interviews or visits to the community, she was welcomed by listeners.

From its inception, the radio station was essentially owned and embraced by members of the community. The learning promoted by Alfaz-e-Mewat enhanced civic participation. By providing a platform for marginalized communities to speak out, the foundation was able to gauge community interest in specific issues and increase awareness of citizens' rights.

Pooja and the Communications team worked hard to strengthen the station's financial sustainability and ensure ongoing innovative programming by taking part in various networking committees and developing professional media partnerships. The first to join in partnership with Alfaz-e-Mewat was Sesame Workshop India Trust. *Galli Galli Sim Sim*, an Indian version of the American television series *Sesame*

Street, produced by Sesame Workshop India and adapted by the radio team to include local voices, became a popular children's series that helped increase school attendance and promote awareness of health and sanitation, particularly for girls. The station was an excellent vehicle for celebrating events, such as International Women's Day, International Day of the Girl Child, International Literacy Day, and Children's Day.

Razia and two reporters from the original broadcast team, Arshad Ayub and Javed Hussain, made frequent visits to the health department, meeting doctors and senior officials to create radio program content. Their work on radio programs featuring health issues (*Galli Galli Sim Sim* and *Saaf, Safai, aur Sehat*) and a program about Sufi history and music, called *Sufi Safar,* brought them recognition. All three were honored by being selected to participate in a government campaign on health by the National Rural Health Mission, a poverty alleviation project implemented by the Ministry of Rural Development, Government of India.

When *Good Governance Now!* was first introduced, the foundation team had hoped to see community members take ownership of the initiative. This occurred gradually as the people became more interested in learning about the Mid Day Meal program, Right to Information, and other programs. Trainers were pleased to finally see that the villagers were now choosing topics to address. As more people began practicing good governance, the more it expanded throughout the district.

The number of *Good Governance Now!* trainees was so large in early 2012 (more than 1,200) that the modest incentives originally provided to the participants threatened to become unsustainable. The trainings were being conducted in three centers and involved forty-eight individual sessions. The team brainstormed about the issue and made the decision to discontinue the Rs. 100 training honorarium and condense the number of sessions. Participants were not pleased with this, and attendance went down by 60 percent.

Governance guides were concerned that they would have to spend far more time mobilizing communities and finding motivated citizens who would attend regular trainings. But within three months, attendance gradually climbed back up again. Villagers had already been convinced of the empowering value of the work. Those volunteers who completed the *Good Governance Now!* training understood the benefits of their new knowledge: their families received subsidized food every month, their children received midday meals every day, they received subsidized seeds and agricultural equipment, their families' old-age pensions were processed quickly because they knew how to follow up on any problem with a government program, and all this was reinforced by the support they had from the foundation teams. As *Good Governance Now!* trainees received more benefits, they tended to participate more and monitor the working of government programs more intensively. Good governance activities were spreading to every village in Mewat district.

Every governance guide on staff was busy providing citizens-rights training to community leaders at five training centers. Twice a month, people from fifteen villages at a time came together in a central location for training. Smaller trainings were held in the individual villages. At local meetings in each village once or twice a month, citizens learned more about how to access their specific entitlements. Some meetings were organized spontaneously in the afternoon or evening with about thirty people if a particular issue was pressing at that moment. To be able to cover so many villages, good governance trainers each conducted two or three meetings a day. Wall paintings that were used so effectively to illustrate Mid Day Meal entitlements now also spelled out entitlements in several other programs, such as Right to Information, Public Distribution System, and Mahatma Gandhi National Rural Employment Guarantee Act. People could see who was responsible for what, and then they learned the steps to take to request and receive their entitlements.

CHAPTER 11

Grassroots Engagement

Good Governance Now! produced such excellent results in a relatively short period that it was propelled into a flagship initiative of Sehgal Foundation. An article written by Ajay Pandey about the collaborative clinical legal education "experiment" conducted by Sehgal Foundation and Jindal Global Law School that was published in *Maryland Journal of International Law*[45] described how law schools and NGOs could work well together to bring about transformational change in rural India by promoting good rural governance through effective citizen participation.

At the second annual good governance conference organized by Sehgal Foundation and Jindal Global Law School, in November 2012, the keynote address was delivered by Professor N. R. Madhava Menon, who praised the *Good Governance Now!* program and the concept of law in governance as an idea whose time had come. He made a powerful statement about the potential for the model, and for the involvement of law students in helping to fulfill the intentions outlined in the Indian constitution with regard to a citizen's right to a dignified life.

Referring to the journal article, Dr. Menon asserted, "Professor Ajay Pandey deserves our appreciation for not only offering up an idea on law-in-governance, but also for developing a model to operationalize

45. Ajay Pandey, "Experimenting with Clinical Legal Education to Address the Disconnect Between the Larger Promise of Law and its Grassroots Reality in India," *Maryland Journal of International Law,* Vol. 26:135. November 17, 2011. In the article, Sehgal Foundation is referred to as IRRAD.

it under clinical legal education, connecting the law school with the community. For quite some time we have been asking ourselves, and we were being asked by others, what are the objectives of legal education? The simple answer has been to train lawyers and judges. A further question was raised: For what are they being trained? The simple answer to that was to help resolve disputes and maintain order in society. That was perhaps a sufficient answer for a colonial regime, but not for a constitutional democracy committed to socioeconomic transformation based on rule of law and human rights. It is, therefore, imperative for law schools in India today to acknowledge the larger purpose of legal education, which is to serve the goals of law-in-governance or law-in-development. Law schools have to organize teaching and research not only to enable its graduates to do conventional lawyering, but also to engage themselves in programs empowering citizens to live a life of dignity by participating responsibly in democratic self-governance, now part of the constitutional scheme. This is what rule of law and democracy are about, and what the Indian constitution expects from the legal community."

In spreading the Sehgal Foundation programs beyond Mewat district, one strategy was to piggyback good rural governance programming onto every water management and agricultural development project undertaken with donor funds. The move into the neighboring district of Alwar, Rajasthan, fit well with the foundation's organic growth strategy. The first contacts were made by Pawan Kumar, the program leader for Agricultural Development, who traveled to Alwar with Pooniaji in 2011 to evaluate potential NGO partnerships. Pawan handled the due diligence, making sure any partner NGO in consideration was in compliance with federal regulations and checking NGO longevity and track records with self-help groups.

From a shortlist of four or five contenders, Pawan and Pooniaji identified an attractive opportunity to partner with an Alwar-based NGO, Ibtada, which focused on empowering women primarily through their work with women's self-help groups that were already organized. In Alwar's Hindu villages, empowering women had evolved more naturally and quickly without the conservative religious influence the foundation team found in Mewat. Pawan described empowering women as his "most rewarding" work and the work with the most potential for making a difference.

With financial support from Ibtada and a leading Egyptian seed company, Misr Hytech Seed,[46] the foundation began a project in 2012 called *Krishi Chetna* (agriculture awareness). Work began with women farmers in eighteen villages to build their capacity to actively participate in agriculture-related decision making by providing them with scientific knowledge. The project conducted demonstrations on wheat, mustard, and millet, and gave milk-animal farmers information about balanced animal nutrition.

Lakshmi Jatwa, an illiterate smallholder farmer from a self-help group, was one of eight women selected to receive training as part of the Krishi Chetna initiative to become a *krishi sakhi* (farmer's friend). Then, as a co-leader of Krishi Chetna, Lakshmi worked to expand the reach of self-help groups, teaching basic reading and writing, facilitating soil tests and field demonstrations, and encouraging women farmers. She spread awareness to other farmers about the benefits of crop diversity and the critical importance of soil health. Lakshmi, once a woman whose husband did not allow her to leave the house, earned respect for her knowledge, inspired her daughters to further pursue their own educations, and made her husband proud of her skills. Motivated to inspire other women, Lakshmi said, "A woman can bring about changes in India if she is able to stand on her feet."[47]

For sustainability, Ibtada organized a block-level women farmers' association and provided funds that could be used by women in the project villages to purchase agricultural services and inputs (equipment, feed, seed, energy, and so on). A similar project was sponsored by K+S Fertilizer Ltd. *Unnat Krishi* (agriculture improvement) involved a group of women farmers growing mustard and millet in ten villages in Alwar district. A crops sustainability fund was created for the farmers to purchase inputs and services after the educational aspect of the project ended.

The foundation's krishi partnerships were created to serve as a tool to demonstrate how to increase agricultural productivity in a sustainable

46. Suri Sehgal founded Misr Hytech Seed International, in Cairo, Egypt.

47. Lakshmi Jatwa was featured in the book *Poetry of Purpose: A Portrait of Women Leaders of India*. See http://www.poetryofpurpose.org/.

way—but the overarching goal, to empower farmers, included arousing the entrenched bureaucracy. The *Krishi Vigyan Kendras* (KVKs), agricultural extension centers financed by the Indian Council of Agricultural Research, had been mandated since 2004 to provide information and training services to farmers in every district in the country. Their work was not reaching any rural villages in Mewat and only reaching a few villages in Alwar district.

Intending to remain catalysts in this process, the foundation's Agricultural Development team wanted to make sure that KVKs provided accurate and sustainable information. "But," Suri affirmed, "each program in water or agriculture needs to establish a committee somewhat similar to the school or health committees at the village level and empower the members with sufficient knowledge so that they can awaken the government bureaucracy. If the bureaucracy delivered the services it is mandated to deliver, the village development process would be greatly accelerated."

The potential for taking the foundation's Agricultural Development program into Bihar was first discussed after a "Good Rural Governance and Citizen Participation" conference was presented there in 2012. Bihar, one of the least-developed states of India, was located more than a thousand kilometers from Mewat. The foundation team agreed that establishing a pilot project in Bihar was a good idea. An intern was tasked to prepare a shortlist of districts where the foundation might be able to replicate successful agricultural development models if donor funds could be found.

The criteria for choosing a district in Bihar included an identified need for Sehgal Foundation expertise in agriculture and governance, and making sure there was no excess of NGOs already working there. The ideal choice of region for agriculture projects would have available freshwater but not be flood-prone. The district chosen had to be connected to public transportation, reasonably safe, and not a Naxalite area.[48] Misr Hytech was a possible donor partner, as was a Sehgal-owned seed company, Hytech India, in Hyderabad. Pawan Kumar and

48. A Naxalite area was any extremely impoverished area where violence and social unrest was common, and armed, antigovernment militants, called Naxalites, wielded influence. Most were Maoists associated with India's Communist Party.

Bihar native Vikas Jha visited the region to determine the best place in Bihar to begin work.

Though good village governance programs reached all 431 villages in Mewat in 2012, by December of that year the team faced intractable difficulties in twenty-eight of those villages. In some communities, influential moulvis objected to promoting education for girls and training women. These religious leaders refused to give their consent for any outside organization to work in their villages, saying it would "spoil" their society. A few other villages were entirely unresponsive to any offers to meet or be provided with information or training, despite every effort made by the team. The villagers were willing to let the foundation file complaints for them to improve government programs in their communities, but they refused to participate in the process. The foundation team would not begin work in any village unless the community was willing to take part and assume ownership of their own development.

The most serious issue in some of the twenty-eight villages concerned actual threats made by elected representatives in gram panchayats. Some representatives said openly that they wanted no changes in the delivery of government programs, such as Mahatma Gandhi National Rural Employment Guarantee Act and Public Distribution System. They had spent money to win elections and wanted to recover their investments from the programs by a sufficient margin. These panchayat members made threats, saying team members "will have broken legs" if they attempted to work in their villages. On occasion, members of the field staff had been pushed around and threatened.

Caution in this area was essential to ensure the physical safety of the field staff, thirteen of whom were women who might occasionally travel alone in the villages.[49] Considering the power of these panchayat members and the lack of law and order in the villages, including rampant corruption and insufficient enforcement of laws or even of police investigation, the governance team decided in 2013 not to work in those villages. Thus only 403 of the 431 villages in Mewat were part of the good governance program.

Despite the difficulties faced in those twenty-eight Mewat villages,

49. Female staff usually traveled with male colleagues.

the *Good Governance Now!* initiative and the capacity-building activities being used to strengthen village-level institutions were a powerful combination that made up the Sehgal Foundation's full-scale approach to good rural governance. In 2013 the Rockefeller Foundation named Sehgal Foundation among the 100 Next Century Innovators with its project "Strengthening the Demand and Supply for Better Village Governance."

The Capacity Building team was about two years into its more formal training program with panchayats in 2012 when a proactive approach suggested in a Panchayat Advisory Group meeting resulted in the introduction of microplanning in five villages. Microplanning, a form of community action planning, was a participatory and interactive process. The overall objective was to initiate community-led development in an environment of unity and good governance by promoting decentralized planning at the grassroots level. The idea was for the selected communities to prepare development plans themselves based on the particular needs of their villages.

To achieve success, all sections of the community had to be fully involved participants, including women, people with disabilities, and the poorest and most disenfranchised citizens. The sarpanches in several villages—Untaka in Nuh block, Mamlika in Punhana, Shakarpuri and Mundaka together under the Firozpur Jhirka panchayat, Sarai in Taoru—were ready to support this experiment in participatory planning. The village of Khedli Khurd in Nagina block was included later. Their full involvement was needed in strengthening panchayati raj institutions and promoting the transparency and accountability of gram panchayats and the Block Development Office. Involvement of the block development officer was important since this person served as the organizer and coordinator of the various government programs for his or her block.

The microplanning process took between four and six days in each village. Making sure they were being sensitive to local customs and traditions, the field team walked through each village looking for people who would be willing to take part. The team was conscientious about including even the most isolated citizens. They explained the objectives and were careful not to make promises.

Anjali Makhija explained, "We had four teams. We gathered history from village elders, constructed a resource map for each village (i.e., water, roads, etc.) and a social map (households, facilities, etc.). Facilitators made sure that all concerned had a chance to share their views. To help identify issues, we wanted to be sure to hear what women needed. We organized a gram sabha for women, called *mahila gram sabha*, where women were free to speak without fear or the influence of men."

Once needs and problems were identified, the village groups identified their highest priorities for required interventions and created an action plan for each. In addition to individual villagers, other stakeholders were invited to participate—members of the Communications team, panchayat members, representatives of the bank, and any local institutions with specific interests, such as in agriculture or water. The next step was to verify the findings so that links could be made with the appropriate government departments, and expenditures could be calculated related to each identified issue. A final document was submitted to the district office through each village's panchayat. A follow-up plan with each department was carried out by the panchayats.

The issues in all five villages included some combination of the same problems: the unavailability of safe drinking water in homes and schools, lack of proper sewage disposal, unhygienic conditions, damaged electricity wires, and poor road conditions. (Eighty percent of the roads were *kutcha* [dirt] roads.)

In Sarai, a village of 222 homes, a woman named Vimla Devi had been the sarpanch for four years. When the Capacity Building team began working with Vimla in 2011, she did not speak out on her own behalf. The men in her family spoke for and represented her in her panchayat work. With support, her enthusiasm and desire to make a positive difference in her village inspired her to overcome her illiteracy and lack of self-confidence and to speak for herself. She said, "I used to be a little apprehensive talking to government officials, as I do not know how to read or write. But slowly, as I started meeting them more regularly, my confidence grew. Now I never send my husband or son to execute my panchayat-related work. I always talk to the concerned authorities on my own."

Vimla served as an inspiration to other women council members in surrounding villages. She proved that women could be equally effective in leadership roles in governance.

When Sehgal Foundation first began work in Sarai, the village was a typical underdeveloped community—dirty, with very few toilets, open defecation, and poor roads. Vimla walked door to door with the Capacity Building team to help educate villagers about the ill effects of open defecation. By using funds from the *Nirmal Bharat Abhiyan* (Clean India Mission) government program, the village was able to install toilets in 175 houses.

In January 2013, when the panchayat undertook the microplanning exercise in Sarai, the entire village participated in developing the microplans. The panchayat then submitted applications to the district administration and received government funds to construct paved roads in the village, install solar tube lights in the streets, and put water tanks and individual toilets in more homes.

Vimla's efforts integrated School Management committees and Village Health, Sanitation, and Nutrition committees with the village council, so that all village-level institutions worked together for holistic development in Sarai. As sarpanch, she actively participated in all monthly committee meetings. She conducted surprise visits at the school on a regular basis to ensure that teachers were present, that children were being taught properly, and that hygienically cooked Mid Day Meals were received on time.

Vimla continued to attend the panchayat training programs conducted by Sehgal Foundation, acting as a motivator for other women who still functioned as proxy council members, encouraging them to take the reins of village development in their own hands. She told them, "When you don't have the confidence, you have to slowly build it. Only when you seek information will you get educated and empowered to realize the power of your own potential."[50]

As a result of the microplanning process in the five villages during 2012 and 2013, village leaders, committees, and individual citizens made positive changes in their communities. Their actions and decisions

50. Vimla was featured in *Poetry of Purpose: A Portrait of Women Leaders of India*. See http://www.poetryofpurpose.org/.

resulted in the receipt of government funds to construct roads in almost every village. Money was also provided for installing toilets, rainwater-harvesting systems, and water tanks. Soak pits were built. Boundary walls were constructed around schools, burial grounds, and ponds. Old electricity wires were replaced in half the villages. Though the issue with safe drinking water was not fully resolved, the citizens of all five villages increased their involvement in gram sabhas to continue the improvements in their communities.

The foundation team recognized and utilized radio as a powerful communication tool. The team posted its radio programs on community radio platforms so that other stations could play them as well. Some of Alfaz-e-Mewat's programs were organized as call-in campaigns. One such campaign, *Asha ki Kiran* (Ray of Hope), held in early 2013, asked listeners to nominate local women to be recognized for their efforts and achievements in their villages. As a result of the campaign, 150 people gathered at the Sehgal Foundation community center to celebrate International Women's Day, and sixty-five women achievers in Mewat, identified by their peers, were honored as a way to motivate others in their community. Following the success of *Asha ki Kiran*, a new call-in campaign on "closing the gender gap" began. Local leaders, officials, artists, and distinguished listeners served on the advisory committee for the community radio station.

CEO Jane Schukoske encouraged the Communications team to expand the outreach to more communities, students, and NGOs. The station began serving as a training ground for interns and volunteers from urban and rural areas, many of whom have gone on to introduce the mission of Alfaz-e-Mewat in national and international forums.

In light of the microplanning successes in the five villages, the team turned new attention to Sehgal Foundation's first "model" or demonstration village: Notki. A foundation task force consisting of both core and field team members reviewed the status of Notki in April 2013 and prepared a report noting what was and wasn't functional in the village. Five of the seven soak wells were functional, but soak pits had become defunct, the road was in bad shape, only two solar tube lights still worked, and the school infrastructure was in disrepair. The resulting action plan involved establishing a committee to work with the panchayat and the governance group in the village to maintain and improve what was already built.

To empower Notki villagers to actively participate and accept the responsibility for their community, the foundation teams and field-level committees worked with individuals and village-level institutions to teach them how to access government funds and services that could solve some of the village's issues that were being addressed. Field team members on the committee held regular meetings in the community and worked with the panchayat to have more toilets built under Nirmal Bharat Abhiyan. With the government's help, every home in Notki finally had a toilet. The sarpanch took the initiative and built a soak well. Villagers were finally beginning to seek help that was available from the government.

Notki was not fully refurbished until 2014. Five other model villages had surpassed Notki by that time. Though a collective decision was finally made for maintenance of the Notki orchard to be fully assumed by the panchayat, the village-level institutions were still not fully active. Recognizing the difficulties of trying to change the dynamic further with the current panchayat leadership, the governance team decided to wait for the 2015 panchayat election. With each panchayat election, held every five years, the hope was always that newly elected members would bring new perspective and a development-oriented sarpanch.

What had happened over the years in Notki was clear proof that the team had to build and strengthen the capacities of community leaders and village-level institutions from the start in every single project in every single community where Sehgal Foundation worked. Communities had to be inspired, motivated, and prepared to manage for themselves and sustain the results of any improvements made. Because the Notki community had been so dependent on Sehgal Foundation for so long, more time was needed before Notki villagers would reach that level of sustainability. The governance training and support provided to village-level institutions by the Capacity Building team had been essential in the development of the model villages.

Individual citizens and village-level institutions, with *sushasan* champions[51] as active partners, had worked well with the government.

Renaming the capacity-building initiative to Strengthening Village-Level Institutions (SVLI) was one of several important changes made in the overall organization of Sehgal Foundation throughout 2014 to focus even more on social change. Sehgal Foundation simplified its organizational structure to focus on the most effective program models: Water Management, Agricultural Development, and Good Rural Governance, which was now inclusive of *Good Governance Now!* and SVLI shifting away from "centers" for activities and toward specific project orientation and creating adaptive technologies would more easily facilitate the integration of all program activities and result in greater impact on communities.

Sehgal Foundation had evolved from its adolescence and was now incorporating more sophisticated and effective organizational components. Anjali Godyal was made group leader for Externally Funded Projects with overall responsibility for concept papers, project proposals, project implementation, progress reporting to donors, and final reports. All proposals in the pipeline would now be her responsibility.

The Rural Research team developed questionnaires, baselines, and analysis tools, which included maps and convergence diagrams that illustrated the foundation's work program by program in each geographic area. These maps and diagrams showed the numbers of Mewat villages where interventions overlapped. A needs-assessment survey was aimed at determining existing problems in the villages where the teams envisioned future work. This helped them understand the acuteness of problems so they could design village interventions according to the requirements and priorities of the communities.

The name IRRAD was finally dropped formally in favor of "Sehgal Foundation."[52] The Communications team strategy included a refinement of the vision, mission, core values, and branding guidelines. The website was revamped and social media activity increased.[53]

51. Good governance trainees were now called *sushasan* champions.
52. The attempt to change the name had never worked, and the term "institute" suggested that the foundation was primarily a formal educational organization offering coursework, which was not accurate.
53. Mick Minard of REEF Reports assisted the team in refining the foundation's vision and mission statements and branding guidelines.

The radio station team had catalogued more than 600 hours of innovative programming for listeners in at least 183 villages. Due to the integration of mobile phone technology, the program reach of Alfaz-e-Mewat was able to extend beyond the broadcast range of the transmitter. By using toll-free phone numbers and an integrated voice-recording system, programming was accessible by cellphone. Of the more than 18,000 callers to the radio station, 20 percent were women—a significant number considering that although more than 94 percent of the families in Mewat had cellphones, most were owned and used by the male members of the family.[54]

Coordination across field and core teams and subject specialist teams on governance, water, and agriculture was enhanced by trainings, including field team cross-training and quarterly meetings with field and core staff. Additional meeting minutes and training materials were prepared or translated into Hindi to further team focus and learning. Several experienced field team members were deployed to leadership positions in Alwar and Samastipur, where the team conducted leadership training of twenty-five senior field staff members. All staff participated in annual gender sensitization trainings.

The role of governance guides now had an action component. Trained to work in five programs related to key laws regarding consumer rights and services, they were now responsible for monitoring and evaluating the functioning of each program in 150 villages. Each governance guide was responsible for twelve to fifteen villages in Mewat. Leaders in twenty-five villages were mobilized in 2014. Monthly meetings with *sushasan* champions maintained the momentum, helped them stay in touch, and kept everyone abreast of new government program updates and information. This continued with each new batch of leaders.

Since each program model was directly related to empowering women, a formal mandate was implemented so that every type of training facilitated by the foundation included at least 50 percent

---

54. A research monitoring report from 2013 showed that within a year of the radio station launch, more than 50 percent of households in Mewat had radio capabilities on their mobile phones and 17 percent of households owned radios. This number was an increase of almost 4 percent. Qualitative discussions in villages revealed that Alfaz-e-Mewat was a factor in the increased popularity of radios.

women participants. This had been successful with *Good Governance Now!* and would now be part of every initiative. Women comprised 54 percent of the participants in good governance training for twenty-eight gram sabhas. SVLI teams now worked with 440 women in five *mahila sangathans* (women's collectives). These women were active leaders who represented panchayats, School Management committees, and Village Health, Sanitation, and Nutrition committees. They had been provided knowledge, training, and skills for undertaking development activities in their own villages by the SVLI team, with help from other active women leaders.

The sarpanch of Sarai, Vimla Devi, attended the trainings to encourage and motivate more women to participate in the governance process. Vimla stood and shared her own empowerment story and told the women, "Nothing will happen unless we step outside our houses; for any change we need to come out and work together." Women listened and stepped forward.

Anjali Makhija observed, "When women come together as a collective force, they get tremendous strength and inspiration from each other. I have seen how they felt resigned even when they were members of village-level institutions. The sangathan has given them 'power' and a sense of belonging."

With the participation of the mahila sangathans, the five model villages (Mundaka, Jatka, Untaka, Sarai, and Khedli Khurd) had become open-defecation-free. The team was heartened to see that Good Rural Governance was effective in all five villages. More villages undertook microplanning and implemented projects according to their own identified priorities. Sehgal Foundation used donor funds to implement some projects in these villages if financial resources were not available from village-level institutions, including school renovations, roof water-harvesting structures, water tanks, and providing agriculture inputs.

The team facilitated interface workshops with state government officials so that village leaders had access to them directly. Synergy with government decision-makers was an important part of a strategy for building relationships, since those are the people with the funds. When the foundation team provided support to get projects implemented, the result was a win-win for all concerned: the government, the community, and Sehgal Foundation.

In the case of Village Health, Sanitation, and Nutrition committees, most of the members were women who did not even know they were members. That meant unutilized funds. SVLI support to revamp the committees and make members aware of their authority helped make them more active. The women accessed and spent the allocated funds, mobilizing their communities to build toilets, undertake sanitation activities, and promote immunizations. More women like Vimla became active panchayat members, rather than having their husbands or sons act as their proxies. Mahila sangathans activated projects in thirty villages.

Working with communities to revitalize the defunct government-mandated School Management committees, the foundation filled some gaps in services in order to get more kids to attend school. Schools that received some simple but important interventions—separate latrines for boys and girls, access to drinking water, and a platform for sanitary food preparation for the school lunch program—saw student attendance go up, particularly for girls.

Teachers were initially reluctant to work with the School Management committees. They had typically selected the committee members and wanted to maintain control of the funds. The foundation team contacted the principal secretary of Education and organized interface workshops with her, which produced good results. District education officials gave written approval for Sehgal Foundation to provide training to School Management committees. Building their capacities and organizing general meetings for all members made candidate selection and utilization of funds more transparent.

The Strengthening Village-Level Institutions initiative expanded to 100 villages in Mewat in 2014. The foundation team created an informal forum of NGOs, corporate foundations, and government bodies, called the Haryana Education Forum. Anjali Makhija coordinated three meetings that year; future meetings would take place annually. The Panchayat Advisory Group continued to meet annually, providing ongoing guidance and support. The SVLI team was invited again by the Haryana Institute of Rural Development to train panchayats. Being invited as experts by HIRD and the Ministry of Panchayati Raj for numerous meetings to prepare curriculum and training material for panchayats underscored Sehgal Foundation's credibility. Similar training for other NGOs on specific village-level institutions brought additional endorsements. The District Rural Development Agency in Bilaspur, a city and district in the neighboring state of Himachal Pradesh, requested and received Sehgal Foundation training for panchayat members.

The governance team noticed that a critical mass of about twenty-five *sushasan* champions was needed to bring about real change in governance in any village. So the *Good Governance Now!* training was offered to twenty-five trainees at a time in a single village. Work was done simultaneously with sarpanches, panchayats, and community members.

Ten legal literacy camps were organized at the village level in 2014. Prior to that, camps were organized on the block level, covering from fifty to eighty villages at one time. The team determined that village-level camps that covered only four or five villages were easier to manage logistically, and governance guides could provide more personal attention to attendees and more appropriate follow-up. By that time, attorney Navneet Narwal had been successful in establishing linkages with District Legal Services Authority (DLSA). Eight of the ten camps held that year were organized in collaboration with DLSA at their Legal Care and Support centers. Paralegal volunteers from DLSA were present in the camps and their Secretary and Chief Judicial Magistrate attended each camp.

Good Governance Now! was now embraced by 403 villages in Mewat District, Haryana; fourteen villages in Alwar, Rajasthan; and eleven villages in Samastipur, Bihar. No other Sehgal Foundation initiative had reached more than fifty villages. Through good rural governance, effective citizen participation demonstrated the tremendous power citizens could have. The Sehgal Foundation team reaffirmed its vow to make "Good Rural Governance" an all-India movement.

Navneet observed, "Awareness and hand-holding support gives villagers confidence and the power to solve their own problems by knowing their rights and using them properly without fear of the authorities. The way in which people have changed is absolutely magnificent and gives confidence that the system will buckle and will become better under the pressure of people who are striving toward improving it."

The Corporate Social Responsibility (CSR) provision of the Companies Act 2013 went into effect in April 2014, mandating that profit-making companies in India that had a prescribed net worth, turnover, or net profit must spend at least 2 percent of their average net profits during the past three financial years on CSR initiatives.[55] By endorsing sustainable development, the new law promised to make a powerful impact on the lives of India's poor. The foundation team was ready to utilize each new opportunity for multiplying the impact of Sehgal Foundation programs. Getting the word out about basic challenges facing the poor in rural India to businesses, corporations, government, and other NGOs and foundations included an open invitation to work together in partnerships with communities to bring about positive social, economic, and environmental change.

Jay Sehgal mobilized the Des Moines, Iowa, chapter of Sehgal Foundation to support a campaign to promote and create rainwater-harvesting systems in schools in India. The Resource Mobilization and Partnerships team[56] engaged with more than thirty corporations to attract additional support for Sehgal Foundation initiatives. The team began crowd-funding campaigns on the website.

Though the team submitted several proposals, few materialized into actual CSR projects. The general consensus was that less money was being spent on this initiative than originally estimated. Speculation was that companies were cautious about taking on new partners for certain CSR projects due to the overall goal of transparency. When a proposal to train a corporate CSR team on good governance was shelved, Jane Schukoske said, "An employer was concerned about the potential risk involved in teaching their workers about governance. Educated employees would be more apt to speak out about their rights and might focus their newly developed skills on their employers. There is a perception that it is safer for companies to pay for educational improvements in schools, for example, rather than teach governance. But in fact, good governance helps the citizenry properly identify and communicate with the government offices that have mandates and funding to deliver

55. See http://www.mondaq.com/india/x/305620/Corporate+Commercial+Law/Corporate+Social+Responsibility+Mandating+Companies+To+Contribute+Towards+Society.
56. Aparna Mahajan with assistance from Sam Kapoor.

basic public services. That benefits both industry and residents in a community."

The team did not slow down in their efforts to attract CSR funds, though the process was lengthy. More proposals continued to be developed on a case-by-case basis in order to engage partners with shared values. Jane explained, "The CSR law has opened the doors for a significant infusion of new funds for development work in rural India. Our focus remains on creating and fine-tuning innovative models of rural development and testing them in different geographical, geological, and sociocultural settings. The government has the capacity to implement these models across rural India. Partnerships between government, communities, corporations, NGOs, and other voluntary groups are important to achieve the shared goals. A win-win situation is possible for each."

Indian Prime Minister Narendra Modi took office in May 2014. Over the course of his first year in office, he cited goals that appeared to be in line with Sehgal Foundation development efforts. One after the other, the programs launched by the prime minister seemed to be the same key programs the foundation was working on. In October 2014 Modi created *Saansad Adarsh Gram Yojna*, an ambitious plan to develop 800 model villages. Under this plan, each member of Parliament was to choose a village in his or her jurisdiction to enhance development in the areas of health, education, housing, repair of infrastructure, and strengthening their village-level institutions while promoting transparency and accountability. Though India's leaders had talked about similar ideas in the past, the Sehgal Foundation team accepted this news with hope and offered to share their own significant learnings about developing model villages. The team published articles acknowledging this truly ambitious effort and asserting that it would be successful only if the people in the chosen villages were empowered, engaged in the process, and able to plan collectively—and if the plan was inclusive of *all* members of the community, such as youth, the disenfranchised, and especially women. They repeated as often as possible, "Just as women played a dynamic role in all aspects of the development of villages in Mewat, their leadership will be essential to Mr. Modi's plan. Individual citizens and members of village-level institutions must be empowered, trained, and engaged meaningfully in the process for any development activities to be sustained."

Sustainability in general would depend on continuous community buy-in and ongoing evaluations of progress. As Suri affirmed, "A village is only a model village if the panchayat is active and the community is empowered and demanding." He added, "The trainers need to be people with compassion. Leaving the training of trainers to officials will not work. Too many bureaucrats in India are *babus*[57] without the necessary compassion.

Prime Minister Modi offered further support for good governance by declaring Christmas Day 2014 as Good Governance Day. He used the occasion to launch new information and communication technology (ICT) to help bring information about government services to the people. He vowed to provide "transparent, effective, and accountable governance."[58] He was quoted on his Internet portal, saying, "Success of democracy is impossible without participation of the people."[59] The foundation teams were heartened, of course, to imagine a growing national movement against government corruption in India and a call for transparency in fiscal affairs.

In July 2015 the prime minister introduced a five-year, multi-billion-dollar water management initiative called *Pradhan Mantri Krishi Sinchai Yojana* to help ensure adequate water for crop cultivation for all farmland and to promote water conservation, precision-irrigation technologies, and aquifer recharge. Model villages, good governance, water management to help farmers—Suri observed, "The prime minister is advocating what is absolutely needed in the country and what we are already doing!" but also added, "I hope it is not all talk and something really happens in the field."

Again, along with the hope was the knowledge that such huge initiatives would not succeed without the engagement of citizens, especially women, at the community level.

Lalit Mohan Sharma described the complexity of the issues the foundation teams faced in each of its programs: "Development involves

---

57. *Babu* or *baboo* is a native Indian civil servant.
58. See http://timesofindia.indiatimes.com/india/Modis-good-governance-drive-keeps-some-babus-busy-on-Christmas/articleshow/45644440.cms.
59. See http://india.gov.in/spotlight/mygov-citizen-participation-towards-good-governance.

a multitude of factors. Efforts in one direction are often countered by forces from another. For instance, it is not sufficient to conserve water without addressing equitable distribution of that water. Water collection, augmentation, and conservation go hand in hand with water security issues. We must move from scarcity to security. There is no life without water."

To that end, the Water Management team now engaged with and provided training to Water User Groups (WUGs). These groups consisted of direct and indirect beneficiaries at the village level of any given water-augmentation project. WUG members assumed responsibility for the management, operation, and maintenance of water management structures and intervention projects carried out in their communities. WUGs generally included ten to fifteen members from the panchayat, School Management Committee, anganwadi center, and other active community groups. Members could include Mid Day Meal cooks and workers, auxiliary nurse midwives, teachers, retired government employees, and youth active in social work. Community contributions raised for the operation and maintenance of a project were deposited in a bank account, which was overseen by two WUG-nominated group members. The foundation team conducted frequent water literacy sessions and training programs to build the groups' capacity around each project intervention to help maintain active engagement. Individual empowerment, community ownership, and the availability of funds (without dependence on funding from any agency, the foundation, or the panchayat) offered the best chance for the interventions to be sustainable in the long term. Trained WUG members would be able to leverage funds from various government programs and schemes for water projects and other developmental work in their villages.

Though Sehgal Foundation's vital programs and activities to promote Good Rural Governance took the lead in 2014, the initiatives in Water Management and Agricultural Development remained strong. Each of the foundation's three main programs would always move along at a different pace and depend on the continued engagement of partners of every kind in this process. By necessity, every Sehgal Foundation plan would be well thought out with respect to its short-term and potential long-term outcomes. Successful outcomes were tied to awareness, education, and the integration of all the related aspects of a community's needs.

Jay Sehgal explained, "The results of true progress are rarely immediate because development is such a slow process. Impact can only be measured over time. This dynamic is important to keep in mind when establishing partnerships for funding that is required for particular initiatives."

Jay put the concept in simple terms: "There are two types of impact: immediate, such as changing the paint color in a room, and long-term, which is something very different. We evaluate our impact based on our mission and also on the mission of our partners. We are careful to read and understand our partners' mission statements, so that any work done by Sehgal Foundation will also help our partners meet their own stated goals. A company with a sincere interest in water augmentation, such as Coca-Cola, wants to see an immediate impact—for example, to create recharge wells that make more drinkable water available. Using donor funds, we can create the desired facilities and infrastructure, but our perspective must also be in line with our mission in order to achieve true prosperity for the communities of rural India. We must maintain a balance: the donor's immediate impact will occur, but so will our focus on that long-term goal. We will keep instilling our vision in crisscross themes in the implementation of every project. Our ultimate goal is positive change, to see the people in rural India leading secure, prosperous, and dignified lives. This kind of change, which includes the empowerment of women, will not happen tomorrow; it could take a generation to see our mission realized. We can't ask our large multinational corporation partners to wait thirty-five years to see the results of their investment. So we will continue to take an integrated, comprehensive approach to the work. Our ultimate goal remains intact; we never forget what we are about."

In September 2014 it was announced that Sehgal Foundation had received the Millennium Alliance award from FICCI, USAID, and the Technology Development Board, Department of Science and Technology, Government of India, for the innovation of a pressurized recharge well for storing freshwater in a saline aquifer. This same project and Good Rural Governance had been shortlisted for Millennium

Alliance awards the previous year. The award included funds that would make it possible to take the Water Management team's innovation to more communities in need. The process of bringing this technology from the concept stage to the point of recognition involved many levels of development and many talented people doing lots of brainstorming and hard work refining the concept, building multiple prototypes, testing, troubleshooting, and problem solving. Foundation consultants, engineers, water experts, proposal writers, and field staff played a part in the outcome. Several team members attended the award ceremony, celebrating the achievement and the opportunity to help more villages.

Earlier in the year Suri Sehgal had been recognized by the Indian Confederation of NGOs with a Global Indian Karmaveer Puraskaar Lifetime Achievement Award, a Global Award for Social Justice and Citizen Action. Suri took a moment during his acceptance speech to first acknowledge and thank Edda for her ongoing support in this work before calling on other genuinely active NGOs in India to join Sehgal Foundation in endorsing transparency, accountability, credibility, and good governance practices in their work. He asserted, "If all NGOs in India stopped squandering resources and betraying the people they were tasked to serve, they could bring a profound change to India."

Sehgal Foundation remained a vanguard institution, a hallmark of integrity, with strict policies against bribes and dishonesty, and always working to stay credible, scrupulously transparent, and accountable in daily operations. Suri Sehgal, typically straightforward about the outside realities, said, "Key barriers remain. Corruption is still an intrusion in all government systems. Government programs to alleviate policy are often like a sieve. Lots of funds pour in, and only a small part reaches the intended beneficiaries. Corruption makes people afraid. There are good laws on the books, but there is a lack of law enforcement. Good Rural Governance plays an important role in creating a fleet of local people who constantly monitor local service delivery to keep it on track and help correct the deficiencies and conquer the barriers."

CHAPTER 12

Looking Back and Looking Ahead

Looking back over the growth and development of Sehgal Foundation, starting with its inception in 1999, Suri Sehgal was occasionally tempted to wonder why each step toward progress in development in rural villages seemed to take so long. Each time this thought nagged at him over the years, he prompted the team to once again assess their current efforts against the foundation's mission and consider the impact being made. With this in mind, the team decided in 2014 to compile and acknowledge a collection of successful accomplishments and lessons learned and spend some time celebrating those achievements more formally. A fifteenth-anniversary celebration, including special events and festive gatherings, would start in June 2014 and continue through the early months of 2015. The first gathering was held at the Ghaghas Community Center with the entire field team and the Gurgaon staff. Every foundation-sponsored get-together during that period—every radio program, book launch, and conference or workshop on good governance, gender, water, health, education, or agriculture—made special mention of the milestones at fifteen years.

In collecting information about the foundation's achievements through 2014, the Rural Research team compiled their regular monitoring reports and gathered additional materials and stories from everyone throughout the organization in order to evaluate the accomplishments as thoroughly as possible. The team paid particular attention to any overarching lessons learned that brought Sehgal Foundation to its present point, recognizing that the most important learnings would help evaluate current strategies and pave the way for the organization's future direction. While this information was being assembled and analyzed, current initiatives continued to move forward at their own paces in the Water Management, Agricultural Development, and Good Rural Governance programs.

In reviewing the work done through 2014, certain realities were evident. For every good idea that proved to make an impact, the team had experimented with lots and lots of other ideas. In each case traditional knowledge was combined with modern technologies, tested in multiple locations, and further improved before it was promoted for wider applications. Learning by doing taught the team powerful lessons about which programs or interventions created maximum impact at minimal cost and in the shortest time frame. Big projects were beautiful and brought significant impact but they were also capital-intensive, whereas the right small interventions proved cost-effective, had big impact, and offered a higher possibility of adoption in the communities. Both were still necessary. Because government was the biggest delivery system in the country for essential services (health, education, sanitation, and so on), the foundation remained in the role of catalyst in empowering citizens to demand that mandated services be delivered. Certainly the most obvious overarching lesson, proved again and again, was that no initiative would be sustainable unless it was community-led.

By the end of 2014, Sehgal Foundation was actively involved in implementing numerous complex and integrated projects. Multiple proposals were in process, and concept notes and expressions of interest had been submitted to various entities to invite collaborations. Systematic steps had been taken to include the tools, strategies, and processes proven to be most effective in making an impact. For example, in preparation for further expansion, the team had scouted and studied several new districts within geographic reach of current programs, primarily in Haryana, Rajasthan, and Bihar, and for potential new partnerships in Madhya Pradesh, Maharashtra, and Uttar Pradesh. Each new region being considered was evaluated according to essential ingredients for success. Enthusiastic participation by the people in the communities was essential not only for the sustainability of whatever was created or built but, more importantly, for empowering villagers to take responsibility for their own development. Other factors considered for expansion included whether reputable NGOs had been or were still working in the area, whether government officials were supportive, if an agricultural profile and understanding of the physical terrain were available, and if expert reviews of draft proposals were positive.

With so much focus year after year on water conservation and promotion of safe drinking water, Sehgal Foundation was becoming known as a center of excellence in rural water management. The foundation's award-winning water-related initiatives had evolved primarily from listening and taking villagers' expressed needs seriously. Water security remained the most basic and critical necessity in villages throughout India. To improve the agricultural productivity of rain-fed areas, or even maintain the current agricultural productivity, more water infrastructure—lakes, check dams, village ponds, and wells—were needed to store water and charge the aquifers.[60] Though integrated water management projects were capital-intensive, the foundation's inventive team had created cost-effective and replicable models for water collection, conservation, storage, recharge, and filtration. Scaling up was necessary to widen the beneficiary base in more villages and more states to trigger an all-India movement to create water security. This would ensure the availability of water for irrigation under drought conditions.

By 2014 most of the foundation's water management projects were externally funded. The plan moving forward was to replicate already-developed models in more partnerships with corporations, government, and other like-minded organizations and individuals—and to create water-literate and conservation-conscious communities by supporting the formation and strengthening of Water Management committees, Water User Groups, and village-development committees. The team envisioned an empowered Water Management Committee in each village to ensure water security throughout the country.

Water Management program interventions incorporated a sophisticated series of valuable modules that reflected the integration of lessons learned over the years about what worked best. These began with needs

---

60. On 4,500 arid acres at ICRISAT in Hyderabad, the critical need for water storage structures prompted the foundation to fund a water storage project there in 2009. The resulting body of water was named Suri Sehgal Lake.

assessments and problem identification, baseline surveys, focus-group discussions, village-level meetings with local citizens, interactions with government officials, and literature reviews. Once suitable sites for implementation were identified, certain prerequisite ground conditions were sought for maximum water-harvesting potential.

For community mobilization and awareness, the team had developed informational materials, conducted water literacy sessions, water marches, rallies, and street plays, as well as painting competitions and essay-writing contests for schoolchildren. Project implementation included local artisans and labor. Proper management and long-term sustainability of any intervention included a committee of active and interested people from all sectors, with heavy emphasis on the involvement of women. In any project, infrastructural components depended on local needs and ground conditions. Activities related to agriculture, livelihood, and village infrastructure development were incorporated as required for each project. Decisions on structures to be built and their projected costs were finalized only after experts visited the areas and discussions were held and agreements reached with local people. Regardless of the project or the nature of the collaboration, the crucial ingredient to accelerating progress in the villages was in the promotion of effective citizen participation in governance.

Interventions were monitored and evaluated periodically for their performance and to assess their impact. Most interventions were successful but, as each project progressed, the team knew to expect some fine-tuning or midcourse corrections, which would always be done only after discussion with the funding partners.

Certain parallels could be seen in the evolution of Sehgal Foundation's integrated agriculture initiatives. The most valuable lessons and impact had come by creating farmers' groups and providing them with education, information, and awareness in the form of demonstrations that illustrated more effective and sustainable methods for improving crop productivity and increasing their incomes. The three "krishi" project partnerships had the potential to lead to the formation of active Agriculture Development committees, which the foundation team wanted to see in each village, inspiring surrounding villages and serving as catalysts for prompting the thousands of poorly functioning Krishi Vigyan Kendras (agricultural extension centers) to actually carry out their government-mandated responsibilities. Finding creative ways to empower farmers to demand those much-needed services from extension centers remained critical for establishing food and nutrition security.

Each of the krishi partnership projects in place as of 2015 involved training modules being carried out over a period of four years. Projects were interrelated and included infrastructure building components and collaborations with other programs and teams. For example, the first two years of work with Krishi Jyoti in partnership with The Mosaic Company focused on cereal crops, a third year focused on vegetable crops, and a fourth was spent on basic governance training and capacity building so the development progress would be sustained while the team phased out of the village. During that same period, a water augmentation project was completed and improvements were made to schools in those villages. Though crop demonstrations, generating awareness, and capacity building were common to the krishi partnerships, other aspects were tailored to each community's needs. Components such as the number of crops, the timespan of each project, beneficiaries, and partners differed from project to project.[61]

An effective ICT (information communication technology) tool was offered to Krishi Jyoti farmers in Mewat in 2014 as part of a larger National Bank for Agricultural Development project to promote rural prosperity. The idea had evolved partially from lessons learned from the 2009 pilot program carried out in partnership with One World South Asia. Voice messages recorded in-house were broadcast to mobile phones, providing farmers with valuable information in their local language about projects and farming practices.

The Good Rural Governance team used an ICT tool starting in September 2014 to widen the reach of governance initiatives. They established a Citizen Information and Support Center (CISC) in the Sehgal Foundation office in Nuh using an integrated voice-response

61. To estimate the number of beneficiaries of Agricultural Development programs through 2014, the Rural Research team extracted the government census count (31,667) of the farming population for the 107 villages where the programs had a presence. Primary beneficiaries received direct training, farm demonstrations, and projects implemented with assistance from foundation teams. Secondary beneficiaries were household members of primary beneficiaries, and tertiary beneficiaries were farmers in the vicinity who benefited from observation of demonstrations.

system (IVRS) and toll-free number. The cloud-based platform made it possible for villagers in Mewat to make a call on any basic mobile phone and ask questions about government programs. Even in the poorest villages, mobile phones were typically available. A facilitator with a smart phone responded to the IVRS calls and held meetings with villagers when they needed more detailed information or assistance. From September 2014 to May 2015, two thousand calls were answered and four hundred villagers visited the center seeking guidance on solving problems related to the Public Distribution System, on claiming pensions under the social security programs, on *Ladli yojna* (the protection of girl children[62]), on *Indira Awaas Yojana* (housing for rural poor), and on Right to Information applications.

Advantages of the new CISC service were noted at a meeting with Umra villagers in the Nuh block in February 2015. Daily-wage workers shared that the center's service hours (9:00 a.m. to 6:00 p.m.) were particularly helpful. Two villagers who learned from their call that the wives and children of people with disabilities were eligible for monthly financial aid each applied for the pension funds and submitted their papers to the block development officer. Villagers from Tusaini in Punhana block of Mewat became aware of provisions in Prime Minister Modi's clean India drive, *Swachh Bharat Abhiyan,* for claiming up to Rs. 12,000 per household for the construction of toilets. An online link to the program facilitated payments directly to beneficiaries' bank accounts, speeding up the process. Direct deposit to individual bank accounts had the added advantage of preventing the siphoning away of money before it reached intended beneficiaries. A government initiative begun in 2014 encouraged all Indian citizens to have bank accounts so that such funds, including pension funds, scholarship money, and so on, could be directly deposited into them. Governance guides helped villagers obtain IDs and open their accounts.

A pilot program that began in September 2014 with a like-minded development organization showed excellent potential for scaling up. With training providing by Sehgal Foundation, the Swades Foundation

62. Delhi Ladli Scheme launched in 2008 was designed to empower girls by linking financial assistance to their education up to the senior secondary level.

was successful in replicating the *Good Governance Now!* initiative in 360 gram panchayats in six blocks of Raigad district, Maharashtra, about 1,450 kilometers south of Mewat. The Good Rural Governance team had provided a three-day training of trainers course with forty program staff from Swades Community Mobilisation and thereafter provided a staff member to stay at Swades for two months to ensure the program's proper functioning. Trainees were encouraged to adapt the components of the *Good Governance Now!* model to fit community needs in Raigad. The group created a one-year action plan to begin work on problems with specific programs. Legal literacy camps focused on those programs.

Community leaders in Raigad learned that vigilance committees were mandated by law to monitor distribution of food grains under the Public Distribution System. The state government constituted vigilance committees at various levels, including village, block, municipal council, municipal corporation, and district. At the village level, vigilance committees led by the sarpanch consisted of thirteen members, including official and non-official members. With their new learning, the Swades team went on to train 674 community leaders who produced impressive results within six months. Vigilance committees were formed in villages where none existed before, and dormant vigilance committees were reactivated. The committees reported to food supply officers at the district level who took vigilance committee reports seriously and took action accordingly. The Raigad community, now better informed about the provision of the law, requested that depot dealers display quota details, rate lists, and a list of Ration Vigilance Committee members by name. They requested receipts for items bought, which deterred false records by shop owners. The governance trainees inspired other community leaders to be active as well.

This single initiative with Swades more than doubled the reach of Sehgal Foundation's *Good Governance Now!* program. The exciting results inspired the foundation team to set a goal for identifying more nonprofit organizations with the potential for replicating good governance initiatives in their own areas across rural India and in more areas where the team was already working. As with every partnership, profiles of organizations' missions and visions were reviewed for commonality of interest, synergy, and the potential for an action plan.

Good Governance Now! outcomes had been tracked quantitatively by the Rural Research team as of 2013. Though it was difficult to determine exact numbers of beneficiaries of *Good Governance Now!* trainings that resulted in the construction of infrastructure, such as roads, drains, and ponds, the team could now demonstrate the number of citizens who benefited from better delivery of services from the Public Distribution System, Mid Day Meal program, Integrated Child Development Services, and other programs.

Another area of impact that would continue moving forward came when governance guides encouraged sushasan champions to seek election to School Management committees. The twelve to twenty members of School Management committees had the power to monitor the schools, check teachers' attendance, check quality of Mid Day Meals, and supervise school budgets. Members were elected for two-year terms by the parents of schoolchildren. As a result of their willingness to join these legally mandated committees, a record 751 sushasan champions were selected to be members of School Management committees in Mewat in 2015. Of these, 107 were selected as chairpersons, and fifty-one were selected as vice chairs. For such a large number of sushasan champions to be motivated to this extent was a significant achievement.

A good example of the sushasan champions' ability to create change was the result of their monitoring of School Management committees' accounts. State governments had been allocating Rs. 400 per student to government schools. School uniforms were supposed to be distributed twice a year to children in classes one through eight. Each boy was supposed to be given a shirt, long pants, a tie, socks, shoes, a belt, and one woolen pullover sweater. Each girl should have received a *salwar kameez* (traditional dress), a *chunni* (headscarf), a tie, socks, shoes, and one woolen pullover sweater. But some schools were not distributing uniforms because committee members were siphoning off the money. Intervention by the newly elected committee members (sushasan champions) facilitated the appropriate distribution of school uniforms to the students.

Community radio continued to be a powerful tool for spreading good governance messages in the Mewat district and in partnerships with other community radio stations in other districts. The Alfaz-e-Mewat team played a leadership role in community radio by sharing their innovative programming packages with leaders in sister stations that didn't have the same type of creative professional staff available. Radio outreach and law talk programs spread to universities, institutes of rural development, and district legal services authorities, and aroused the interest of more foundations, corporations, and NGOs.

A people's movement toward good rural governance in India was the definitive achievement the team was aiming for. Replicating the Good Rural Governance program by nonprofit organizations, university social science departments, law schools, and Indian institutes of higher education, and promoting it through community radio and publications, with support from legal services authorities across India, were valuable strategies for empowering citizens to participate in making their village-level institutions functional and improving the operation of key government programs. The ideal represented by the Good Rural Governance program was to enhance effective citizen participation for the advancement of truth, justice, dignified human existence, rule of law, democracy, and human rights. This ideal could only be realized through involvement of citizens everywhere. General development practitioners and those interested in development work, social justice lawyers, human rights workers, jurists, law school professors and students, legal aid workers, street law practitioners, paralegals, legal literacy and empowerment missionaries, social scientists, and economists were some of the people the team recognized as most likely to realize the importance and uniqueness of the model. Their appreciation and support was essential for the realization of the Good Rural Governance program throughout India.

Law students were ideal candidates for helping to strengthen legal aid clinics, create petitions, and strengthen support services but, unfortunately, they received no academic credit for that type of work. Law faculty members were generally not acknowledged in any way for their good governance efforts either. Though law institutes in India were mandated by bar councils to assist legal aid clinics as part of their curriculum, this was more on paper than in practice. Until the legal aid clinics actually existed, the foundation team was challenged to consider what corrective steps could be made to overcome this constraint by pushing for policy changes at the top so that incentives and rewards were created. The team would actively support any government programs that made legal services available and they would strengthen those that showed promise on paper but were yet to become fully functional.

While moving forward on the law school front, the team was exploring the interests of academic programs in social sciences, which actually had community outreach programs as part of their curriculums. The Strengthening Village-Level Institutions program was a natural fit for social sciences departments. In many universities, students pursuing master's degrees in this area received credit for community outreach. Faculty members would be responsible for handling assignments in adopted villages where the villagers themselves identified the priorities, prepared plans, and undertook development of their communities holistically. An advantage in persuading social science departments to replicate Good Rural Governance initiatives was that the program engaged with communities and achieved results without much capital investment. Universities did not typically have funds for capital investment anyway, but they had human resources in the form of bright students and faculty members with the skills to conduct community-level trainings.

Unnat Bharat Abhiyan, a program to uplift rural India, was a promising opportunity for the foundation to collaborate with technical institutes to promote Good Rural Governance. Launched in November 2014 by the Ministry of Human Resource Development, Government of India, the program asked all central/state government-funded institutes to adopt a cluster of backward gram panchayats for development.

Law schools and university social sciences departments supported promoting Good Rural Governance initiatives in principle, but the potential for actively replicating the models remained to be seen. The team's plan was to continue to organize legal literacy camps, collaborate with law schools and other educational institutions, partner with other NGOs and corporations to share foundation program templates and written training materials, utilize the power of community radio, promote functioning legal cells, and train and inspire individuals and groups. Components of good rural governance would be embedded in every Sehgal Foundation proposal and agreement with corporations on every project, whether in water management, agricultural development, or any other initiative, because the team knew that real change would not take place until Good Rural Governance became an all-India movement.

Sehgal Foundation would continue to promote honest and wholesome fundamentals in the face of rampant corruption within government entitlement programs—a barrier that continued to prevent so many people in desperate circumstances from receiving the help they needed for basic survival. Other challenges to the expansion of good governance came from some leaders in the corporate sector who opted to provide "safer" community services such as health camps and school supplies rather than the potentially threatening idea of empowering communities with information and skills for expressing their demands. Manufacturing plants that employed 200 or 300 laborers expressed fear that if their workers became more educated on legal issues they might strike for higher wages. Some NGOs did not want to change the political dynamics that allowed them to maintain the status quo. Such was the reality of power. The Sehgal Foundation team was determined to keep their attention focused on finding solutions to any constraints.

Looking back, the Sehgal Foundation team had never turned away from a challenge. Their work began in a part of rural India that many NGOs had written off—even government reports had once called Mewat "development resistant." But the team had proven that Mewat was not development resistant. Real change had occurred and was continuing to occur on a daily basis because the team had never given up and there was always more potential to be realized.

A significant feature of the Sehgal Foundation celebrations of 2014–2015 was the publication of a biography about the founders. *Seeds for Change: The Lives and Work of Suri and Edda Sehgal* by Marly Cornell was originally intended for a small audience of family, friends, and the Sehgal Foundation team. However, by the time the book was printed in October 2014, Suri and Edda Sehgal were finally convinced to allow the book to be made available to the public. Deeply humble by nature, Suri and Edda Sehgal had never even told their own children about the hardships of their childhoods, their refugee pasts, or the historical figures and events that were part of their remarkable lives. Upon reading *Seeds for Change*, lifelong friends and colleagues of the Sehgals expressed their wonder at the astonishing information that provided new insight into why Suri and Edda were so committed to making a positive difference in the lives of the rural poor in India. Missouri Botanical Garden Press offered to distribute the book, the biography won multiple literary honors, and Sehgal Foundation added award-winning publisher to its accolades. Launch parties for the book were held in conjunction with Sehgal Foundation's fifteen-year anniversary celebrations in Hyderabad and Gurgaon.

At the Hyderabad book launch on April 15, 2015, several people attended who had worked for the Sehgals at Proagro. More than one person commented to Suri that Proagro's greatest contribution was in training people. One gentleman, with tears in his eyes, said that those years at Proagro were the "most happy times" of his life. Several agreed that without that company's human resources, the growth of the seed industry in India would have been much slower—that every key figure in the seed industry had some connection to Proagro. Touched by hearing these comments, Suri thought hopefully, *In a few years, perhaps the same can happen in the social sector with the help of Sehgal Foundation.*

Sehgal Foundation activities in the United States on behalf of Sehgal Foundation in India were driven by a small staff and several members of the Sehgal family who provided funds and a variety of skills and support. Key successes in recent years had been in attracting excellent volunteers and interns—highly educated, motivated, and productive individuals who brought strong energy to rural India. An informal Sehgal Foundation group in Iowa raised awareness of and funds for the work. Sharing a dedication to community and to making a difference, various members of the Sehgal family had been part of the staff in India and had worked in an assortment of supportive roles stateside as consultants or liaisons to the foundation and to a range of other organizations devoted to conservation and biodiversity in India, the United States, and around the world.

Describing a goal still to be met, Suri said in 2015, "We have not been able to do enough to raise the awareness of NRIs (nonresident Indians) to feel some level of obligation toward their country of origin, especially for the highly subsidized educations they received in India that helped qualify them for their successes achieved in the United States. A growing number of CEOs of major companies in the US and globally came from India. The same has been true in every financially lucrative profession from medicine to investment banking. It will be rewarding to engage these individuals so they are inspired to make some sort of contribution in funds or in kind—perhaps share their expertise—but do something to give back to India. India has the largest number of malnourished children and anemic women in the world. The need for help is so great."

On April 24, 2015, one last formal anniversary celebration, "Celebrating 15 Years of Working Together with Rural Communities," was held at Sehgal Foundation campus headquarters in Gurgaon. The foundation team and international attendees included trustees, advisors, partners, representatives of academia, and diplomats. The program, which included entertainment, conversation, cocktails, and dinner, opened with classical Indian vocalist Vidya Shah. Suri Sehgal welcomed the guests on behalf of himself and Edda and thanked all the team members, partners, and others in attendance.

In his brief remarks, Suri said that each of Sehgal Foundation's primary programs—water management, agricultural development, and good rural governance—directly and indirectly address social justice, and most importantly the critical issue of gender equality. He said, "When we started our work in India, we made three important decisions to ensure impact. First, we must be credible, transparent, and accountable. We must rekindle hope, to help change the villagers' mind-set from despair and hopelessness to hopefulness—to show them that change is possible. And finally, anything we do must be measurable, scalable, and sustainable." He underlined that "development must be community-led to be sustainable" before adding that the most overarching truth learned in fifteen years was the power of empowerment. "An empowered individual can create miracles if given an opportunity, guidance, and support." He reminded guests of Margaret Mead's certainty, "Never doubt that a small group of committed citizens can change the world; indeed, it is the only thing that ever has."

Suri concluded with what he called a "humble request": "Let

us work together to meet the unmet needs of the rural poor. Let us rekindle hope where there is despair. Let us offer the poor clear paths to prosperity, justice, and human dignity."

CEO Jane Schukoske continued the welcome, describing the Sehgal Foundation campus and its platinum LEED-certified Green buildings as a hub for innovative thinking and problem solving. She offered a few highlights of the foundation's programs and interventions over the past fifteen years that had created opportunity, built resilience, and provided solutions to pressing social, economic, and environmental challenges in some of India's poorest communities. She acknowledged the talented foundation team and thanked the many partners who she said were "critical to our expansion and learning." She ended her remarks with an invitation to create more partnerships to further the empowerment of rural India. After a short video about Sehgal Foundation work, guests were treated to traditional Rajasthani folk music by Umer Farroq and his ensemble.

Jane's four-year anniversary as CEO of Sehgal Foundation was soon after the last fifteen-year anniversary event. In her annual report to the team, she wrote about the "critically important work" still to be done with village communities and reaffirmed, "We have what it takes." She quoted Suri, saying, "We are clear on our mission and vision and have a clear plan. We have solid, eager partners. We have sound experience, a good reputation, and an able team. We realize that results matter."

When asked what part of her work she particularly enjoyed, Jane said she loved working with the team on a shift in orientation from activities to results. "We have strengthened our planning and tracking of success by bringing in new perspectives from partners, external experts, academics, and interns."

Carrying forward her lifelong commitment to access to justice, Jane expressed joy at the foundation's new work with the Legal Services Authority, and her opportunities to train judges and speak at law schools, serve on editorial committees of law journals, and spread the idea of good rural governance in her publications and law review articles. She said her meetings with the women on the field team were "empowering for all of us." Jane was glad to see that formalizing gender policies had inspired ideas from others on the team to do more to empower women in a range of areas. She noted that pushing to learn more about women-led water management had ultimately resulted in the 2015 publication of a groundbreaking book, *Gender Issues in Water and Sanitation Programmes: Lessons from India.*[63]

Suri said about Jane: "She has been effective and successful in continuing to raise the professionalism of the Sehgal Foundation staff with solid team development and training that is heavy on communication, dialogue, and consensus building—the same respectful, participatory approach she has brought to community development. She has established vital academic and diplomatic linkages that are benefiting the organization, assisting in creating more partnerships, and furthering good rural governance. She has added vitality to Sehgal Foundation."

When Suri and Edda Sehgal were asked to consider Sehgal Foundation's legacy as of mid-2015, Suri began, "To create sustainable social impact requires a combination of invention, innovation, and entrepreneurship. Invention is the creation of new ideas, science, or technology. Innovation is applying an idea or invention to a product or service that creates value. Entrepreneurship is the replication or scaling up of an innovation to create sustainable social impact. Sustainability of projects or programs is a challenge every NGO and business faces. We have seen this dilemma whenever something completed was not sustained by the community. Good rural governance was an internally generated idea. The application of the idea and initially testing it in six villages was the innovative step. The entrepreneurial application on a large scale (now over 450 villages and more than twice that counting Swades' reach) has had a huge social impact. Furthermore, it assures the sustainability of the projects by the community."

Edda added, "We were tackling something complex from the beginning. Some organizations build one hospital or one school, one simple thing. Our goal was not to create a 'lovely' village; we basically wanted to develop the people. Developing skills in people is growing in momentum, but that takes time. India is a big and complex country. Suri thinks of the foundation like running a business. Yes . . . , but it's

63. Published by Sage Publications, Aidan A. Cronin, Pradeep K Mehta, and Anjal Prakash, editors.

not a business. The people with whom we work don't see it that way. They work with their hearts. Everyone was so busy doing so many simple concrete things that it took time to adapt to an understanding of the larger mission. Over time and many meetings in small groups, we figured out where we were going. Prior to 2011, the sense of hope was vague. But then we really saw the potential. The employees saw the benefit and so did the people in the villages."

She continued, "Seeing some village women become leaders reinforced hope in the community. Our feelings and attitudes made the big difference, whether it was with employees or villagers. A smile goes a long way, particularly when we are strangers. The attitude we convey is so important in not making someone feel inferior. We need to be careful not to offend. Respect is crucial. Feelings are very strong. Face-saving is an important cultural imperative in India as elsewhere in Asia or the Middle East; one misstep can reflect on one's family. This is strange for us in the West to understand. In rural India, blame is always placed on women, and women are supposed to accept this. But citizen participation is in direct conflict with that acceptance. Changing mind-sets is slow, especially with multiple generations living in the same household and strong elder influence. Women in the rural villages still have no economic independence or economic security. Even if they earn a paycheck, the money goes to the men. Obedience and independence work at cross purposes."

Suri agreed, adding, "Development is a slow process. Experimentation takes time. Did we take too much time in experimenting with ideas before deciding on what to scale up? There have been detours and changes along the way, which have been confusing to employees at times, but I don't think we could have done anything differently." Offering a metaphor from his experience as a seedsman and scientist, Suri explained, "In corn breeding, we look for one 'crown jewel'—an inbred line that combines well with other inbred lines to create a high-yielding hybrid. We screen hundreds of thousands of samples to find one. Similarly, to find a model that creates effective impact that is scalable and sustainable is like finding a needle in a haystack. When we find what really works in the villages, adoption by the communities can be relatively quick."

He continued, "Getting people involved is the trick to sustainability. Interaction is not just teaching; participation is necessary for people to see results. Once people begin to see results, change begins to happen. Sehgal Foundation has many strengths—grassroots knowledge, some financial security, a professional and committed core team—and we have more focus than ever with the Good Rural Governance program. This is a key element in the total development strategy."

Edda observed, "I am supportive of new ideas and welcome trying new things. Suri has sometimes dismissed ideas initially because he can quickly evaluate the potential in the big picture and visualize where an idea might go. His idea is to dream and dream big, have big goals, but be realistic and pragmatic with our resources."

Suri continued the thought, "We learned from Notki that appropriate capacity building involving the entire community is the key to sustainability. Every single initiative in the Water Management and Agricultural Development programs must involve capacity building of citizen groups (Water User Groups, agricultural committees, village-level institutions, etc.) for sustainability. We are now on the right track; we have models to implement. We will continue to seek more partners, demonstrate our credibility, implement projects as perfectly as possible, finish them on time, and keep our donors fully satisfied. Changing mind-sets is a slow process, not easy. We must keep our own minds open, be willing to change but stick with what works. We use no textbook model at Sehgal Foundation. We learn by doing."

He added this reflection: "We have collectively developed a shared mission and vision at Sehgal Foundation. Both are powerful. All of us firmly believe in them and enthusiastically support them. The two concepts, community-led and empowerment, are mantras that drive us. We have seen what an empowered individual or community can achieve. We have seen how any program can be sustained if it is community-led. *Good Governance Now!* is a sophisticated tool for creating hope—teaching the rural poor about their entitlements, sensitizing them to identifying problems, and voicing their concerns to appropriate authorities. By teaching villagers about good rural governance, citizens can see results of their own actions. They are engaged, enabled, and empowered to take responsibility for their own development. Villagers' despair is transformed into hope. There is power in empowerment. This is our strength—our legacy. This has the potential to awaken the entrenched bureaucracy and, with it, change rural India."

Sehgal Foundation will continue to invest in excellent people and technology and state-of-the-art facilities to go on serving as a premier learning platform for rural development and poverty reduction in India. The strategic alignment process will continue from year to year to help keep the organization's purpose, values, models, processes, responsibilities, culture, and people together and to attract more partners to the effort. As Suri Sehgal often reminded the team, "Development is work in progress. The obstacles created by bureaucracy are many, but these can be overcome with tenacity and perseverance."

An Invitation

Sehgal Foundation's achievements in rural development arise from the collective action of people in many roles, and each accomplishment is the result of collaboration and teamwork.

Our entire team—starting with visionary founders, Suri and Edda Sehgal, who continue to provide ongoing motivation and strategic direction drawn from a lifetime of achievement in agriculture and institution building, globally and in India; our eminent and committed trustees, who provide vital multidisciplinary perspectives to Sehgal Foundation goals; our technical and implementation partners, including local government, nongovernmental organizations, academia, and corporate affiliates; our in-house experts and service-oriented field staff who work directly with rural communities, converting ideas into reality with their hard work; and the external specialists, interns, and steadily increasing stream of volunteers, donors, and partners with whose assistance the important work is expanding—strives to achieve our vision of empowered rural people leading more secure, prosperous, and dignified lives.

Each of us owes a salute to the villagers in rural communities who have placed trust in us. Community members' undaunted spirit and openness to adopt new ways continue to be essential for sustainable development.

We invite everyone committed to improving the lives of millions of people in rural India to join with Sehgal Foundation in its mission of strengthening community-led development. When individuals and organizations in all sectors of society work together with the community, contributing time, skills, expertise, and/or funds, rural India will flourish.

Please join us, and together we will empower rural India.

Jane Schukoske, CEO
Sehgal Foundation
Summer 2015, Gurgaon, India

SEHGAL FOUNDATION is a true partnership between donors, volunteers, interns, employees, researchers, and rural communities.

SEHGAL FOUNDATION
100 Court Ave, Suite 211
Des Moines, Iowa 50309-2256
USA
Phone: 1 515 288 0010
email: sff-usa@smsfoundation.org

Sehgal Foundation is a US-based 501(c)(3) tax-exempt private foundation. Donations are deductible for US tax purposes as allowed by law.

S M SEHGAL FOUNDATION
(Sehgal Foundation)
Plot No.34, Sector 44, Institutional Area
Gurgaon, Haryana 122003
INDIA
Phone: 91-124-4744100
email: smsf@smsfoundation.org

S M Sehgal Foundation has 80G status in India.
All donations made within India are 50% tax deductible.

With support from donors and partners, Sehgal Foundation works together with India's rural communities to manage water resources, increase agricultural productivity, and strengthen rural governance through citizen participation and emphasis on gender equality and women's empowerment.

Join the team and see what we can do together!
www.smsfoundation.org

More About the Sehgal Foundation Team

The Sehgal Foundation team embraces the core values of integrity, excellence, professionalism, and optimism, along with the belief that, with appropriate support from civil society organizations and the government, rural communities will be mobilized to develop their own vision for development and transform their awareness into action.[64]

Integrity: We value honesty and consistency of character in our actions and attitudes.

Excellence: We encourage a culture of innovative thinking and creative collaboration.

Professionalism: We practice and promote professional standards in our work.

Optimism: We believe in passionate optimism and continuous learning to realize our vision.

The team culture at Sehgal Foundation evolved from the core beliefs of founders Suri and Edda Sehgal. From their previous successes in business, they brought a strong belief in what Suri has referred to as a "loose and tight" organization, that is, tight on the principles of honesty, integrity, transparency, and fairness, and somewhat loose and flexible with regard to day-to-day operations. The team learned by example to stay focused and never deviate from principles. Promises must be honored with commitment. The Sehgals transferred the same approach to Sehgal Foundation.

In their business model, leadership defined the big picture and provided the staff with ample opportunity to create innovative solutions to achieve overall goals. Sehgal Foundation teams were given a free hand

64. United Nations Research Institute for Social Development noted that nongovernmental organizations and institutions, called civil society organizations (CSOs), "emerged in the 1990s as increasingly influential actors in national development. In one area in particular, the provision of basic services, CSOs have in many countries assumed a major responsibility." http://www.unrisd.org/80256B3C005BCCF9/search/19AB2640214382A380256B5E004C94C5?OpenDocument.

to test ideas, learn, and grow. They were encouraged to experiment with what worked in the villages and "learn by doing."

Mistakes were inevitable, but the stated expectation was for people to use each mistake as a learning tool to move forward. The founders knew that time was needed to create ideas and technology, to see what worked, to put useful structures in place, and find ways to replicate successes.

Envisioning a nonhierarchical "flat" organization as ideal, the Sehgals also knew that, as the foundation grew, it would not be possible to remain entirely flat. Their preference for decentralized, solution-oriented management and a strong team culture remains paramount. From the part-time drivers to the full-time CEO, equal treatment and consideration for every person at Sehgal Foundation is important. Each person, whether an executive leader, a laborer, housekeeper, or staff member, is an equal partner in the work and is treated with the same respect.

This philosophy motivates people and allows them to feel authentic ownership of their work. The Sehgals understand that ownership is key to job satisfaction in any field, but it is particularly important in development work, which is difficult, sometimes unpleasant, and requires great patience and persistence to achieve even a small victory.

Administrative director Ramesh Kapahi explained, "The atmosphere within Sehgal Foundation is one of trust and respect. You can't buy that. That is something that must be practiced to be felt by people. Staff members have told me they don't experience such respect anywhere else."

To illustrate the type of commitment, ownership, and engagement felt by team members, Ramesh described an incident that occurred in the early summer 2015 during an informal meeting with the housekeeping staff who pointed out a need. The water storage tanks for the building were almost empty, and the monsoon rains were due. Contractors hired to remove the silt from the tanks had not shown up. Sehgal Foundation housekeepers volunteered to come in that weekend to do that work. Ramesh said, "Of course they were compensated for the extra work, but the point was that they noticed the problem and were motivated to do something about it. They felt ownership. With such mutual respect, we motivate each other collectively."

From the organization's beginning, the priority for hiring new people to Sehgal Foundation was to identify those who fit well with the team and had mutual respect for the key issues represented by the foundation. Being good at what one does is important, of course, but being a fit with the team and the mission is essential.

It is perhaps no surprise that several Sehgal Foundation team members worked in the past with the Sehgals at their former business, Proagro Group. In the work environment at Proagro, people continued to think, learn, evolve, and grow. Suri and Edda sincerely believed that every team member's success was a shared success—and every team member felt vested in successful outcomes. This had been a goal at Proagro, at the Sehgals' other businesses, and at Sehgal Foundation. International visitors were often amazed to hear the same goals articulated by each team member when they met them on a one-to-one basis. Everyone was clear on the mission.

People who fit well on the Sehgal Foundation team are solution-oriented, always looking for possibilities rather than barriers—what can be done rather than what is wrong—and they readily take action. There is no room for naysayers. All team members, including executives, trustees, managers, researchers, consultants, trainers, interns, students, volunteers, administrators, support staff, experts, and partners of every sort, are invited to and expected to engage in open discussions, voice opinions, and share suggestions.

Such a model requires strong leadership—people who pull the team together, motivate them, and make sure the team remains focused and clear on the messages. Core leaders are tasked with making sure that all team members have the necessary support and resources needed to do their work and continue to learn. Leaders take everyone's aspirations into consideration; the paths to upward mobility are defined through horizontal or vertical expansions of responsibility.

Sehgal Foundation leadership clearly articulates the organization's vision for the future and where employees and departments fit into the big picture, reinforcing objectives that need to be fulfilled by the team as a whole. The goal is for the decisions and behavior of all the organization's teams to be in sync with the shared vision of the organization. Strategy meetings emphasize interdepartmental decision making. Being involved in the organization's operational design fosters a strong team spirit and positive morale that translates to achievements in the field. Sehgal Foundation's dedicated staff know the organization deeply and are passionate about their work; they typically enjoy being out in the field, interacting within the community.

People who are part of Sehgal Foundation teams naturally became familiar with each other's work, help one another, and work both collaboratively and independently as needed in their given roles. Some gaps will always develop, but the focus on legal and ethical correctness and finding good solutions to any problem keeps Sehgal Foundation moving forward.

Sehgal Foundation and its teams evolved over the years as more systems and procedures were put into place. As village partnerships became more numerous, Suri and Edda continue to be invited to villages to meet people and see the work firsthand. The Sehgals share the excitement felt by people in the villages in showing their successes. They participate in as many visits, events, and celebrations as possible during the weeks they spend each year in India. They listen to team members, collect qualitative information, hear suggestions and complaints, mentor and motivate, and facilitate and build team spirit as they keep a finger on the pulse of the organization.

The manner in which Sehgal Foundation's teams work, together and within the rural villages and with partners throughout the world, has been a dynamic process that continues to develop and change. People working with and for the foundation don't experience boredom, because there is constant growth and transformation. Even though job titles and project names have changed from time to time, Sehgal Foundation's overall mission and vision have remained the same.

In addition to the core staff, field staff, and research staff, people frequenting the foundation have included a range of visitors. From 2010 to 2014, Sehgal Foundation hosted more than 130 interns and volunteers, including high school students and undergraduates from colleges and universities in the United States and Canada. A continuing stream of interns is in the pipeline. Guidance has been provided to students pursuing master's degrees and advanced studies from esteemed academic institutions, such as Georgetown University's McDonough School of Business, University of Nevada-Boyd School of Law, and Harvard Law School in the United States; the University of York in the United

Kingdom; and EHESS/School for Advanced Studies in the Social Sciences and the Toulouse School of Economics in France.

Sehgal Foundation has also attracted the interest of highly skilled professionals who share their expertise in a volunteer capacity. One such volunteer found her way to Sehgal Foundation by way of a meeting with Suri when he and Edda were in Tokyo in March 2011 to meet with potential funding partners. The devastating earthquake and tsunami that struck on March 11 brought the larger plans to an abrupt halt. Research scientist Satoko Okamoto was one of only eleven people to show up for what was to be a large reception that evening in Tokyo. Satoko ended up traveling to India and staying for two full years with Sehgal Foundation, sharing her skills with the Rural Research team, organizing events and seminars, and assisting with grant proposals. CEO Jane Schukoske credited Satoko's precise work on an application with the eventual receipt of a grant from the Embassy of Japan.

Dutchman Jan Dirk Geertsema is another esteemed international volunteer. A human resources consultant, he provided yearly training workshops from 2004 until 2010 (and as needed thereafter) to Sehgal Foundation teams, which assisted in promoting a work culture with strong principles. His skills in the areas of strategic alignment and leadership principles helped to keep the team in sync with the foundation's stated goals. Anjali Godyal partnered with him from 2006 onward, conducting behavioral change and leadership workshops for the field team.

Satoko and Jan Dirk are only two examples of many, many talented people who have shared their hearts and skills with Sehgal Foundation. The trustees, consultants, associates, and advisors over the years have been a treasure trove of astonishing human beings, benefactors of the highest degree who share the foundation's values and vision for the people of rural India.

Sehgal Foundation has played a part in the career development of village champions, governance guides, and other field staff, many of whom are from the villages where the work is being done and who have been subsequently recruited for coveted government jobs. Their ongoing commitment and excellent work is a source of great satisfaction for the entire team.

Razia, the first radio station manager for Alfaz-e-Mewat FM 107.8, whose extensive work at Sehgal Foundation was described in Chapter 9, is an example of someone who came directly from the villages of Mewat, worked at the foundation for several years, and served as a powerful role model for her community. She and two others from the original broadcast team, Arshad Ayub and Javed Hussain, created such impressive radio programming on health and hygiene that their skills and talents were sought by the National Rural Health Mission (NRHM). Razia accepted a job at NRHM as district coordinator while still remaining active on the radio station's community advisory committee. These are some of at least eight Sehgal Foundation employees hired by NRHM.

One of the first trained village champions, Mubarik Husain, was initially assigned to the village of Notki. Over the next five years, his excellent work there was rewarded with two promotions, first to block facilitator with oversight of other village champions, and then as an assistant program leader. After three years in that role, Mubarik accepted a position with Haryana State Rural Livelihood Mission (HSRLM), which implements NRHM programs at the state, district, and block level. Mubarik was hired as the district program manager of training and capacity building. He is one of three people trained and employed by Sehgal Foundation to go on to work at HSRLM.

Community mobilizer and sociologist B. R. Poonia, who has been with Sehgal Foundation from the start, spoke with warmth and pride about these talented former employees who continued to do development work elsewhere. Good work done by Sehgal Foundation "alumni" from the village communities is evidence of the efficacy of their training and experience. He included Mubarik Husain, Razia, Arshad Ayub, Javed Hussain, and many others who are now elsewhere contributing and making an impact in the development field, and are part of the "legacy of the Sehgal Foundation."

Members of the field team have been instrumental in every successful foundation endeavor. The courage and heroism of this well-trained and high-quality group of people who came from the local villages have been evident at every critical juncture. Their intervention was essential again and again in overcoming obstacles, ignorance, and complacency.

Vikas Jha, group leader for Governance and Policy Advocacy, described an incident in 2014 that illustrated the bravery and resolve of field team members even in the face of hostility. Field staff members were conducting training of community leaders in a Tauro village when an Integrated Child Development Services (ICDS) worker was angry about her ICDS center being checked regularly by community leaders. She physically attacked a female governance guide, tearing at her clothes. The injured governance guide filed a complaint with the police. The ICDS worker colluded with police in filing a false complaint alleging that she was the one attacked. Both sides ended up withdrawing their cases. Such was considered a typical result when dealing with local criminal justice systems.

As of mid-2015 there were about 125 members of the field team, seventy on the regular payroll and the rest part of a contractor team brought in for specific projects. Some worked in Water Management, some in Agricultural Development, and some were governance guides. But all were trained in good rural governance, and could be relied upon to articulate their shared mission.

The empowerment generated by Sehgal Foundation's respect-based, nonhierarchical business model extends beyond each of the employee teams. The community feels it, too. Foundation team members work to earn the respect of the people in the villages.

Respect has always been modeled first by founders Suri and Edda Sehgal. Team members agree that Suri Sehgal is a thorough gentleman whose subtle and humble manner makes those around him feel comfortable and valued. Team members describe Edda Sehgal as a thoughtful and stabilizing force in all circumstances. In team meetings she is an attentive listener who discreetly conveys advice. She has a talent for analyzing and synthesizing complex information and expressing it briefly and simply. She always "makes sense." Like Suri, Edda is also known for remembering small personal details about others, such as a team member's preference for a certain type of treat, and will months later perhaps show up with that treat as a gift.

Suri and Edda Sehgal's focus on people and their growth and development is a key component of every Sehgal Foundation decision and action. Each training, whether a field training, leadership sessions, or time spent on capacity building, is an investment in people. According to Suri, "When you build up people's capacity, human capital will deliver."

The appreciation people involved with Sehgal Foundation feel for each other and for their work is evidenced by the way so many who have been involved, from every level within the organization, continue to stay connected to the foundation in various ways. By mid-2015 several members of the original core team were still with the foundation, still humble and still determined, as they continued to adapt to the evolving needs of the communities and the scope of the work required to meet those needs.

Achievement Examples Over the Years

This summary is intended to convey a select assortment of activities carried out in key focus areas, including short-term and experimental initiatives along with those that proved more sustainable.

SEHGAL FOUNDATION INFRASTRUCTURE sites include two Platinum LEED (Leadership in Energy and Environmental Design)-certified buildings, which house the organization's headquarters, business offices, and guest areas; and the Ghaghas Community Center, with its training center and the community radio station Alfaz-e-Mewat FM 107.8.

GOOD RURAL GOVERNANCE training and mobilization began in 2008 and used two complementary program approaches that continue to work hand in hand: *Sushasan Abhi!* (*Good Governance Now!*) and Strengthening Village-Level Institutions (SVLI).[65]

Between 2008 and 2014, Sehgal Foundation rural governance programs trained 8,625 *Sushasan* champions and 942 members of village-level institutions, mobilizing 428 villages in Mewat, Rajasthan, and Bihar, and strengthening 98 panchayats in 131 villages.

From the start, reviving village-level institutions was a priority for sustaining programs and projects undertaken in partnership with individual communities. Such partnerships involved assisting in the building of three community libraries, eight school boundary walls and nineteen school latrines (nine for males/ten for females), and the hiring of seventeen schoolteachers (four male/thirteen female) as short-term appointees to cover vacant positions.

From 2010 through 2014, strengthening village-level institutions resulted in activating 109 Village Health, Sanitation, and Nutrition committees, which added 2,535 more new latrines. This brought the total number of latrines constructed or facilitated by Sehgal Foundation

65. Initially referred to as capacity building.

teams working in Mewat communities to 3,939. Activating 199 School Management committees made possible the building of fifteen school boundary walls and thirty-four schoolrooms, and entailed beautification efforts such as whitewashing eighteen schools and landscaping with plants around the schools.

Good rural governance training was provided to twenty-eight *gram sabhas*, in which women comprised 54 percent of 3,796 participants, and to five other organizations. Training to 607 participants in five *mahila sangathans* (women's collectives) began in 2014. SVLI training and support was essential in the development of six demonstration model villages.

Over a four-year period (2011–2014), legal literacy camps had more than 33,000 participants, with some returning for additional training.

Over a two-year period (2013–2014), the team was able to track and quantify the number of individual citizens (35,582) who benefited from better delivery of government programs, including Public Distribution System beneficiaries (27 percent), Mid Day Meal beneficiaries (44 percent), Integrated Child Development Services beneficiaries (21 percent), and miscellaneous recipients of old-age pensions, subsidized housing, agriculture equipment, and school uniforms.

A Citizen Information and Support Center was established in September 2014 in Nuh, using an integrated voice response system and toll-free number. In the first eight months (through April 2015), trained facilitators responded to 1,764 calls and four hundred visits from villagers seeking guidance related to problems in government services.

WATER MANAGEMENT projects in seventy-four villages through 2014 included assistance to individual households and farms as well as community-based initiatives that also benefited other villages in close proximity. Integrated water-augmentation systems included twenty-six check dams and thirty village ponds, ninety-five recharge wells, and forty-five nallah bund structures for groundwater recharge in forty-three villages in Mewat and Jyotisar district of Haryana and Alwar district of Rajasthan.

Other projects included ninety-seven rainwater-harvesting systems for community water collection and storage, and for community centers, hospitals, schools, private buildings, and individual households; and 1,389 soak pits and ninety-nine soak wells for sanitation and wastewater disposal. Individual projects included reviving a *baoli* (step well) and installing a *wudukhana* (a place for ablution).

In addition to individual models for useful items, such as in-home latrines and biosand filters, innovative models included pressurized wells for creating freshwater pockets in saline groundwater areas.

AGRICULTURAL DEVELOPMENT work from the beginning through 2014 focused on helping farmers by improving crop productivity at the farm level and educating farmers about balanced fertilizer application and soil health management. Promotion of sustainable agricultural practices to enhance farmers' income was carried out in 124 villages, which entailed more than 12,000 demonstration plots on a crop-specific package of practices, hundreds of exposure tours, farmers' meetings, and field days. Other demonstrations showcased methods of composting, vermicomposting, drip irrigation, sprinkler irrigation, and the use of effective microorganisms for good-quality manure. Trainings (640) were organized for teaching modern farming practices. Information communication technology (ICT), in the form of mobile telephone recordings, provided voice messages to thousands of farmers on crop and livestock management.

Partnership projects of differing lengths were created between farmer groups and NGOs that varied by crop, strategy, location, and beneficiary: *Krishi Jyoti* with mostly male farmers in forty-five villages in Mewat and Alwar; *Krishi Chetna* with women in eighteen villages in Alwar, and *Unnat Krishi* with women in ten villages in Alwar.

More than 35,000 native plants were planted in catchment areas, check dams, ponds, and school boundaries.

CROP IMPROVEMENT work by Sehgal Foundation scientists and researchers housed at ICRISAT resulted in recognition as a Scientific and Industrial Research Organization by the Department of Scientific and Industrial Research, Ministry of Science and Technology, Government of India. This research, informed by Suri Sehgal's expertise as a crop scientist, is driven by a commitment to identifying elite germplasm that would help scientists in public and private sectors to develop new and improved varieties and hybrids. Achievements noted here refer to the identification of elite genetic materials having qualitative or quantitative traits as source material. Because the potential must be realized in the field, decades of research are needed to show real results. But once such hybrids or varieties are identified, they have a great impact.

By the end of 2014, at least one hundred public- and private-sector scientists had participated in each of four mega maize field days sponsored by the foundation. More than 10,000 seed packets of inbred lines and segregating materials were supplied by request to scientists.

The research team successfully deployed doubled haploidy (DH) technology to develop 283 DH inbred lines of corn.

Disease tolerant/resistant sources were identified for turcicum leaf blight (27), stalk rot complex (21), polysora rust (38), and multiple disease resistance (21). This work, initially based at ICRISAT, was relocated near Bangalore, a geographic and climatic location more conducive to disease development, allowing good selections of disease resistant/tolerant plants.

More than 1,000 germplasm accessions were genetically fingerprinted using SSR markers, 500 germplasm accessions were screened for diseases, and 2,799 germplasm accessions were stored in the gene bank.

EDUCATION AND SKILL BUILDING initiatives included individual training of 208 villagers in mobile phone repair, electricity, computers, or community radio. More than 2,000 villagers participated in Life Skills Education programming (until 2010).

INFORMATION/AWARENESS OUTREACH AND INTERVENTIONS

In-house trainings, government programs, water literacy trainings, and door-to-door health, hygiene, and sanitation campaigns reached 250,000 people in 428 villages in Mewat, Rajasthan, and Bihar through 2014. Events included annual immunization drives, health camps, disability testing camps, and the creation of two delivery huts for safe childbirth. This work plus agriculture programs expanded the foundation's reach to 464 villages.

Issue-related events and celebrations brought attention to important issues, helping to mobilize communities to take part in their own development. These included:

Environment Day
Green Gala for Environmental Awareness
Independence Day
International Women's Day
Kriti Kendra Inauguration
Street Theater on Girl Child Education, Water Awareness, Sanitation
Water Awareness Walk (*Jal Chetna Yatra*)
World AIDS Day
World Breastfeeding Week
World Water Day

TRAINING WORKSHOPS, singular events and in series, brought attention to important development focus areas. These included:

Community Radio
Field Team Gender Training
Gender Inclusive Research Methodology in Agriculture and Water Roundtable
Gender Perspectives in Research Roundtable
Good Rural Governance through Community Radio
Government Programs Implemented Through Panchayats (with district administration)
Kisan Sammelan (gathering about farming)
Panchayat Sammelan (gathering about village councils)
Partnering for Rural Development: Experience Sharing and Idea Generation (with CII and Times Foundation)
Promoting Hygiene and Sanitation (with district administration)
Roadwork for Development Brainstorming
State Forum on Education
Village-Level Legal Literacy Camps
Waste Management Training
Water Crisis
Youth Personality Development

CONFERENCES AND SEMINARS brought the community together with experts in key areas:

- Good Rural Governance and Citizen Participation, and *Good Governance Now!* (annual/multiple locations)
- Citizen-District Administration Dialogues
- Forum on Institution Building and Rural Development Panel Discussion
- Indo-Japan Partnership Potential in Rural Development Roundtable
- Indo-Japanese Dialogue
- MGNREGA Consultation
- National Conference on Women and Water
- Strengthening Mid Day Meal and Public Distribution System in Villages Panel Discussions
- *Rubaru*: An Interface with Sarpanches of Mewat, and Notki Visit: A Public Private People's Partnership (PPPP)
- Rural Government Prospects and Challenges Panel Discussion
- Rural Voices Conference
- Safe Drinking Water Seminar
- Strengthening the Right to Education Consultation
- Working Together to Mitigate Climate Change and Eradicate Poverty in India/India Development Coalition of America (IDCA) Conferences

MEDIA (on air, online, and in print) proved to be a powerful tool for sharing important information, providing a platform for village voices, empowering and mobilizing individuals and communities, and bringing information to potential partners in rural development. Examples include:

Alfaz-e-Mewat FM 107.8 MHz radio station (begun 2012 through 2014) with many episodes freely available to other stations on Internet sites such as EDDA and Manch. Community radio staff includes trained community members. Regular programming, thirteen hours daily includes:

- *Kisse Kahani* (old stories from Mewat): one hour
- *Hello Farmaaish* (live phone-in program): one hour

Guftgu (interviews with subject experts): half hour

Jal Jangal Jameen (Our Heritage/Water, Forest, Agriculture): half hour

Mausiki Mewat (local folklore): half hour

Saaf Safai Aur Sehat (Cleanliness, Sanitation, and Health): fifteen minutes

Krishi Khabar (agriculture news): ten minutes

Sufi Safar (Sufi history and music): half hour, three times a week

Humse Hai Shasan (Toward Good Governance): half hour, three times a week

Gaon ki Chaupal (Live Discussion of Village Issues): half hour, three times a week

Waqt Hamara Hai (By and For Schoolchildren): fifteen minutes, three times a week

Radio School: fifteen minutes, twice a week

Series programming includes:

Aas (Hope): Twelve episodes about TB patients, medical challenges, and proper treatment involving medical practitioners in the program—supported by Resource Group for Education and Advocacy for Community Health.

Dastak (The Knock): Six programs on women and governance—a partnership between Alwar Ki Awaaz radio station and Alfaz-e-Mewat, supported by Ideosync Media Combine.

Galli Galli Sim Sim: 104-episode series (Indian version of Sesame Street) promoting literacy, numeracy, emotional well-being, health, and hygiene, including local voices—supported by Sesame Workshop India Trust.

Kanoon Ki Baat (Talk About Law): weekly pilot by three stations in Haryana; supported by National Legal Service Authority of India.

Humara Ration Humara Haq (Our Ration Our Right): Twelve episodes by five community radio stations in five states—supported by Sehgal Foundation.

Nai Dishayen (New Directions): Thirty programs on panchayati raj and social security programs relevant to villagers—supported by Haryana Institute of Rural Development.

Panchayat Ki Baat, Tai Ke Saath (Discussion on Panchayats with Progressive Village Aunt): Twenty episodes—sponsored by Ministry of Panchayati Raj, Government of India.

Shochalay Mere Angana (Toilet at Home): Ten episodes on open defecation, health effects and challenges to women—supported by Commonwealth of Learning, Canada. Another ten episodes started in the summer 2015.

Udaan (Flight): Sixty episodes about unsung women heroes and stories of change through self-help groups—funded by National Rural Livelihood Mission.

Website: smsfoundation.org
Blog: smsfoundation.org/blog/

Newsletters

Connect (online newsletter about Sehgal Foundation news): produced quarterly

Sushasan Patrika (governance newsletter): quarterly distribution 5,000

Vikas Patrika (development newsletter): quarterly distribution 5,000

Books and Book Chapters

Empowering Women in Developing Countries: ICT Applications and Benefits, "Harnessing the power of New ICTs for Rural Women in India: NGO Roles," chapter by Jane Schukoske, eds. Finarya Legoh and Suman Kapur, Daya Publishing House: New Delhi. 121–137, 2015.

Gender Issues in Water and Sanitation Programmes: Lessons from India, eds. Aidan A. Cronin, Pradeep K. Mehta, and Anjal Prakash, Sage Publications, 2015.

Interlacing Water and Human Health. "Water Quality and Human Health in Mewat: Challenges and Innovative Solutions," chapter by Lalit Mohan Sharma, Aravinda Satyavada, and Archana Chowdhury, Sage Publications, 200–229, 2012.

Legal Aid: Catalyst for Social Change, "Achieving Socially Relevant Legal Education through Rural Legal Aid Clinics" by Jane Schukoske and Latika Vashist, eds. Raman Mittal and K. V. Sreemithun, University of Delhi, 167–189, 2012.

Seeds for Change: The Lives and Work of Suri and Edda Sehgal by Marly Cornell, Sehgal Foundation, 2014.

Booklets

Good Governance Now! Guidelines on Key Government Programs

Krishi Jyoti (enlightened agriculture) a new dimension to NGO corporate partnership

Mapping Soil Fertility of Mewat, Haryana

Panchayat Se Ek Mulaqat (meeting with village *panchayat*) (pictorial)

Ready Reckoner on Grievance Redressal Mechanisms

School Management Committee Information

School Management Committee: A Step Toward Model School (pictorial)

The Right to Education Act

The Right to Information Act

Village Health, Sanitation, and Nutrition Committee Information

RURAL RESEARCH (since 2010) included thirty-three monitoring, learning, and evaluation studies (needs assessments, baseline surveys, midterm monitoring, and impact evaluation), and eighteen thematic research studies.

Recognition for the foundation's research quality was reflected in major studies, including a collaborative research study called "An Assessment of Convergence of Sarva Shiksha Abhiyaan with Selected

Central and State Government Schemes" completed in May 2012 and sponsored by the National Resource Centre for Women, Ministry of Women and Child Development, Government of India; and a research study called "Identifying Backwardness of Mewat Region in Haryana: A Block-Level Analysis" completed in June 2015 and sponsored by the Research Division of the National Institution for Transforming India Aayog (NITI Aayog)—formerly the Planning Commission, Government of India.

ACADEMIC PUBLICATIONS have documented the work of Sehgal Foundation and demonstrated the organization's potential as a knowledge institute. Select examples include:

Godyal, Anjali and Anjali Makhija, "Empowering Meo-Muslim Women in Mewat: Experiences and Challenges." *Women's Link*, Vol. 18:1. 36–42, Jan–Mar 2012.

Hussain, Rukshat, and Bhawna Mangala, "Toilet as an Asset: Necessity Versus Luxury," *Developing Country Studies*. 4:9, 2014.

Mehta, Pradeep Kumar, "Farmers' Behaviour Towards Risk in Production of Fruit and Vegetable Crops," *Journal of Rural Development*. Vol. 31:4. 457–468, October–December 2012.

Murada, Pooja O., and Arti Manchanda Grover, "Women's Voices: Engaging the Excluded. *Review of Market Integration*. Vol. 6:1, 114–130, 2014.

________, and Charu Khanna, "Power in Empowerment: Role of Community Media in Bringing Governance at Local Level." *ICT for Development*. Vol. 4:2, 61–81, 2014.

Palacios, Alison C., and Pradeep Kumar Mehta, "Role of Gender in Food Security of Agricultural Households in Rural Mewat." *Asian Journal of Development Matters*. Vol. 7:1, 121–135, June 2013.

Pandey, Ajay, "Experimenting with Clinical Legal Education to Address the Disconnect Between the Larger Promise of Law and its Grassroots Reality in India," *Maryland Journal of International Law*. Vol. 26:1. 135–158, 2011.

Schukoske, Jane, "Engaging with Communities for Access to Justice," *e-Pg Pathshala: Social Sciences: Law: Paper 2 Access To Justice, Module 17*, Ministry of Human Resource Development National Mission on Education through Information and Communications Technology, 2015.

________, "Book Review of *Legal Education in Asia*," *Asian Journal of Legal Education* 2(1), 78–80, 2015.

________, and Roopali Adlakha, "Enhancing Good Governance in India: Law Schools and Community–University Engagement," *Journal of Indian Law and Society*, Monsoon issue. Vol. 3, 206–232, November 2012.

Sharma, Lalit Mohan, "Innovation for Making Potable Water Available in Saline Groundwater Areas," *Journal of Water Resource and Protection*, Vol. 6:14, 1284–1289, 2014.

________, and Rashmin Kaur Joshi, "Reverse Osmosis is not a Viable Option for Water Purification in Water Stressed Regions of India,"' *IOSR Journal of Environmental Science, Toxicology, and Food Technology*, 8:8, 23–27, 2014.

Sehgal Foundation Partnerships

1999–2015

Support from partners and donors makes it possible for Sehgal Foundation to design and promote rural development interventions that create opportunities, build resilience, and provide solutions to some of the most pressing challenges in India's poorest communities.

This partial list of short-term, long-term, and ongoing partnerships, including academic, technical, strategic, funding, public, and private, is presented with profound gratitude and sincere appreciation for their part in empowering rural India. In addition, the Sehgal Foundation team thanks the many individuals from all parts of the world who have made contributions during the foundation's first fifteen-plus years in rural India.

Advit Foundation, Haryana, India
Aga Kahn Foundation, New Delhi, India
Aide-et-Action Private Ltd., Chennai, India
Amity University, Manesar, Haryana, India
Amity University, Noida, Uttar Pradesh, India
An Association for Development of Harmony and Action Research (AADHAAR), Dehradun, Utarrkhand, India
Animal Husbandry Department, Haryana, Government of India
Aravalli Vikas Sangathan (ARAVIS), Gurgaon, India
Ashoka Trust for Research in Ecology and Environment (ATREE), Bangalore, Karnataka, India
Asian Broadcasting Union, India
Assam University, Silchar, Assam, India
Astha Sansthan, Udaipur, Rajasthan, India
Australian National University, Canberra, Australia
Azim Premji University, Bangalore, Karnataka, India
Birla Institute of Management Technology, Greater Noida, Uttar Pradesh, India
Birla Institute of Technology and Science, Pilani, Rajasthan, India
Borlaug Ruan Internship/The World Food Prize Foundation, Des Moines, Iowa, USA

Boyd School of Law, University of Nevada, Las Vegas, Nevada, USA
Center for Development and Population Activities (CEDPA), Washington, DC, USA
Central University of Hyderabad, Hyderabad, Andhra Pradesh, India
Centre for Affordable Water and Sanitation Technology (CAWST), Calgary, Canada
Chanakya Law University, Patna, Bihar, India
Chungath Family Foundation, Des Moines, Iowa, USA
Clinton Global Initiative, New York, New York, USA
Coca-Cola India Foundation (CCIF; AKA Anandana), Gurgaon, India
College of Agricultural and Life Sciences, University of Wisconsin, Madison, USA
Commonwealth Educational Media Centre for Arts (CEMCA), New Delhi, India
Community Radio Alwar ki Awaaz, Alwar, Rajasthan, India
Community Radio Rim Jhim, Gopalganj, Bihar, India
Confederation of Indian Industry (CII), New Delhi, India
Deepalaya, New Delhi, India
Delhi Council of Child Welfare (DCCW), Orthopaedic Center, New Delhi, India
Delhi School of Economics, Delhi, India
Delhi School of Social Work, University of Delhi, India
Delhi University, New Delhi, India
Department of Education, Government of India
Department of Panchayats, Haryana, India
Department of Science and Technology (DST), Government of India
Des Moines Community Fund, Iowa, USA
Development Alternatives (DA), New Delhi, India
Dharma Vana Arboretum (DVA), Andhra Pradesh, India
Directorate of Audio Visual Publicity (DAVP), New Delhi, India
District Administration, Bahraich, Uttar Pradesh, India
District Administration, Sirsa, Haryana, India
District Rural Development Agency, Bilaspur, Himachal Pradesh, India
Dr. Shroff's Charitable Eye Hospital, Haryana, India
École des Hautes Études en Sciences Sociales (EHESS) Paris, France
Engineers Without Borders, San Francisco, California, USA

Federation of Indian Chambers of Commerce and Industry (FICCI), New Delhi, India
Food Nutrition Board, New Delhi, India
G. D. Goenka World Institute, Gurgaon, Haryana, India
Georgetown University McDonough School of Business, Washington, DC, USA
Global Compact Network India, New Delhi, India
Global Development Network, New Delhi, India
Gokhale Institute of Politics and Economics, Pune, Maharashtra, India
Government and People of Japan, Embassy of Japan, India
Great Indian Dream Foundation, New Delhi, India
Gujarat National Law University, Gandhinagar, Gujarat, India
Harvard Law School, Cambridge, Massachusetts, USA
Haryana Agricultural Department, Government of India
Haryana Agricultural University, India
Haryana Education Department, India
Haryana Government Health Department, India
Haryana Institute of Public Administration, India
Haryana Institute of Rural Development (HIRD), India
Haryana State Rural Livelihoods Mission (HSRLM), Chandigarh, India
Hindu College, Delhi, India
Horticulture Department, Government of India
Human Welfare Foundation, Moradabad, Uttar Pradesh, India
Humanities Research Council of Canada (SSHRC), Ottawa, Ontario, Canada
Ibtada, Alwar, Rajasthan, India
ICICI Fellowship Programme, India
ICICI Foundation for Inclusive Growth, Mumbai, India
Ideosync Media Combine, Faridabad, Haryana, India
India Development Coalition of America (IDCA), Willowbrook, Illinois, USA
Indian Institute of Management, Kashipur, Uttarakhand, India
Indian Institute of Plantation Management, Bangalore, Karnataka, India
Indian Institute of Public Health/Public Health Foundation of India, Gurgaon, Haryana, India

Indian Institute of Technology, Guwahati, Assam, India
Indian Institute of Technology, New Delhi, India
Indraprastha College for Women, University of Delhi, New Delhi, India
Indraprastha University, New Delhi, India
Institute for Conflict Analysis and Resolution, George Mason University, Fairfax Co., Virginia, USA
Institute of Rural Management Anand, Gujarat, India
Institute of Technology and Management, Delhi, India
Integrated Child Development Services (ICDS), Haryana, India
International Crops Research Institute for the Semi-Arid Tropics (ICRISAT), Hyderabad, India
International Development Research Centre (IDRC), Ottawa, Ontario, Canada
International Management Institute, New Delhi, India
Iowa State University, Ames, Iowa, USA
Jamia Millia Islamia University, Department of Social Work, Delhi, India
Jamsetji Tata National Virtual Academy for Rural Prosperity, Chennai, India
Japanese International Cooperation Agency (JICA), New Delhi, India
Jawaharlal Nehru University, Delhi, India
Jindal Global Law School, Sonipat, Haryana, India
JSS Law College, Mysore, Karnataka, India
K+S Kali GmbH Fertilizers (India) Pvt. Ltd., Gurgaon, Haryana, India
Key Management Group Foundation, Gurgaon, India
KMG Foundation, USA
Krishi Vigyan Kendra (KVK), Mandkhola, India
Lady Bamford Charitable Trust, Faridabad, Haryana, India
Lady Irwin College, Delhi, India
Maharaja Agrasen Institute of Technology, Delhi, India
MAMTA Health Institute for Mother and Child, New Delhi, India
Mandikhera Hospital, Mewat, Haryana, India
Maraa—A Media and Arts Collective, Bangalore, India
Mewat Development Agency, Haryana, India
Mewat Social and Educational Development Society (MSEDS), India

Millennium Alliance (USAID, DFID/UKAID, FICCI, DST-GoI, ICCo India, and ICICI Foundation for Inclusive Growth
Ministry of Agriculture, Government of India
Ministry of Panchayati Raj, Government of India
Ministry of Tourism, Government of India
Ministry of Women and Child Development, Government of India
Misr Hytech Seed International, Cairo, Egypt
Narsee Monjee Institute of Management Studies, Mumbai, Maharashtra, India
National Bank for Agriculture and Rural Development, India
National Institute of Research on Jute & Allied Fibre Technology (NIRJAFT), West Bengal, India
National Institute of Technology, Warangal, Karnataka, India
National Law University, Delhi, India
National Law University, Jodhpur, Rajasthan, India
National Legal Services Authority (NALSA), New Delhi, India
Navjyoti India Foundation, New Delhi, India
Ohio State University, Columbus, Ohio, USA
One World South Asia, New Delhi, India
Pardada Pardadi Educational Society, Uttar Pradesh, India
Participatory Learning and Action Network (PLANET KERALA), Kerala, India
People in rural communities in the Alwar District, Rajasthan; Mewat District, Haryana; and Samastipur District, Bihar, India
Planning Commission, Government of India
Population Foundation of India (through Vardaan Consultants), New Delhi, India
Practical Action, Rugby, Great Britain, UK
Primary Health Center, Mewat, Haryana, India
Public Health Department, Government of India
Rajiv Gandhi National Institute of Youth Development, Chennai, India
Resource Group for Education and Advocacy for Community Health (REACH), Chennai, India
Rural Development and Self-Employment Training (RUDSET) Institute, Gurgaon, India
Rural Development Department, Rajasthan, India

S. P. Jain Institute of Management and Research, Mumbai, Maharashtra, India
School Health Annual Report Programme (SHARP), India
School of Planning and Architecture, Vijayawada, Andhra Pradesh, India
Sesame India Workshop Trust, New Delhi, India
Sir Ratan Tata Trust (SRTT) and Navajbai Ratan Tata Trust, Mumbai, India
Sitaram Jindal Foundation, New Delhi, India
Social Science and Humanities Resource Council, Ottawa, Ontario, Canada
Society for Promotion of Youth and Masses, New Delhi, India
Sri Venkateshwara College, Delhi, India
St. Catherine University, St. Paul, Minnesota, USA
Students of the World, San Francisco, California, USA
Sukarya, Faridabad, Haryana, India
Swades Foundation, Raigad, Maharashtra, India
Swaraj Sansthan, Bhopal, India
T. A. Pai Management Institute, Manipal, Karnataka, India
TERI University, Delhi, India
The Coca-Cola Foundation, Atlanta, Georgia, USA
The Energy and Resources Institute, New Delhi, India
The Mosaic Company, India, Gurgaon, India
The Mosaic Company Foundation, Plymouth, Minnesota, USA
The Restoring Force (TRF), Gurgaon, India
Times Foundation, New Delhi, India
Times of Money Ltd., Mumbai, India
Toulouse School of Economics, France
Transparency International India, New Delhi, India
Trees for Life, Wichita, Kansas, USA
Tribal Department, District Koriya, Chhattisgarh, India
UKAID, Government of United Kingdom
United Nations Children's Fund (UNICEF), New Delhi, India
United Nations Development Program (UNDP), New Delhi, India
United Nations Educational, Scientific, and Cultural Organization (UNESCO), New Delhi, India

United Nations Information Centers (UNIC), New Delhi, India
United States Aid for International Development (USAID), New Delhi, India
University of Baltimore School of Law, Baltimore, Maryland, USA
University of Florida, Gainesville, Florida, USA
University of Iowa, Iowa City, USA
University of Montana, Missoula, Montana, USA
University of Pune, Department of Women's Studies, Maharashtra, India
Vardaan Consultants, Gujarat, India
Varun Myneni Fund, USA
Vasant Valley School, New Delhi, India
West Bengal National University for Juridical Sciences, Kolkata, India
William L. Brown Center (WLBC), Missouri Botanical Garden, St. Louis, Missouri, USA
York Law School, University of York, North Yorkshire, England, UK
York University, Toronto, Ontario, Canada
Zila Panchayat, District Koriya, Chhattisgarh, India

Membership Affiliations

Sehgal Foundation is uplifted by associations with those who share the commitment to making a positive difference in the world. This is a partial list of membership affiliations from 1999 to 2015.

Central Ground Water Authority (CGWA) District-Level Committee in Mewat, since 2010.

Confederation of Indian Industry (CII), 2007–2008.

Clinton Global Initiative (CGI), New York, USA, since 2005.

Credibility Alliance, New Delhi, India, since 2005.

Department of Science & Technology (DST), Government of India, Panel of Experts for Water Technology, Mission for Water Programme, since 2010.

Guidestar India, Mumbai, India, since 2012.

ICRISAT Hybrid Parent Research Consortia on Pearl Millet, Sorghum and Pigeon Pea, since 2004.

India Development Coalition of America (IDCA), founding member, since 2003.

Indian Green Building Council (IGBC), Hyderabad, India, May–December, 2011.

Institute of Rural Management (IRMA), Anand, designated organization, since 2004.

Mewat Development Agency (MDA), Haryana, India, since 2008.

Swasthiya Kalyan Samiti, Mandikhera Hospital, Mewat; and District Health Society, Mewat, since 2010.

UN Global Compact India, NGO member, since 2009.

UN Global Compact, Network Training Subcommittee, 2010.

United Nations Development Program (UNDP) and the Government of India's Endogenous Tourism Program, 2005–2010.

United Nations Economic and Social Council (ECOSOC), since 2005.

Awards and Recognitions

The work done by the Sehgal Foundation team alongside many partners has been honored in various ways over the years. The team is humbled by these awards and recognitions, which serve to reinforce the commitment to the foundation's vision, mission, and values.

WE ENVISION every person across rural India empowered to lead a more secure, prosperous, and dignified life.

OUR MISSION is to strengthen community-led development initiatives to achieve positive social, economic, and environmental change across rural India.

Sehgal Foundation (S M Sehgal Foundation), and in some cases Founder and Chair Suri Sehgal or other staff, were presented with awards. Some awards between 2008 and 2014 were presented in the name Institute of Rural Research and Development (IRRAD).

2002

ICRISAT "Best Friend of ICRISAT" Trophy from Director General Dr. William Dar.

2005

Bharat Samman Excellence Award, NRI Institute, New Delhi, India, to Sehgal Foundation.

Bharat Samman Excellence Award, NRI Institute, New Delhi, India, to Dr. Suri Sehgal.

Centre for Development and Population Activities Recognition to Better Life Options Program for adolescent girls in India.

United Nations Economic and Social Council (ECOSOC) Special Consultative Status awarded to Sehgal Foundation

2006

Department of Scientific and Industrial Research (DSIR), Government of India, New Delhi, India, R&D Recognition for Crop Improvement.

Institute of Directors, New Delhi, India, Golden Peacock Award for Philanthropy in Emerging Economies, Finalist.

Samaj Gaurav Samman National Award, Manav Dharm Mission, New Delhi, India.

2007

Pinnacle NRI Award, NRI Institute, New Delhi, India.

Rashtriya Samaj Gaurav Samman (Pride of Nation) award to Jay Sehgal.

2008

Mewat Development Agency, Haryana, India, recognition as Premium Organization for Undertaking Water Resource Management in Mewat.

Water Digest and UNESCO Best Water NGO Award, New Delhi, India.

2009

Bharat Samman Life Time Achievement Award by NRI Institute, New Delhi, India, to Dr. Suri Sehgal.

Information Integrity Coalition, USA, Award Finalist for Excellence in Information Integrity.

Times Foundation and FICCI Women Achievers Award, New Delhi, India, to Sehgal Foundation health specialist Shaheena Khatoon.

Water Digest and UNESCO Best Water NGO Award, New Delhi, India.

2010

CII Woman Exemplar Award to Kamlesh Sherawat, Block Facilitator, Taoru, Mewat District, Haryana, for her contribution in the field of education.

Japanese Award for Most Innovative Development Project (MIDP), Global Development Network, Bogota, Columbia, Third Place for *Good Governance Now!* model.

National Ground Water Augmentation Award, Government of India, Ministry of Water Resources, New Delhi, India.

Sehgal Foundation model project "Improving Sustainable Livelihood Security Using Proven Solutions to Land Degradation in Semiarid Regions of India" selected in top-30 most innovative projects, at 2010 Global Conference on Agriculture, Food Security, and Climate Change, The Hague, Netherlands, organized by Dutch, Norwegian, and Ethiopian governments, FAO (UN), and the World Bank.

U.S. Green Building Council, Platinum certification under Leadership in Energy and Environmental Design (LEED) for New Construction, Phase I building, Gurgaon.

Water Digest and UNESCO Best Water NGO Award, New Delhi, India.

2011

American India Foundation, New York, USA, Leadership in Philanthropy Award to Dr. Suri Sehgal.

Department of Education, Haryana, India, Letter of Appreciation for participation in Dastak-e-Taalim Program.

Indo-US Education Conclave and D. Y. Patil University, Pune, Maharashtra, India, recognized Sehgal Foundation CEO Jane Schukoske for her "Significant Contribution to Indo-US Education Cooperation."

2012

Bhaskar Foundation Jal Star Award, Dainik Bhaskar Group, New Delhi, India.

2013

Arcelormittal, New Delhi, India, Special Recognition for Women's Empowerment to Kamlesh Sherawat, Block Facilitator, Taoru, Mewat District, Haryana, India.

Arcelormittal, New Delhi, India, Special Recognition for Women's Empowerment to Devika Batra, Project Coordinator, Gurgaon, Haryana, India.

Arcelormittal, New Delhi, India, Special Recognition for Women's Empowerment to Sehgal Foundation Communications Director Pooja O. Murada, for providing a grassroots platform for women to share their voices and document their cases.

Global Indian Karmaveer Puraskaar Lifetime Achievement Award to Dr. Suri Sehgal, a Global Award for Social Justice and Citizen Action, from the Indian Confederation of NGOs (iCONGO), New Delhi, India.

Manthan Award Asia Pacific Finalist, Community Radio Alfaz-e-Mewat FM 107.8.

Indian Green Building Council, Platinum certification under Leadership in Energy and Environmental Design (LEED) for Core & Shell, Phase II building, Gurgaon.

Rockefeller Foundation Top 100 Next Century Innovators Awards Short List, Sehgal Foundation IRRAD project, "Strengthening the Demand and Supply for Better Village Governance."

FICCI Water Award, NGO Category First Prize, New Delhi, India.

Water Management Forum, Institution of Engineers, Chennai, Tamil Nadu, India, Recognition for Outstanding Work in Water Conservation.

2014

Amity University, NOIDA, Uttar Pradesh, India, Woman Achiever award to Sehgal Foundation CEO Jane Schukoske for her "Outstanding Accomplishments and Contribution in the Social Sector."

Benjamin Franklin Awards silver award winner in two categories, biography and multicultural, The 27th Annual IBPA Benjamin Franklin Awards™ sponsored by IBPA for *Seeds for Change: The Lives and Work of Suri and Edda Sehgal* by Marly Cornell, published by Sehgal Foundation.

DNA & Stars of the Industry Group, Mumbai, India, Innovative B-School Award in Education Leadership.

Felicitation certificate to Sehgal Foundation from Chief Minister, Haryana, as one of the partners in Haryana Education Department event on Haryana Shiksha Utsav, held at Bohra Kalan, Haryana, India.

Foreword Reviews Indie Fab Book of the Year Award, silver award winner in biography, sponsored by *Foreword Reviews* magazine, for *Seeds for Change: The Lives and Work of Suri and Edda Sehgal* by Marly Cornell, published by Sehgal Foundation.

ICRISAT Plaque of Appreciation and Thanks from Director General Dr. William Dar, 42nd Anniversary Celebration.

Midwest Book Awards first place winner in two categories, social science and cover design, sponsored by Midwest Book Publishers Association (MIPA), for *Seeds for Change: The Lives and Work of Suri and Edda Sehgal* by Marly Cornell, published by Sehgal Foundation.

Millennium Alliance (FICCI), India, Technology Development Board, Department of Science of Technology, Government of India, and USAID), New Delhi, India, Millennium Alliance Award for Outstanding Work on Pressurized Recharge Wells for Creating Fresh Water Pockets in Saline Ground Water Areas.

National Indie Excellence Awards (NIEA) 9th Annual Indie Awards first place winner in biography for *Seeds for Change: The Lives and Work of Suri and Edda Sehgal* by Marly Cornell, published by Sehgal Foundation.

World Women Leadership Congress & Awards, Mumbai, India, Women Leadership Award to Sehgal Foundation CEO Jane E. Schukoske.

2015

Best Learners Award, Namati Global Justice Prize, Special Category Winner for a project that focuses on demand and supply or local governance and justice.

Glossary

20 to 200 to 2000. Sehgal Foundation catchphrase introduced in 2005 represented goal of increasing scale and impact from 20 villages to 200 villages to 2000 villages.

73rd and 74th Amendment Act of 1993. Amendments that provided constitutional status to local panchayats and municipalities, enabling them to function as self-governing institutions.

Alfaz-e-Mewat. Rural Voices of Mewat. The name of the Sehgal Foundation sponsored community radio station.

Anganwadi centers (AWC). *Anganwadi* = courtyard shelter. Childcare centers.

ANM. Auxiliary nurse-midwife.

ASHA. Accredited social health advocate.

Babu. (also *baboo*) A native Indian civil servant.

Babudom. A disparaging term referring to the Indian bureaucracy.

Baoli. Old step well that once numbered in the thousands across India.

CBC. Capacity Building Center; a former Sehgal Foundation team.

CDPO. Child development project officer.

CEDPA. Center for Development and Population Activities.

Chaas. Yogurt-based savory drink.

Chaupal. A community building or space, used as a gathering place especially for men of the village. If not a building, it may be a platform under a tree.

Charpoi. Traditional Indian bed with wooden legs and a woven rope sleeping surface. Also called *manja*.

CHC. Community health center.

Check dam. A dam built between hills to capture rainwater as it flows down the hillsides.

CHW. Community health worker.

CHV. Community health volunteer.

Chunni. Girl's head scarf.

CIMMYT. International Maize and Wheat Improvement Center.

CISC. Citizen information and support center.

Commit Less and Deliver More. Sehgal Foundation catchphrase introduced in 2002 represented a commitment to uncompromising integrity, even in the face of indefinite delays.

Contour bunds. Loose-stone structures placed at specific angles to slow the flow of water, increase percolation into the ground, minimize soil erosion, and improve soil moisture.

CSO. Civil-society organizations. Nongovernmental organizations and institutions that assist in development, particularly in helping the poor gain access to basic services.

CSR. Corporate social responsibility.

Dai. Traditional midwife.

Daincha (*Sebania bispinosa*). A green-manure plant that is able to grow in saline soil.

DLSA. District Legal Services Authority.

Dudhia. Milk collector or middleman.

Darul Qaja. A form of Islamic court.

Farm bunding. Embankments created around farm fields for better irrigation.

FVGA. Fruit and Vegetable Growers Association. A cooperative formed by villagers to pool their agricultural products for sale in the market, making it possible to bypass middlemen.

Four, Four, Four. Sehgal Foundation catchphrase introduced in 2002 represented a goal to achieve and demonstrate satisfactory levels of transformation in four villages, using four programs, within four years. Also called 4 by 4 by 4 or the 4x4x4 model.

Freshwater. Nonsaline water, not necessarily free of bacteria or sediments.

Gabions. Loose stones covered with wire mesh that serve as free-draining walls, used to slow the flow of water, increase percolation, minimize soil erosion, and improve soil moisture. The wire mesh helps hold the stones against high water currents.

Germplasm. Genetic resources of a plant, such as a collection of seeds.

GGN. Good Governance Now.

Good Governance Now! Sehgal Foundation initiative introduced in 2008 represented the demand for accountability in government programs and services and became a foundation program.

Good governance. Concept related to how public institutions can conduct and manage their affairs and resources in order to meet the needs of the people.

Gotra. Tribal cultural lineage, akin to a family name in Brahman, Kshatriya, and Vaishya castes of Hindu social system.

Governance guides. Paid staff whose main responsibilities are training *sushasan* champions, generating community awareness, and providing inter-program work support.

Gram. Village or villages.

Gram panchayat. Village self-governing body.

Gram sabha. Assembled village electorate, assembly of eligible voters.

Gram sachiv. Village secretary.

Gram swaraj. Village self-governance.

Gram vikas sanstha. Village-level institution.

Groundwater. Water beneath the surface of the ground.

Gulley plugs. Loose stones, placed strategically to slow the flow of water.

Haram. Forbidden by Islamic law.

HIRD. Haryana Institute of Rural Development.

Hizaab or *hijab*. Head covering worn by Muslim women to show modesty.

HSRLM. Haryana State Rural Livelihood Mission.

Ibtada. NGO based in Alwar, Rajasthan.

ICDS. Integrated Child Development Services.

ICRISAT. International Crops Research Institute for the Semi-Arid Tropics.

IDEAS. Acronym the foundation used to illustrate the organization's scalability direction in 2012. Innovate, Demonstrate, Empower, and Assess, to result in Scaling up.

Indira Awaas Yojana. Social welfare program providing housing for rural poor.

IRDP. Integrated Rural Development Program.

IRRAD. Institute of Rural Research and Development. Sehgal Foundation was known by this name while considering a legal name change from 2006 until 2014.

ISVD. Integrated Sustainable Village Development.

ITC. Information and communications technology.

IVRS. Integrated voice response system.

Jal Chetna Yatra. Water awareness mobilization campaign.

Jalsa. Public gathering of Muslims.

Jhola or *jhola chhap doctor*. An untrained medical practitioner, or quack; a charlatan conducting medical practices without the required degree or license.

Juma. Friday sermon in Islam.

Kisan gosthees. Farmer meetings and training events.

Kisan mitras. Farmers' friends, volunteers.

Krishi Chetna. (krishi = agriculture, chetna = awareness). Farmer training program launched by Sehgal Foundation and Ibtada in Alwar, Rajasthan.

Krishi Jyoti. (krishi = agriculture, jyoti = light). Training program launched by Sehgal Foundation and The Mosaic Company India Ltd.

Krishi sakhi. Farmers' friend.

Kuchcha roads. Dirt roads.

Kutumbs. Ancestrally linked families.

KVKs. *Krishi Vigyan Kendras.* Agricultural extension centers financed by the Indian Council of Agricultural Research.

Kutcha. Crude, temporary, like a dirt road.

Lead by Example. Sehgal Foundation catchphrase introduced in 2006 represented the intent to practice what we preach regarding responsibility for the environment, while the new LEED certified building was under construction.

LEED. Leadership in Energy and Environmental Design.

Loose-stone structure. Similar to gabions without any wire mesh covering, constructed on gentle slope channels to increase water percolation into the ground, minimize soil erosion, and improve soil moisture.

Madrasa. Educational institution, school.

Mahila. Woman.

Mahila Gram Sabha. Gathering of village women voters.

Masjid. Mosque.

Meo. Muslim tribal culture of Mewat (majority population of Mewat).

Meoni. Mewati woman, in the local dialect.

Mewat. A district as of 2005; formerly part of Gurgaon and Faridabad districts of Haryana.

Mewati. Dialect spoken by Meos.

MGNREGA. Mahatma Gandhi National Rural Employment Guarantee Act.

Moulvi or *Maulvi*. Muslim religious leader, Muslim scholar.

MPLADS. Member of Parliament Local Area Development Scheme.

MP. Member of parliament, similar to a US senator.

NRI. Non-resident Indian.

Mufti. Islamic scholar who gives legal opinions.

Nallah bunds. Use of bricks or stone masonry on slopes and water catchment areas to slow or divert water in order to increase percolation of water into the ground (arresting silt, improving soil moisture, and reducing erosion).

Namazees. Readers of the prayers in Islam.

NCPCR. National Commission for Protection of Child Rights.

Needs-based approach. NGO strategy of responding to expressed needs in a village.

NGO. Nongovernmental organization.

Nirmal Bharat Abhiyan (NBA). Clean India Mission. Previously called Total Sanitation Campaign (TSC), a program following the principles of community-led total sanitation (CLTS).

NRHM. National Rural Health Mission, a poverty alleviation project implemented by the Ministry of Rural Development, Government of India.

NRLM. National Rural Livelihood Mission.

NRM. Natural Resource Management.

Nukkad natak. Street theater.

Pal. Meaning protector; tribal culture/clan. Used like a surname for those with unique clan identities.

Panch(es). Member(s) of the panchayat, elected as representative by a geographical subset of voters.

Panchayat. Panch = five. Ayat = assembly. Participatory local self-governing body; wise elders.

Panchayati Raj. Mahatma Gandhi's concept of local government (AKA Gram Swaraj).

Patrika. Indian local newspaper.

PDS. Public Distribution System.

PGA. Policy, Governance, and Advocacy.

PHC. Primary health center.

Power in Empowerment. Sehgal Foundation catchphrase introduced in 2008 represented strength associated with empowering people.

PRI. Panchayati raj institutions.

Purdah system. Purdah means curtain; pertains to the tradition of the veiling and seclusion of women.

Rights-based approach. NGO strategy of empowering villagers by raising awareness of rights and developing their knowledge and skills to assert them.

RRC. Rural Research Center. A team within Sehgal Foundation.

Rs. Rupees.

RTE. Right to education, referring to an Act of the Parliament of India.

RTI. Right to information, referring to an Act of the Parliament of India.

Rubaru. Face to face, or soul-to-soul meeting.

RWH. Roof water-harvesting or rainwater harvesting.

Salahkar parishads. Community advisory groups.

Salwar kameez. Traditional girl's dress.

Sarpanch(es). Elected head(s) of a village-level self-governing institution, similar to a mayor.

Service-based approach. NGO strategy of providing basic services within villages.

SGSY. Swarnajayanti Gram Swarozgar Yojana. A program launched in 1999 to help the poor.

SHG. Self-help group.

Shramdaan. Voluntary manual labor.

Small Interventions, Big Impact. Sehgal Foundation catchphrase introduced in 2002 reflected the team's preference for "fulcrum-like" interventions, those small actions that made a big difference in changing direction, the way a small rudder changes the direction of a big ship.

Small Is Beautiful, But Big Makes Impact. Sehgal Foundation catchphrase introduced in 2005 reiterated value of small actions that make a big difference, but supported the need for greater impact.

SMC. School Management Committee.

Success Builds Success. Sehgal Foundation catchphrase introduced in 2002 reflected the criteria for selecting a model village with the greatest potential for success.

Sushasan Abhi. Sushasan = good governance. *Abhi*= right now. Good Governance Now!

Sushasan champions. Good governance trainees now acting in unpaid community leadership roles, monitoring government programs in the villages and improving access to government programs.

Sushasan karyakartas. Good governance activists.

SVLI. Strengthening Village-Level Institutions. The complementary initiative that, along with *Good Governance Now!,* is part of the Sehgal Foundation's Good Rural Governance Program.

Swachh Bharat Abhiyan. Clean India Mission.

Swasthya sakhis. Community health volunteers.

Sweet water. Potable (drinkable) water.

Tehsildar. Block-level official.

TOT. Training of trainers.

Ulemas. Elite Muslim religious scholars.

Unnat Bharat Abhiyan. Government program to uplift rural India in collaboration with engineering institutes.

Unnat Krishi. (*unnat* = improvement. *krishi* = agriculture. Farmer training program launched by Sehgal Foundation and K+S Fertilizer in Alwar, Rajasthan.

USGBC. U.S. Green Building Council.

VC. Village champion. Young person from village communities selected for development advocacy training.

VHSNC. Village Health, Sanitation, and Nutrition Committee.

Vikas Patrika. Development newsletter.

VLI. Village-level institution.

VLS. Village-leadership school.

Water-augmentation system. Term to include the integrated infrastructure components used in combination for the collection, conservation, storage, and recharge of water.

Water Is the Engine Which Drives All the Programs. Sehgal Foundation catchphrase introduced in 2006 represented a new emphasis on water management.

Where Water Is Running, Make It Walk; Where Water Is Walking, Make It Crawl; Where Water Is Crawling, Make It Stand. Sehgal Foundation catchphrase introduced in 2006 used to address water crisis and the need to capture and percolate water into the ground.

WHBPI. World Heritage Biodiversity Program for India, a United Nations Foundation program.

Wudukhana. A washing station for ablution, ritual cleansing before prayer.

Acknowledgments

The paramount goal of *Together We Empower* was to create a reliable and accurate account of Sehgal Foundation's first fifteen-plus years of direct work. This endeavor entailed countless interviews and the gathering of stories, reports, correspondence, and other materials, official as well as personal, from foundation team members, associates, and volunteers at all levels in the organization. In every case, the people involved provided gracious assistance and cooperation along with their enthusiasm and support for making sure the facts were right, even when interpretations of some events appeared to be contradictory. Readers from inside and outside Sehgal Foundation provided feedback to each draft of the material, which made it possible to ask more questions, uncover more complete details, and make sure that this book is a true description of the organization and its development over time.

Humility runs deep within those associated with Sehgal Foundation. Their tenacity and steady commitment frequently calls to mind Mahatma Gandhi's comment, "In a gentle way, you can change the world." I am grateful to each of those gentle and committed people, those who allowed me to use their names in the book and also for the many others not specifically named who, through their work, continue to fulfill the Sehgal Foundation vision of helping people in rural India lead more secure, prosperous, and dignified lives.

My special thanks to Dr. Ellora Mubashir, whose writings and research served as a valuable reference, and to Dr. M. S. Swaminathan for writing the Foreword. For all of their indispensable assistance, my sincere thanks goes also to Saheed Ahmad, Dr. Kiran Bedi, Tad Cornell, Ryan Clutter, Janet Gage, Jan Dirk Geertsema, Anjali Godyal, Debika Goswami, Arti Manchanda Grover, Nasir Hussain, Zafar Hussain, Dr. Vikas Jha, Dr. M. L. Kansal, Ramesh Kapahi, Sam Kapoor, Pawan Kumar, Mayapriya Long, Aparna Mahajan, Anjali Makhija, Dr. Pradeep K. Mehta, Dr. N. R. Madhava Menon, Voncille Meyer, Jaan Mohammad, Patricia Morris, Pooja O. Murada, Navneet Narwal, Kari Niedfeldt-Thomas, Dr. Ajailiu Niumai, Dr. Kevin O'Brien, Ajay Pandey, B. R. Poonia, Dr. Kiran Prasad, Ambassador

Kenneth Quinn, Dr. D. R. Prasada Raju, Padmavathi S., Salahuddin Saiphy, Niti Saxena, Jane Schukoske, Dr. Ben Sehgal, Jay Sehgal, Veena Sehgal, Vicki Sehgal, P. Vani Sekhar, Anne Seltz, Kamlesh Sharawat, Lalit Mohan Sharma, Dr. Prem Sharma, Bhamy Shenoy, Dr. Deep Shikha, Roy Skodnick, Maureen Smith, Dara Srykin, Geert Van Brandt, and every other partner and team member of Sehgal Foundation.

My profound appreciation and admiration go to Suri and Edda Sehgal for everything they do to help others, for the privilege of partnering with them in sharing the wonderful work of their foundation, and particularly for their unwavering commitment to empowering rural India.

About the Author

Marly Cornell is an American artist, writer, and social justice advocate. She has a BFA from Moore College of Art in Philadelphia and an MA from St. Mary's University of Minnesota. For thirty years, she worked in the corporate nonprofit sector in healthcare, mental health law, behavioral services, and physician recruitment. She is the author of award-winning books: *Seeds for Change: The Lives and Work of Suri and Edda Sehgal* (Sehgal Foundation, 2014) and *The Able Life of Cody Jane: Still Celebrating* (LightaLight Publications, 2011). She lives with her husband Ernie Feil in Minneapolis, Minnesota. www.marlycornell.com

Index

Bold typeface indicates the entry is a photograph. Page numbers followed by an "n" refer to the footnote on that page.

The body text for *Together We Empower* is set in Adobe Garamond Pro, a contemporary typeface family based on the Roman types of sixteenth-century French type designer Claude Garamond and the italic types of Robert Granjon. The title and chapter numbers font is Serlio LH.